Billy was there.

Prone on the floor.

His pig eyes stared into eternity, mouth agape as if cut off in midsurprise. A rough circle of rust stained the carpet underneath him.

And, oh yes, sticking in his chest, like an arrow shot into a bull's-eye, dirt scattered all about, clay pot off to the side, was the spear point of Okawa's bare wood bonsai, rammed up to the hilt of the first wired branch.

———————————— ★ ————————————

Forthcoming from Worldwide Mystery by
PETER ABRESCH

KILLING THYME

BLOODY BONSAI

PETER ABRESCH

WORLDWIDE®

TORONTO • NEW YORK • LONDON
AMSTERDAM • PARIS • SYDNEY • HAMBURG
STOCKHOLM • ATHENS • TOKYO • MILAN
MADRID • WARSAW • BUDAPEST • AUCKLAND

For Annemarie whose love and faith have sustained me

BLOODY BONSAI

A Worldwide Mystery/September 1999

First published by Write Way Publishing, Inc.

ISBN 0-373-26321-X

Copyright © 1998 by Peter Abresch.
All rights reserved. No part of this book may be reproduced
or transmitted in any form or by any means, electronic or
mechanical, including photocopying, recording or by any
information storage and retrieval system, without permission
in writing from the publisher. For information, contact:
Write Way Publishing, Inc., 10555 E. Dartmouth, Suite 210,
Aurora, CO 80014 U.S.A.

All characters in this book are fictitious, and any resemblance to
actual persons, living or dead, is purely coincidental.

® and TM are trademarks of Harlequin Enterprises Limited.
Trademarks indicated with ® are registered in the United States
Patent and Trademark Office, the Canadian Trade Marks Office
and in other countries.

Visit us at www.worldwidemystery.com

Printed in U.S.A.

Acknowledgments

Tom Orem and Marijka Unlanowicz for critiquing this book; Michael Kuegler for advice on physical therapy; Tina Pleake-Tamm and Bert Brun for their encouragement; and, of course, Dorrie O'Brien for her editorial work and taking a chance on me.

PROLOGUE

"HEY, YOU CRAZY?"

He stared at the miniature tree, peeled end pointed at him like a stick.

So what was this, a joke?

He shifted his look to the wild eyes glaring back at him.

What could you do with a three-foot bonsai tree?

But then it was thrust at him like a spear.

"Hey, get away—no!"

It caught him in the chest, smashed against his rib cage and shoved him back a step. The spear point slipped inside, and the shock of it sent him plunging down a deep hole. He flailed his arms for something to grab onto while the bottom rushed up and slammed him in the back.

Air exploded from his lungs. He sucked it back in a wheeze. A gurgle bubbled up from down where the bonsai tree nailed him to the floor like a pin through a butterfly.

Okay, enough was enough.

Pull the damn thing out and get a doctor.

The joke was over.

But the wide-screen TV of his mind shrank down to a far star of light, and it came to him, for a brief moment, the joke might be on him.

Then the star winked out.

ONE

YOU'LL HAVE A really good time, they said.

You'll learn lotsa stuff, they said.

You'll meet people, they said.

Yeah, right.

Jim's two-year-old blue Lincoln smoothed out the thump thump of the low bridge's expansion joints so they hardly disturbed the instrumental of "Somewhere Over the Rainbow" playing in the tape deck. Off to the side, sending up bursts of dirty spray, a twenty-foot sport fishing boat plowed through the slate gray bay, complimenting the slate gray sky, as two men huddled against the cold in the lee of her cuddy cabin.

Jim glanced at his watch.

One o'clock, probably heading in for a late lunch.

Houses lined the barrier island shore as far as he could see, with a yacht basin just to the left as he came down off the bridge onto 130th Street, the main drag of Bolder Harbor, New Jersey. "North of Cape May and not far from Stone Harbor," the brochure had said, and: "Bolder Harbor, despite our name, is a gracious family resort where boldness is our vision and violence is unknown."

It looked like most of the town's businesses were centered on this one street: bay side restaurants in the short first block; quaint gift shops, a Ben Franklin, and a firehouse in the second; the statue of a revolutionary war soldier, life-size plus a half, stood in the middle of the intersection; and in the third block, a library, post office, hardware store, a theater advertising the movie *Ping Pong,* liquor store, combination bar and café, and the police station. The number of cars angle-parked at the curb was less than he could count on his toes; this was a summer resort caught in the chill of early spring. Plus, it was Sunday.

Jim brought the Lincoln to a full stop at the corner of 130th and Ocean Boulevard, glanced in the rearview mirror to see no one behind, then rummaged through the papers on the passenger seat and pulled out the motel brochure. He slipped on his reading glasses and read the address, Ocean Boulevard between 110th and 111th Streets.

So, left or right?

He sucked in his breath, letting it out in a long sigh, and turned north, rolling along the lonely road, relaxing as he noticed the cross streets ticking off in descending order. Empty motel parking lots along the shore on his right, deserted beach houses to the left. New leaves, not yet blossomed to full size, clung to trees buffeted by a fresh breeze that sent low clouds scudding overhead.

The Windswept Dunes Motel sign announced, in block slide-in letters: Welcome Elderhostelers.

Yeah, right.

Shouldn't have come.

Uncle George's fault.

"C'mon," he phoned from Richmond, "you haven't been anywhere since Penny passed away. It will be good for both of us. I need a roommate and someone to drive me, and you need to get away with your really super uncle."

Except that two months ago, on the very day Jim got his Elderhostel confirmation, Uncle George had canceled out of everything.

Seems like he'd attended a lot of funerals lately.

So maybe it was really God's fault.

Somewhere over the rainbow...

He turned into the parking lot. The four-story motel was L-shaped, half running along the beach in front, half along 111th Street on his right, a drive-under portico at the front entrance. He pulled the Lincoln into one of the empty spaces—few cars, lots of spaces—and cut the engine, draping his arms around the steering wheel and staring out the windshield.

Or maybe it was Ceecee's fault.

"Go, Dad, you already paid your money." It went on for two months. Getting her brothers to gang up on him. "You need to get away. You haven't gone anywhere since Mom died."

Did any of them ever wonder that maybe he hadn't wanted to go anywhere after Penny died? And on top of it, two to a room, he would be paired up with a stranger for a roommate.

Great, really great.

He climbed out of the car, got his bag from the trunk, and lumbered across to the entrance.

The lobby extended clear through the building to a patio and pool on the other side, the beach and Atlantic Ocean beyond. Two couches and two easy chairs mated up with a wall to form a conversation area on the right, where two women and a man were whispering. On the left was the check-in desk.

"I have a reservation. Dandy, James P."

A redheaded man, looking too young to be working, ran his hand over a computer screen, and blinked. "I don't see a reservation. Are you with the Elderhostel?"

"Yes, I am."

"That's a different register." He typed in a few keys and the computer monitor flickered. "Ah, yes, here you are."

"Is it true what the brochure says about Bolder Harbor? Where boldness is your vision and violence is unknown."

The redheaded man glanced sideways at him. "Oh, yeah."

Jim raised his eyebrows. "It's not? What, the bold vision or the violence—"

"I'll deny I told you if the chamber of commerce asks," the man typed on the computer, "but four months ago we had a grisly murder right down on the main drag. A computer nerd by the name of Bixby Boyd was stabbed to death like he had a stake through his heart."

"Maybe I want to go home."

The man shook his head as he ran his hand down the monitor. "That's been the only real trouble we've had since I came here."

"They ever catch him?"

"Nope. If the murderer was even a 'him.'" He took a key from a rack of square holes attached to the back wall. "Personally, I think it was a drifter, although the police have other ideas." He handed over the key. "Okay, you're in room Two Oh Four, Mr. Dandy."

"James Dandy?" barked a new voice.

Jim turned to see a man coming from the patio, unzipping a leather bomber jacket. He was taller than Jim, six two or three, hard brown eyes, bushy brown eyebrows; close-cropped brown hair rimmed a nearly bald head.

"Are you James Dandy?" The man held himself erect, like he had spent too many hours on a military parade ground. "Two Oh Four?"

"Yes," Jim nodded.

"I'm General Sopwaite, U.S. Army, retired." He stuck out his hand. "Barney, to you. I'm your roommate."

Jim stuck out his own hand and had it engulfed in the big man's firm grip. "Good to know you, Barney." He caught the unmistakable reek of cigarette smoke clinging to the man's clothes.

Oh great, really great.

"Guess you're here to learn about bonsai," Barney said, pronouncing it "bone sigh."

"I'm going to give it a try," he answered.

Not that he cared if Barney smoked. He had a right to his own life, but he sure didn't want it in his bedroom.

As if reading his mind, Barney gave him a square grin. "I'm a smoker."

Big revelation there.

The retired general wore a plaid shirt with a string tie under his leather bomber jacket. "I guess you don't smoke," Barney said, shaking his head. "No sir. Dirty habit really. Most everyone I know has already quit. Our generation, huh? But I figure, what the hell, if I made it this far along, why should I deprive myself of the pleasure of it now, right?"

What was the guy telling him?

He wanted to smoke in the room?

"I thought," Jim glanced toward the glass doors as four women blustered in from the parking lot, "I thought there was no smoking in the motel?"

The grin faded to cool. "Oh, you can smoke in your room, if both parties agree to it?" the General ended the sentence in a hopeful question. "Well, I guess I can smoke out on the balcony, if I have to? It's not that cold."

"Do I have to sign in somewhere else," Jim asked, ignoring the bait, "or is this it?"

"Oh, no sir," Barney turned and pointed across the lobby, where full-height windows separated the parking lot from a hallway. "You register with the Elderhostel down there. I'm already checked in. The room is the same way. Can I help you with your bags?"

"I only have the one," he answered, pocketing his key and picking up his bag.

"Well, sir," Barney zipped up his bomber jacket and smoothed the rim of brown hair encircling his head, "I'm going to head out and get the lay of the land. Glad to meet you, roommate."

Jim watched the general march out, like he was keeping cadence under his breath.

Going out to get the lay of the land.

Well, hell.

If the guy didn't smoke in the room, he'd probably end up liking old Barney...

What was the last name—Sopwaite? General Sopwaite?

See, that was another thing, he could never remember people's names. Probably forget "Barney" by morning and have to end up calling him—oh God—*Roommate.*

He shouldn't have come.

Shouldn't have allowed himself to be talked into it.

You'll have a really good time, they said.

You'll learn lotsa stuff, they said.

You'll meet people, they said.

Helloooo Barney!

TWO

JIM GLANCED THROUGH the glass doors at the back of the lobby. A closed-for-the-season sign sat on a round patio bar with an imitation palm roof; a wind chime hanging from a support beam struggled to be free. Mottled water lived in the deserted pool. And a wood walkway led to the beach where a gray sky faded into a gray sea out on the horizon.

"Oh, look," came a husky woman's voice. "This must be the way to the beach."

He turned to see frosted-blond hair, green eyes, a mouth too large for her face, which was all teeth when she gave him a passing smile. Rugged trail clothes that could have come from L. L. Bean hung snugly on a five-foot-nine body broad enough to plow through the woods with the best of bears. A string tie hung from her neck with a plastic name-tag—Kelly Massey—for a slide.

Jim put her age somewhere in the early forties.

"It is indeed so," said her companion, her voice sounding like she was rehearsing for a part in a British-India movie. A multicolored sari, string tie name-tag of Vasantha Powell, complimented the accent, as if she had just stepped off a plane from Bombay or Calcutta, except for a white angora sweater underneath. "Brrr," lips turned down on her dark olive face, dusky pools for eyes, "it looks cold, does it not?" She carried her thin five-foot body, a single braid of black hair reaching to her waist, like a young girl, making her age more difficult to guess.

But no way could either of them, stretching it, be over forty-five. So how did they get on the Elderhostel?

Maybe they weren't.

Through an open double-door on his right, he saw the cheery sight of two coffee urns set up in the motel restaurant, a sign between them announcing, "Welcome Elderhostelers." He re-crossed the lobby and swung left along a glassed-in hallway, passing the main entrance to the same restaurant, to a woman sitting at a desk outside the door to a conference room. Early thirties, big almond eyes in a round olive face gave her a Eurasian flavor, but she wore a string name-tag tie of Lee Sullivan.

"Hi, my name's James P. Dandy," he said, falling into his habit of always using the formal James P. when he coupled it with his last name.

It hadn't been that way when Penny was alive.

"Hi," she'd smile, "we're Jim and Penny Dandy."

The Penny part was just the separation he needed to make it work.

"Ah, Mr. Dandy," Lee Sullivan said, without a trace of accent. "You are easy."

Easy?

"Right at the top of my list," she checked him off and handed him a welcome packet. "You're in the bonsai class. Mr. Okawa will be doing a demonstration inside—ah, two more," she nodded up the walkway past him. "Maybe I'll tell you all at once."

Jim turned to see two women.

One was definitely an Elderhosteler, in fact an elder Elderhosteler if there was such a thing. A warm smile rested easy on a well-traveled face, all the wrinkles and laugh lines accommodating it, giving the smile, reflected in watery blue eyes, an air of permanence. She wore a long, dark-green rain coat and walked with a slight limp and a cane, a small bag slung over the opposite shoulder.

The woman at her side, laboring under the weight of a suitcase and a hanging bag, hardly appeared old enough to register for Elderhostel, even with the recently lowered age from sixty to fifty-five. Hair about the color of ripened wheat, eyes blue as cornflowers, she was five-foot-three or four, dressed in a navy corduroy jacket and blue slacks, and had a smile reminiscent of the older woman's, but the face lacked the wrinkles.

"Hi," Lee Sullivan looked up from her desk, "I'm the coordinator for the Elderhostel this week. I thought I might explain it to you all at once. Save a little air." She took a quick breath, like she had been talking for hours, and smiled.

Everyone was smiling.

So why wasn't he smiling?

Because he should have stayed the hell home is why.

No, the real problem was Penny wasn't along. Quick to smile, she had always been the one to make instant friends, including him as part of the package.

We're Jim and Penny Dandy.

Without the Penny part he was a joke.

"Mr. Okawa," Lee Sullivan said, "our bonsai master for the week, will be doing a demonstration inside"—she hooked her thumb to the conference room behind her—"in about an hour. Workshops really start tomorrow, but this is a preview of some of the things you'll be learning. Dinner is in the Whispering Sands Restaurant at six, and we'll have an orientation at seven-thirty for those who want to attend."

"Were we supposed to bring anything?" asked the older woman. "The brochure didn't say."

"Everything is provided for the workshop, but Mr.

Okawa will have tools and books for sale at the end of the course.''

"The stairs are this way?'' Jim motioned past her down the hall.

"One more thing,'' she said, holding up an index finger. "The motel is getting ready for the start of the season and there will be men working on the patio door locks during the day. There was a mix-up in the weeks we would be here, really my fault, so if we could be patient with them it would be a big help. And yes—'' Lee Sullivan turned and pointed ''—the elevator and stairs are that way. All rooms are on the second floor. We're lucky to have most of them facing the beach rather than the parking lot or One Eleventh Street.''

Jim stuck his packet under his arm, picked up his bag and headed for the elevator.

Top of the list.

Damn.

The top of the list always gets the first questions and ends up making an ass of himself while everyone else has time to figure out the answer.

Weren't there any Abrams or Bakers or Carters?

Maybe he could change his name to Xerox for the week.

He found the elevator next to a public phone and pressed the button.

All he needed was to have one of the few rooms on the street side of the motel. Barney and the parking lot. Just great.

He glanced back to the two ladies, the younger struggling under the weight of two bags.

He should offer to help.

No, then they would want to talk.

What would he say?

Ask some phony questions like—

Ah, dammit!

"Here," he called out, striding towards her, "let me take that for you."

The younger woman looked around. "You mean me?"

"I'll take the suitcase if you like."

"Well, that's very kind of you," answered the older woman, voice a bit too loud, and he could see she was wearing a hearing aid. "There was supposed to be someone at the desk to help us, but Dodee didn't want to wait."

"I can manage, really."

"Now, Dodee, if a gentleman is gallant enough to offer you help, you should be ladylike enough to accept."

The cornflower blue eyes glared at the older lady before giving up the suitcase. "My aunt is from a different era, but thank you."

He picked up the bag.

Sonofabitch.

Probably ten tons.

He should have listened to his first instincts and ignored her.

"My name is Alice Atwater," the older woman said, when the doors of the elevator slid shut, "and this is my niece, Dodee Swisher. Are you taking the bonsai class, too?" she asked, pronouncing it "banzai."

He nodded. "Do they have something else?"

"There's a course on shore birds and one on barrier island ecology," Dodee Swisher answered, blue eyes on the digital lights announcing the floor level.

The elevator jerked to a stop, but it was a door to the rear that slid open, surprising them, and they stepped out into a carpeted hall.

They turned left and his room, 204, was down two doors on the right, the beach side of the motel. Hoo Rah. Jim dropped his bag and car coat in front of it.

"I can take that from you now," Dodee offered.

He shrugged, "I don't mind," and followed Alice Atwater. Four rooms down, also on the beach side, the older lady held the door for him and he swung the bag onto a suitcase rack. "There you go."

"And your name is?" Alice Atwater blinked her watery blue eyes.

"Jim—James. James P. Dandy."

"Well, I'm glad to know you, Jim." She held out her hand, taking his in a surprisingly strong grip. "You're a real light to come into our lives. We'll see you in class?"

"Thank you for carrying the bag," Dodee shook his hand as well, smoother then her Aunt's, but the same strong grip.

He headed back down the hall.

Wait a minute, if the older lady was named Atwater, how could he be at the top of the list? Unless they did it by who signed up first. He shouldn't have signed up at all.

He continued on past the elevator to a cross hall, the street wing of the L-shaped motel. It stretched out on his right until the walls converged like railroad tracks on a Kansas flatland; a couple of red exit signs probably led down to entrances off the parking lot. A door to his left opened onto what proved to be a hospitality room with a sign announcing, "Welcome Elderhostelers," and a view of the ocean through a glass door on the other side.

He turned back to his room, picked up his bag, and unlocked the door.

Barney's suitcase sat on the nearest of two double beds, giving Jim the one by the sliding glass door, which is the way he'd have preferred it, except for the smoker's back-and-forth trips to the balcony. A round table sat beside the glass door, armchairs on either side, two low dressers with a mirror on the right, along with a suitcase rack and an open closet. Immediately to the left, between the entrance and the bathroom, was a below-counter refrigerator with a two-cup coffeemaker sitting on top. He opened it.

If Penny were here she'd be rushing him out to stock it with wine and cheese, or beer and peanuts, or some other little snackies to make the adventure special.

He stared into the empty fridge.

The only good thing was knowing her suffering was over and she was at peace.

But what about him?

Oh no. He shook his head. He would not get back into that funk. He shut the fridge door, crossed over to the window and swung his bag onto the double bed.

Besides, he had made two friends already. Three, if you counted old Barney.

Alice Atwater and her niece, Dodee... Dodee...?

Swisher.

Dodee Swisher.

With eyes bright as cornflowers.

And hair the color of ripened wheat.

The trouble was, not that he would ever have the opportunity, but just suppose for argument's sake, against all odds, that he did have the opportunity, would he be able to do anything? Maybe that was the real reason he didn't want to be here.

He opened the Elderhostel packet, dumped the contents on the bed and put on his reading glasses.

There had not been much doing the last year Penny was alive, and nothing in the two years since unless you counted the joy of last summer's Roto-Rooter job on his prostate.

He looked over the meal and class schedule, a brochure on Mr. John Okawa, bonsai master, and a name-tag string tie to loop around his neck.

So, if the opportunity ever did arise, say like against all odds, would he be able to do any—

Jim Dandy!

Sonofabitch!

Right there on the name tag.

Oh great, really great.

He threw his reading glasses on the bed.

Now he was going to have deal with that for a week.

Well, it's easy to see everything's Jim Dandy with you.

It's a Jim Dandy day, isn't it, Jim Dandy?

Looks like a Jim Dandy bonsai to me.

Yeah, well, how would you like a big fat Jim Dandy punch in your big fat Jim Dandy nose?

He unlocked the sliding glass door, and stepped outside.

Three balconies over, a lithe, redheaded woman, encased in a Spandex body suit, powered through a series of side kicks, hammer punches and karate chops, oblivious to the stiff breeze that whipped the small white puffs of her breath away.

Jim brushed silver gray strands of hair from his brown eyes and looked over the railing.

A tang of sea salt rode on the early spring air while militant waves, streaked with beer foam, marched in from a leaden eternity to rise up like phalanxes against the New Jersey shore, and with a roaring charge came smashing and crumbling and bumbling and bouncing onto the sand, deserted of even the bravest of beachcombers.

Another Bixby Boyd could be murdered down there, despite Bolder Harbor's claim that violence was unknown, and a hundred others right beside the computer nerd, and not a shout would rise above the surf.

May the first be he who wishes him a Jim Dandy day.

Well, for better or worse, he was on his first Elderhostel.

THREE

Mr. John Okawa, bonsai master as stated in the brochure, stood in the center of the exhibition room, behind an eight-foot-long table on which rested a three-foot-high bush in a washtub of dirt, appearing as tall as he. The sleeves of a plaid shirt were rolled up over thick arms to the elbows, and a veined hand, looking strong enough to strangle an ox, polished the rim of the tub, almost a caress, his gold wedding ring scraping on the metal, as he waited for late-comers.

Okawa fit Jim's expectation of the man from his Japanese name—short stature, powerful body, Oriental flap to the eyelid, black hair and eyebrows, round, olive-skinned face—until the man started to speak.

"Ah'm gonna be goin' ovva a lotta terms as Ah demonstrate on this chere bald cypress," he said, his voice as thick as a southern soup of ham hock and beans, *"taxodium distichum."*

Jim did a double-take to jerk the voice and face together. Had it come across a radio he'd never have done it.

A rack of copper-wire spools sat on the end of the table, free-rolling so the wire could be peeled off as needed. Scrawled across an easel, behind and off to the side, in a large artist's hand, was John Okawa's name.

Jim stood behind three rows of ten chairs, aisle down the middle, facing the bonsai master. Alice Atwater, hearing aid in her ear, sat in the front row with her cane at her side. The four women he had noticed arriving in one car sat across from her. Dodee Swisher stood, like him, behind the chairs, a sketch pad resting in the crook of her left elbow, drawing pencil in her right hand, eyes fixed on Okawa.

"Ah gathered this chere tree myself from an area near the Okefenokee Swamp five years ago." Okawa's jet eyes had a jolly glint to them, as if he were listening to a private joke. "It's been sitting in this chere washbasin ever since, one of the things I been meaning to get to."

At the end of the last row, near the wall, sat a heavy man with a chin melding into a fat neck, legs apart to accommodate hefty thighs, a wide-track rear end overflowing the chair. He looked to be in his early sixties, ruddy face, brown crew-cut, heavy arms sticking out of a gaudy Hawaiian shirt, short sleeves in spite of the fact spring had not yet set in. The portly man kept glancing towards the door as if expecting someone.

"So this works out nice in that I get to style this chere tree on this first day of Elderhostel, and you get to see how we turn a collected specimen into a bonsai." Okawa gave a slight bow. "That's pronounced 'bone sigh,' don't you know, like a bone a dowg wants to chew, and a pretty lady letting out a love sigh, 'bone sigh.'" He gave a little laugh and the four women politely joined in. "Yes sir, this chere tree's been saying for the last five years—hey, partner, when ya gonna get to me?"

The portly man turned his ruddy face towards the door and Jim glanced around to see the two women from the lobby, the tall, frosted-blonde with the broad body, and the sari-clad Indian, diminutive next to her muscular friend, her long braid of black hair trailing behind as they took seats in the second row.

So they *were* on the Elderhostel.

"What I'm gonna do here is a little advanced styling," Okawa was saying. "We won't be getting into this on the

trees you'll be working with, but the principles will be the
same.''

Jim scanned the room for his roommate, Barney, but the
General was AWOL. The portly man eyed the door again
as two more people, a man and a woman, arrived.

The man, Simon Crew by name tag, had watery blue
eyes, octagonal glasses, and a mane of silver-gray hair that
flowed into a full gray beard. He looked like an older
Steven Spielberg, say on the topside of his sixties, nattily
dressed in a brown sport jacket, light tan shirt, and plaid
tie.

But it was the man's consort that sucked Jim in.

She was the woman he had seen on the balcony, a statuesque redhead, probably natural from the fair skin of her
oval face, five-feet-six-inches of long legs and shapely
body, borne lightly, like a teenager, and set off in a blue
blouse and red silk scarf, white hip-hugging jeans, white
sneaks and socks, all appearing to be just plucked from the
rack. In spite of having the same last name on her tag,
Tiffany Crew, she couldn't have been over thirty. Was she
his wife or daughter? If they were spouses, only one had
to be older than fifty-five for Elderhostel, but did that apply
to a daughter as well?

So who cares?

Was he the Elderhostel police?

''The first thing we always have to do is find the front.
I have this tub sitting on a turntable that's made specially
for bonsai styling.'' Okawa spun the tree in spurts while
he spoke, completing a circle. ''There's a lock so you can
work on the tree, and then release it to look at all the an-
gles.'' He bent down to inspect it at tree level. ''I'm seeing
maybe two fronts.''

''What's a front?'' called Tiffany Crew, hardly in her
seat.

"The opposite of a back, my dear," quipped elderly Simon Crew, bringing a polite laughter.

"Well, that's sure one way of looking at it," Okawa's face split by a grin. "But usually it is the front we're searching for, the way we'll display our bonsai." He looked up at them. "Now how do we pronounce it, everybody?"

"Bone sigh," the women said in chorus.

"Very good. Banzai means long life. Bonsai means tree in a pot." He cut some of the feathery needles off the bald Cypress for a better look. "The front is the way we'll display our bonsai, so we do our styling with that view in mind." He swung the tree a little bit, tilting his head back to get a better look, then stuck a chopstick into the dirt. "Shazam. This chere tree is saying, 'hey, partner, this is my front.'" And he swung it around to show every one.

He picked up a pair of clippers and started cutting off the lower branches.

"Ideal rule: the height of the tree should be six times the thickness of the trunk at the ground. Second ideal rule," he worked as he talked, "the first branch should be one third the way up the trunk. Taking off the lower branches allows us to see the taper of trunk and any exposed roots, both of which gives us the appearance of age. The second branch up spreads out on the opposite side, and the third is a back branch with a spread of foliage that gives the tree depth. These are general rules the old bonsai masters worked out over the centuries."

He stopped cutting and looked at them.

"Ah'm Japanese, you know that." He grinned, laying on the southern accent this time. "Ah talk the way Ah do cause Ah'm from southern Japan, called Georgia," and he laughed.

And all the women laughed with him.

"What happens if you don't have the branches where you want them?" Tiffany Crew asked.

"Good question. If you don't have a branch where you want it, then you have to work around it, or graft one on. This chere bald cypress, for instance, does not have the branches we need, but that's okay because we are going to make an advanced design. This will become a tree lightning has struck and run down the side and front, leaving it half dead. Where the bark has been stripped off, the wind and rains and sun have weathered it to a silver gray. This is what we call a 'jin'—" he wrote it on the easel below his name "—but even though some of the branches are no longer there, we still have to see them in our mind's eye so we can place the remaining ones in a pleasing position."

Then he began clipping off branches, willy-nilly it seemed to Jim, grimacing as the larger branches took the full strength of his hand, until the trunk slowly began to emerge, and what had been nothing but a bush was now taking on the appearance of a small tree.

Alice Atwater got up from her seat and limped back to her niece, whose wheaten head was bent over her sketch pad.

Jim moved closer, peeking at the drawing, the pencil not only duplicating what Okawa was doing to the bald cypress, but a fair representation of the man as well.

"That's very good," he whispered, voice spilling out almost on it's own.

"What?" the gray-haired woman asked, holding her hand to the hearing aid in her ear.

Jim pointed to the sketch. "Very good," he nodded.

"Oh yes, Dodee's an artist," Alice Atwater said under Okawa's prattle. "She's sold pictures for thousands of dollars."

"One picture, Aunt Alice." Dodee turned her cornflower

blue eyes on him, and he felt a warm glow. "The way Aunt Alice tells it, I'm popping them out all over the place."

"Well, I don't know why you're too modest to admit it," Aunt Alice whispered. "You're selling paintings all the time."

"But not for a thousand dollars."

"Is that how you make your living?" he asked, finding her more interesting than the bonsai for the moment.

"Part of it," she turned the blue eyes on him again, adding a smile for good measure. "I own a small gallery which brings in most of the money. And I teach aerobics to other senior citizens. If I depended on my own art I'd starve to death."

"You are always selling yourself short," Aunt Alice said, looking around. "Excuse me, I want to get some tea."

"I didn't realize I was carrying the bag of a celebrity."

She smiled again, but there was sarcasm in it this time. "Don't be a smart-ass, Jim."

"Sorry," he shrugged, feeling like he had been put down, "I didn't mean to be."

She studied him a moment, as if she didn't believe him, then her checks flushed and she returned to the sketch.

So, what was that about?

You're a jerk, Jim?

Get lost, Jim?

A motel employee, a man in a spotted, white, short waiter's jacket, thick-soled shoes and white socks, rolled in a cart and started setting up water pitchers and glass tumblers on a table by the door. Jim strolled over and poured himself a glass.

"Can you bring me a cup of tea?" Alice Atwater whispered to the waiter.

The man looked like a forty-year-old busboy, short, thin shoulders and chest, a large pot belly and bigger hips, as if he had suffered a partial meltdown and sagged and solidified into a pear with legs.

"Can't do it," he said in a nasal voice. "We're only s'posed to put out water. Gotta charge for anything else."

"That will be fine. What's your name?"

Little pig eyes squinted in a round, jowly face. "Billy Dack. Why?"

"Well, Mr. Billy," Alice Atwater said with a genteel air, "if you could bring me a cup of tea with a little lemon I would be most grateful."

"I gotta charge."

"How much is it?"

The man hesitated a moment. "One dollar."

"That will be fine."

Billy Dack nodded and headed out the door.

Jim turned back to see what the bonsai master was doing. Which was denuding the tree.

FOUR

SOME PAPERS slipped out from under Dodee's arm, dropping to the carpet, and Jim picked them up. She had been making rapid sketches of the various metamorphoses the tree was going through.

"Thank you," she said, as she reached for the papers.

"I'll hold them. Free you up a bit."

"I hate to impose, after carrying my luggage."

"No big deal."

She gave him a smile and turned back to Okawa.

By this time the bonsai master had clipped everything off the top eighteen inches, leaving it lopsided and bare, with only two low branches remaining. If this was suppose to give the impression of an old tree, the effect was utter failure. It looked more like a spear than a bonsai.

A new woman came stealing into the room, and the stout man with the crew-cut hopped out of his chair and waddled to her, screwing his lips to one side of his ruddy face as he spoke, holding out a hand towards Okawa.

The woman folded her arms and nodded a few times before whispering something back.

The fat man wagged his head and led her to his seat.

So what was all that about?

Hey, Wife, I came to this dumb thing because you wanted, and now here I am and where the hell you been?

Billy Dack came back with Alice Atwater's tea, whispering back and forth, a wrinkling of brows, finally a transfer of money from the old lady's purse to Billy Dack's pocket.

He heard the ripping of paper and turned to see Dodee, eyes on the developing bonsai, holding out a fresh sketch to him. He took it like a dutiful servant, but he was no longer happy about holding them.

What the hell was he?

Her flunky?

But Dodee Swisher was already working on a fresh sketch of Okawa butchering what had been a nice little bush.

"Did you grow this tree?" asked Tiffany Crew, who seemed to have appointed herself Group Questioner.

"Ah," Okawa gave her an impish smile, "if you had been on time you would have gained those early pearls of wisdom. No, I've been growing this chere tree in the bucket for five years, but I found it, thick trunk as you see, in Okefenokee Swamp, just off the side of a road."

Dodee jerked around to Jim.

He peered into her eyes, so wide he had the impression he was staring into deep pools, her jaw hanging open enough to air out a pretty pink tongue. Then she snapped out of it, bending close and whispering. "I saw two great bonsai trees on the side of the road. Right here. In Bolder Harbor."

He smiled and nodded.

Who cares?

What did she want him to do, go—

"Can you do that?" asked Tiffany. "If you find something on the side of the road, can you just dig it up?"

"Oh yeah," grinned the bonsai master, Georgian humor flashing in his eyes, "especially if you want free room and board from the state. This one was actually in a fence-line where cows mustta been a-chomping on it, don't you know. So I trucked up to the farmer's house and got his permission to dig it up. Reluctantly, I might add. I thought I was going to have to make a commando raid in the middle of the night, but I talked him into it by promising to let him inspect the spot when I had finished, so he could see there was no damage to his fence, and everything smoothed over so his cattle didn't step into no hole. I say I talked him into it. Actually, I think he felt sorry for my pregnant wife.''

"So you can't—I don't understand,'' Tiffany ran a hand through her red hair. "Can you take trees from the side of the road or not?''

Okawa shook his head. "You can if you can get permission, state or private. Sometimes you can get permission from, like the highway maintenance guys, but it's always easier for them to say no. And I know some friends who just dig them up, but you open yourself up for a hefty fine when you take anything from state land. And if it's a preserve or a national forest, my advice is to not even take a pebble without permission.''

Okawa studied his handiwork, then glanced up. "But if you all are determined,'' he lowered his head between his shoulders and made slits of his eyes, speaking in a stage whisper, "dig it up in the middle of the night.''

Dodee swung to Jim again with the same wide eyes, but this time smiling and nodding. "In the middle of the night,'' she whispered.

He nodded back.

In the middle of the night what?

He could think of a lot of things he wouldn't mind doing in the middle of a cold night, but sneaking out and digging into the side of the road sure in the hell wasn't one of them.

He felt a presence at his side and turned to see Barney Sopwaite smoothing down the hair rimming his bald head. Tall and imperious, chiseled stone face, his clothes stank of burnt cigarettes.

"Did you get the lay?'' Jim asked. Barney turned towards him, knitting his brows. "The lay of the land?" Jim asked. "Didn't you say—"

"Oh," Barney's face cleared, "yes sir, I got it reconnoitered." He glanced to Okawa and back. "By the way, you don't have to worry about me smoking. I was able to talk them into giving me a separate room."

"I have a new roommate?"

"No sir. I had to give up the ocean view for the parking lot, but now we both have a room to ourselves."

Jim gave him a half shrug, trying to register indifference, but inside doing cartwheels. He'd have been willing to move across the hall himself for a single.

Barney nodded towards Okawa. "I believe I'll take in what's doing," and moved forward along the side to slip onto one of the end chairs, his shiny head looking like a monk's.

By now the bonsai master had stripped most of the bark off the tree, ripping it right on down to the base in a few spots.

He was not only denuding it, the guy was killing it.

How the hell was it supposed to end up looking like a bonsai?

Obviously someone else had the same notion.

"Excuse me," said the frosted-blond, Kelly Massey, in her husky voice, "won't that kill the bonsai?"

"I sincerely hope not." Okawa carved the edge of the remaining bark. "I have only these two branches that will remain alive, and I've left enough cambium to safely take care of them." He rested his hands on the rim of the washtub, the three-foot tree now down to two and a half, the top eighteen inches scraped to bare wood. "You are Ms. Massey and Ms. Powell? Right? You're the two that registered independently of the Elderhostel?" Both of the for-

tyish women nodded. "Yes, I thought you looked, that is,
I mean, not as old—elderly as—"

"They are not old bats like the rest of us," Alice Atwater
interrupted, followed by laughter.

"I was trying to put it more diplomatically."

"And failing."

Okawa carved a rounded point on the top of the tree, off
to one side, asymmetrical, giving the impression it had been
struck by lightning and split off. He did the same for a stub
of a high branch, making it appear it, too, had broken off.
He rolled out a length of copper wire from one of the spools
at the end of the table, studied it with a seasoned eye, then
snipped it off. He anchored the wire in the middle by taking
a wrap around the trunk and spiraled one end about the
upper branch.

"You must not wrap the wire so tight it cuts into the
bark. And you have to watch it during the growing season.
Nothing is worse than a branch scarred by wire. And if the
coils are too close together it will impede the flow of sap
through the cambium, killing the branch."

Jim watched him complete the wiring and inwardly
shook his head. If the poor little tree appeared forlorn before, now it looked like pure hell.

Then Okawa twisted each branch, flattening them out,
bending them down at a slight angle, fanning out the bran-
chlettes like the fingers of a hand, like an umpire calling
someone safe at home plate, and tilted them up at the tips.

And a little sigh escaped in the room.

What had started out as a many-spiked bush was now
transformed with a few deft moves from a spear into a tree
growing on the edge of a forest, one that had been around
a long time, a survivor of storms and lightning strikes and
bearing the brunt of all nature could throw at it, the top
half dead and weathered, and still, tenaciously, like an old

man fighting the ravages of time, it spread its needles to the sun.

Okawa peeked at his watch, then, forearm muscles bulging, worked the tree out of the wash bucket, some soil spilling off the table onto the carpet, and held up a red clay pot to its base.

"General rule of thumb, the length of the pot should be a pinch more than two-thirds the height of the tree. And the depth of the pot should equal the thickness of the tree trunk. This pot is oversized because I want to give it a year to grow more hair roots before trimming it down to the proper size. But it will give you the picture, a sort of phony baloney bonsai."

He glanced at his watch again.

"It's just about time for your supper, don't you know, but I'm going to pot this chere tree and I'll leave it so you can come back and check it out. Thank you for your time, and tomorrow morning come ready to work," he rubbed his hands together, "to get dirt under your pretty fingernails, and you'll start on your own—how do you pronounce this again?"

"Bone sigh," came a chorus of voices.

"Tomorrow you start on your own bonsai."

A small round of applause rippled through the room.

Dodee turned to Jim, taking her sketches. "Thanks for holding them," she said, eyes gazing into his. "We'll meet at dinner," she lowered her voice to a sinister whisper, "and discuss our plans."

He blinked as she hurried to help her Aunt.

What the hell had he gotten himself into?

Was she serious about getting those plants?

He turned back towards John Okawa, wondering what the bonsai master would think of it, but Okawa was engaged in a heated discussion with the busboy, Billy Dack.

A familiar kid's saying came back to him from his childhood days: *Don't let your alligator mouth overload your canary ass.*

If the pear-shaped Billy Dack didn't shut his alligator mouth, the powerfully built bonsai master could well squash his canary ass.

FIVE

DINNER TOOK PLACE, buffet style, in the motel's Whispering Sands Restaurant, overlooking the leaf-strewn patio complete with deserted patio pool and patio bar. A wind chime, hanging from the bar's roof, danced like a possessed banshee, while beyond, somber in the onrushing dusk, the Atlantic Ocean railed against the New Jersey shore.

Calendar-wise it was spring. Weather-wise a stroll on the freeze-your-ass-off beach was an open invitation to pneumonia. It would be worse next week with the start of daylight savings, when longer evenings screamed out to work in the garden while the ground remained in permafrost.

Jim got himself a plate and went through the line, starting with a cup of clam chowder and loading up on potatoes, string beans with ham bits, meat loaf and gravy. He skipped the rolls and butter at the end, but even so, his plate looked like a small mountain.

That was the trouble with buffets.

No matter how much he told himself not to take too much, he took too much.

One thing he had to admit, if the rest of the meals were as good as this one—

"Are you some sort of group?"

He turned to see a woman around fifty years old.

"You mean Elderhostel or the bonsai class?"

"Elderhostel?"

Jim added a desert of rice pudding to his tray. "It's like a series of classes, learning events for senior citizens." He looked over to where five ten-person tables had been set aside, Dodee Swisher motioning him to join her. "We have two or three classes here, bonsai, which I'm taking, shore birds and ocean ecology I think is the second, and the third is," he waved a hand, "something else. But the price is extremely reasonable, even if you don't attend the classes."

"Like how reasonable?"

"The five days, including room and meals and classes is three hundred and twenty dollars."

Her eyebrows rose. "And how old do I have to be?"

"Fifty-five."

Her eyebrows rose again, but this time her lips turned down as well. "No, I have a number of years for that, but my husband could go. I'll have to tell him."

"But if he goes, you can go with him."

"Really? How can I find out about it?"

He looked down at his food, and across to where Dodee was motioning, and back to the woman. "I could leave the address at the front desk for you. What's your name?"

"That would be great." She set down her tray, pulled a card out of her pocketbook and gave it to him. "I'm holding you up from dinner. But thank you so much."

Jim made his way between the tables towards Dodee Swisher.

Why was she saving him a place?

Because he had carried her bags, or was she trying to seduce him? He heard about widows trying to do that to widowers. Except he didn't know if she was a widow.

He glanced at her face, vivid eyes and smooth skin, welcoming smile.

Oh yeah, right, seduce him; like he was living on Fantasy Island.

Which was just as well because even if, against all odds, she did, how was he supposed to act? More importantly, what was he to say if Dr. Jekyll turned into old Mr. Floppy?

He shouldn't have come on this damn trip.

Yeah, buddy!

He set his plates on the table, and gave the tray to the pear-shaped Billy Dack who happened to be walking by in his spotted waiter's jacket.

Barney, his nearly-bald almost-roommate, sat across from him, Aunt Alice sat on the other side of Dodee, and in between the two was a tall couple with ruddy complexions, as if they had just come in from a brisk walk on the freeze-your-ass-off beach, the Miettlinens who spoke with a European accent.

"You are taking bonsai also, *ja?*" asked the male half of the couple.

"Yes," Jim answered, spreading a linen napkin on his lap. "What are you taking?"

"Ve are not taking classes," said the female half, raising her chin, "Ve are teaching shore birds and ocean ecology. *Ja,* sure."

He took a forkful of potatoes.

Wow, too bad he wasn't in that class.

Ja, sure.

Dodee leaned close to him, herbal perfume pleasantly coloring the taste of his potatoes. "I thought," she whispered, "when things clear away, we might discuss our plan."

Nooo, it had nothing to do with sexual fantasies. The lady was still serious about digging up plants in the middle of the freeze-your-ass-off night.

Another couple from the bonsai class joined them, the portly man with the wide-track rear end, and his mousey wife. The man set down two plates on the table, both full, both his, one in front of the other, plus a salad, a piece of cake, and a bowl of rice pudding.

"Hi, my name's Clarence Harmony——" shiny round face

beamed with a big smile "—and this is my wife Winifred."
He jerked his thumb to the woman beside him. "We all
call her Winnie." Clarence waited for her to set a modest
plate of food on the table, then handed both trays to the
stubbly-faced Billy Dack and sat down. "I saw most of
you in the bonsai class today."

"Ve are the Miettlinens," said the female half of the
couple, in her European accent. "Ve are teaching shore
birds and ocean ecology."

"Wow, you guys must be pretty smart." He shoveled
meat loaf topped with gravied potatoes in his mouth. "I'm
just a garbage man, myself."

His wife Winnie let out an exasperated sigh. "He owns
it."

"You own the garbage?" The Miettlinen woman
frowned.

"I own the company. Thirty trucks." Another mound of
meat loaf and potatoes disappeared. "Maybe you seen my
trucks if you been to Philly? Harmony Refuse Collection."
His ruddy face lit up. "Our motto: Because Waste is a
Terrible Thing to Mind. Ya get it? Like I turned that other
saying around, like—"

"They get it, Clarence," his wife muttered through
clenched teeth.

"I'm Alice Atwater," the elderly woman said as the two
women in their forties joined them, filling up the ten-person
table. "And this is my niece, Dodee Swisher. We spent last
night in Philadelphia, on our way in from Kansas City."

"Are we into introductions?" asked the tall frosted-
blond, short hair cradling a face that seemed all mouth and
teeth. "I'm Kelly Massey. I saw you all in the bonsai class
this afternoon. Didn't John Okawa do a good job?"

"I am Vasantha Powell," said the dark-skinned woman
in a singsong voice. "I am originally from India, but I

married an American. It is easier to call me Sana, which indeed everyone does.''

The Miettlinens and the Harmonys reintroduced themselves.

"I've seen your trucks," Kelly Massey said. "We're from Philadelphia, too.''

"Lotta trucks, very busy," Clarence stuffed a forkful of potatoes in his mouth. "I wasn't coming here, too much to do, you know, let Winnie come by herself, but when she got her confirmation letter a couple of months ago, I thought—Hey, I never go anywhere and Winnie wants to go, so screw it. Let the kids take care of the business for a couple of days. They're gonna have to do it some day. Right?''

"My name is Dandy, James P.," Jim said.

"Hi, everybody," Lee Sullivan interrupted, coming up to rest an arm on Jim's shoulder. "Everyone happy with the food?" asked the Eurasian Elderhostel hostess. "Oh," she stared across the table, "you two are not with Elderhostel, are you?''

"No." The broad-shouldered Kelly gave her a toothy smile. "Sana and I are staying at the motel and registered independently for the bonsai classes.''

"Yes," Lee looked down at her list, "Kelly Massey and Vasantha Powell? I thought you looked too young to be Elderhostelers.''

"I wouldn't mind being one for a week. We're paying double what everyone else is.''

"One more thing," Lee Sullivan scanned the table. "I told you there would be workmen in your rooms to change the balcony door locks? The motel managed to postpone them until next week, so we won't have to worry about people coming in and out of our rooms all day. Those of you who are on the ocean side, isn't the view great?" Nods all around. "Well, everyone have a good week," she said, "and if there are any problems, let me know." The coordinator moved on to spread cheer at the next table.

"I'm General Bernard Sopwaite, U.S. Army retired," barked Jim's almost-roommate. "Barney is fine, no need to call me 'General.'" But the hard brown eyes and chiseled features gave the impression that he wouldn't object if they did. "Live in Pittsburgh." He nodded to Kelly Massey. "I think Mr. Okawa certainly did an acceptable job on the tree today, but I've seen some real bonsai masters in Japan, so I am not overly impressed."

"You have indeed studied in Japan?" the olive-skinned Sana Powell asked.

"No, not studied, but I visited many times and was stationed there twice, base commander the last time. There is a whole village north of Tokyo where they have nothing but bonsai nurseries. Place called Omiya."

"Is that right?" Clarence exchanged his first plate, now empty, with the full one he had set aside. "Winnie was in Japan, weren't you, Winnie? Yeah, she was over there on a garden club tour. Hey, maybe you guys were over there at the same time."

"No, I'm sure we weren't, Clarence," Winnie said.

Clarence held out his hand, a chunk of meat loaf stuck in the tines of his fork, "Well, you never know." He glanced over at Barney. "You said you've been there many times. For all you know you might have been standing one aisle away from each other at one of these bonsai places and never known it. Yeah, it would have been a big coincidence," he stuck the meat loaf in his mouth, "but it could've happened."

Barney's lips turned down and he wrinkled the brow that extended to the top of his head. "If you want coincidences, I remember once walking down the street in Manila and

coming the other way was my roommate at The Point,
that's West Point. He looked at me and I looked at him
and we both recognized each other, but we couldn't ac-
knowledge it because I was with my wife and he had a
Philippine floozy in each arm. Stopping to chitchat would
have stirred up a whole can of worms," Barney laughed,
"both of us being married, so there was just eye contact
and recognition and that was it. Heard he bought it in 'Nam.
Never saw him again."

"Your wife didn't come?" Alice Atwater asked.

"I lost her ten years ago."

"Oh, I'm sorry to hear that."

"I'm not. Last I heard she was traipsing around with a
man half her age in Louisiana."

"So, what do you do, Jim?" Clarence asked between
bites.

"I'm semi-retired." He set his knife and fork on his
empty plate. "I used to be a full-time physical therapist,
but I only work a couple of afternoons a week now. It
allows me to use all the exercise machines."

"Yeah? You look in great shape," Clarence nodded, rip-
pling all the chins on his fat neck. "Gotta start working out
one of these days myself. Played varsity football in high
school."

"Really?" Jim held out a hand. "I played varsity football in high school. A million years ago."

"Those were the days, wrapping an arm around someone's neck and wrestling 'em to the ground."

"Look!" Kelly Massey said in her husky voice, then bit
her lip. "Excuse me, but there's that other couple that was
in the class." The nattily dressed man in his sixties and the
twenty-something redhead sat down at a table one over.

"So," asked the female Miettlinen, "they are married?"

There was another embarrassed silence, then Kelly gave a small laugh. "Are we all wondering the same thing?"

"She's young enough to be his granddaughter," barked Barney, perhaps a bit too loud.

"They have the same last name on their tags," Alice Atwater said. "Perhaps she's his daughter, late in his life."

"I think they're married," Dodee said. "I saw them holding hands earlier."

"Um," Kelly nodded, "I wonder how much he's worth."

"I think that he is very probably well-off, indeed," Sana said in her British Raj, India accent. "If I am correct, they arrived in a red Mercedes sports car."

Winnie stood up and bent over her husband. "I want to go up to the room before the movie."

"Okay," he answered, scraping his second plate clean and placing his desert on top of it. He forked off a piece of cake, scanning the table as his wife excused herself. "There's a group taking in a flick tonight. *Ping Pong* with Clint Eastwoood and Mel Gibson. Anyone wanna go? Can give you a ride if you need it."

"Sounds good," Kelly said. "We'll think about it and let you know."

The Miettlinens—it turned out they were from Finland— declined. "Ve have to go over our teaching notes for to-morrow."

Alice Atwater also declined. The two-day drive from Kansas City had tired her out and she had a new book she wanted to get into.

"I already have plans," Dodee said. "I'll keep my Aunt company," and she gave Jim a surreptitious smile.

He looked across to Clarence Harmony, wanting to go, but wondering what time Dodee's plan was kicking in, and if he could get out of it. "I'll let you know."

"Well, if you decide, we're meeting in the lobby at seven-fifteen." Clarence hauled himself to his feet. "I'm gonna get some more rice pudding." He patted his big stomach. "I think there's still a little room in here."

At the end of dinner Dodee turned to Jim; only the two of them and Alice Atwater remained at the table now. "When do you want to do it? How about eight?" she rushed on. "Okawa said to do it in the middle of the night, but I think we can go around eight. What do you think?"

He shrugged.

"Did you bring any dark clothes? We should wear dark clothes."

"I have a black sweater, and dark blue corduroys."

"That should do it. I went out this afternoon and got some black ski masks." He blinked at her. "To put over our faces," she said. He blinked again. "So we won't be seen in the dark."

"What are you two talking about?" Aunt Alice put down her cup of tea and fingered the hearing aid in her ear.

"Those trees that we saw this afternoon," Dodee whispered.

"What's that?"

She looked right at her aunt. "The trees. From this afternoon."

"Oh, oh. Yes, yes." But it was obvious the old lady hadn't a clue what Dodee was talking about.

"The trees we saw that would make good bonsai. Remember?"

"Oh yes," Aunt Alice nodded, dawn finally coming up.

Dodee showed him two spoons she had slipped into her napkin, then hid them as the pear-shaped Billy Dack came by. "What do you think?"

"How big are these trees?"

"Hey," Billy said, piling the empty dishes on a tray, "I'm missing two spoons."

Jim glanced up at him, wondering how he could know he was missing two spoons, unless he had seen Dodee hide them.

"Ya know," came the man's nasal voice, Adam's apple bobbing up and down, "I could get in a lota trouble if anything's missing."

Dodee sighed and smiled. "I just wanted to borrow them for the night," she pleaded. "Can we do that? We have to do a little digging."

"Oh, boy." Worry lines on the stubbly face contrasted with the coolness in his little pig eyes. "I could get into big trouble, ya know what I mean?"

"He wants some money," Aunt Alice said in her overly loud voice.

"Shh," Billy whispered. "Maybe I could look the other way. But maybe I could help. How big a hole you gotta dig? There's a shovel in the pottin' shed. But, ah, I take a big chance going in there, you know."

"He wants some money," Aunt Alice said again.

"Shh," Billy repeated, glancing around, then nodded. "If you made it worth my while, sneaking it out of the room, you know."

"How much?" Jim asked.

"Ten dollars?" Jim turned to Dodee. "Hey," Billy continued, nasal voice grating, "it's not much, considering I could get fired. I even have to steal the key to get it."

She rubbed her chin and shrugged.

"Unless these things are tiny," Jim said, "two spoons won't be a lot of help."

"Right," Billy said, "the shovel is much better for digging than a couple of small spoons. How big a hole you gotta dig?"

"Okay," she nodded.

"Ten dollars," Jim looked up to the busboy. "When we get the shovel."

"Gotta be careful, nobody see me taking it outta the pottin' shed, ya know. How about an hour?"

"Eight o'clock," Dodee said. "By the front door."

"Ya got it." He finished piling the dishes on the tray as Dodee put the spoons on the table. "Nah, keep 'em. I'll be outside so no one will see." And he hurried on towards the kitchen.

Dodee held up the two spoons.

Aunt Alice nodded. "He wants money. He's a weasel. After telling me a cup of tea was a dollar this afternoon, when he brought it back he insisted he said two dollars. I gave it just to get rid of him."

Dodee put her hand on Jim's arm. "Can we use your car?"

"Sure."

She stood up, helping Aunt Alice to her feet. "I'll see you at eight then, in the lobby?"

"Eight o'clock in the lobby."

"And wear your dark clothes."

He watched her walk away.

Nice figure.

Probably from teaching aerobics.

He was glad she wasn't trying to seduce him. All she really wanted was to collect a couple of trees. It relieved a lot of anxiety.

But, looking at her body, the relief was sandwiched between disappointment.

SIX

DRESSED IN A black sweater and navy-blue pants, black shoes and socks, his camel hair car coat slung over his arm, Jim came down to the front desk at eight o'clock. It was empty.

The diminutive Indian, Sana Powell, and her friend, Kelly Massey, stood on the other side of the lobby, near the patio doors, listening with intent faces to a dark-haired man with his back to Jim. Kelly's broad figure towered over him. She glanced toward Jim, which the shorter man must have picked up, because he turned around.

"May I help you?"

"Do you work here?"

"I am Ramon Reed, the night manager," he said, coming across the lobby. He had dark eyes and eyebrows, black hair and mustache, and reminded Jim of a thinner Juan Valdez, the Colombian Coffee man. "What can I do for you?"

"A woman was asking me about Elderhostel." He showed Ramon the card she had given him, and the slip of paper on which he had written: Elderhostel, 75 Federal Street, Boston, MA 02110. "I told her I'd leave this address for her."

"I will put it in the lady's box," Ramon said, circling through a lobby door into an office to come back out a second door behind the registration desk. He stuck Jim's message in the room slot. "Is there anything else?"

"That's it, thanks. Hear anything about the weather?"

The night manager's lips turned down, dragging the Juan

Valdez mustache with it. "I think they say it will warm up toward the weekend."

"Just about the time I'll be leaving," he said, resigning himself to the fact that no warm front was moving in to help him out tonight. "Thanks again."

"No problem," the man answered, again circling through the rear office and heading back across the lobby to the two women.

Jim turned away to see Dodee Swisher striding towards him in a black sweater, her figure just as nice from the front as he had admired from the rear. She carried a navy-blue tote bag, a navy corduroy jacket over her arm, and a plastic bag.

"Hi," she whispered, sneaking him a peek at two ski masks in the plastic bag. "Suppose Billy's lurking around outside?"

"One way to find out." He held the door for her as a car drove into the parking lot.

"Hey, I got ya shovel," Billy's nasal voice called to them in a stage whisper from the shadows. "I had a heck of a time getting it."

Jim dug a ten-dollar bill out of his wallet. "Here's your—"

"It's suppose to be fifteen. Man, all the trouble I went through—"

"We said ten dollars."

"That's right," Dodee added, "ten dollars."

"Man," Billy threw his free hand in the air, "I can't take a chance on getting fired for ten dollars. Have some compassion here. And all the trouble I went through."

Jim shook his head. "We said ten dollars. Take it or leave—"

"How you gonna do any digging without a shovel?"

Billy held it up. "I had to steal a key to get it, and I gotta sneak it in when you get back. Fifteen bucks is cheap."

Dodee opened her bag and yanked out a five. "Here."

"Wait a minute." Jim held out his hands. "This guy is trying to con us—"

"We're drawing a crowd," she motioned to those getting out of the car. "Everyone will want to tag along."

"Yeah," Billy passed over the shovel, "ya gotta have some compassion here." He pocketed the money. "How big a hole ya gonna dig?"

"What should we do with the shovel when we get back?" Dodee asked.

"Just sneak it inside the conference room and I'll get it," he answered. "So, what are you gonna put in that hole? You gonna plant a body? Ha ha."

They left the pear-shaped busboy standing there, Jim carrying the shovel alongside his body, trying to keep it out of sight.

"What's going on?" Barney barked in his general's voice, unzipping his bomber jacket. "That man bothering you, Jim?"

"No," he said, "everything's fine."

"Just going out for a walk on the beach," Dodee said, staggering as she stepped into the brisk wind from the lee of the building. "What happened to the movie?"

"The marquee is screwed up," Clarence Harmony said. "*Ping Pong* doesn't start until Wednesday. *Stupid and Stupider* is playing and none of us wanted to see that."

"What's with the shovel, Jim?" Barney asked.

"We told you," Dodee answered, "we're going for a walk on the beach."

"Isn't it cold for that?" asked Winifred Harmony.

"Yeah, and the shovel—"

"We're going to dig a hole and sit in it," Jim said, starting for his car.

How did that sound?

It seemed to have them stumped for a moment, then fat Clarence called after him. "Well, I can see wanting to get out of the freezing wind, but you're crazy. Just to be alone?"

Jim's blue Lincoln was parked next to a red Mercedes 450 SL. He fit the shovel in the trunk, laid his and Dodee's jackets on the back seat, then held the passenger door for her.

"Why did you tell them that?" she asked, getting in.

"Tell them what?"

He slammed the door and walked around to climb behind the wheel.

"Why did you tell the them we were going to dig a hole on the beach?"

He shrugged. "Why did you tell them we were going for a walk on the beach?"

"Because I didn't want them tagging along while we're trying to sneak two trees from the side of the road."

He started the car. "Well, we had to tell them something."

"Makes it sound like an assignation. Are we going to get the trees or just sit here?"

"Are you going to tell me where to go, or do I just pick a direction and strike out?"

"I can do that. We have to go down to Seventy-fifth Street."

He put the Lincoln in gear and cruised out of the parking lot, turning right. "Why are you being so secretive about this?"

"I told you. I don't want a crowd around when we're digging them up. Someone will be sure to notice us. Besides, there're only two trees, and I'm wondering if they're as good as I remember.''

"When did you see them?"

"This morning. Aunt Alice and I spent the night in Philadelphia and arrived too early to check in, so we just drove around to see what was here.''

"Like getting the lay of the land.''

"We stopped over on the bay side to look at the water. Two cedar trees were growing in a grassy strip near the sea wall. They look like they've been cut over by a lawn mower for years. I just hope they're as nice as I remember. I thought at the time they looked like bonsai in the ground, but I didn't examine them that closely.''

"You didn't draw a sketch?"

"No, I didn't think of it at the time. I'd feel better if I had done a quickie.''

"I know I'd feel better.''

"What do you mean?"

"If I had a quickie,'' he smiled.

"Ah, but can your body keep pace with your fantasies?''

He glanced over at her.

If she had deliberately sought to poke a finger in a festering wound, she couldn't have picked a better target—

"Turn here, turn here!''

He swung the wheel over, snapping on the brakes, and barely made the corner, running over a low curb.

"What the hell! This isn't Seventy—''

"I remember we came out by that motel. Maybe it isn't Seventy-fifth Street.''

"You have any idea where we're going?"

"Yes. I think.'' An apology caressed the uncertainty in her voice. "I'm pretty sure it's straight up this street. And a block to the right at the water. Is that okay?''

"I guess.''

He gripped the wheel.

Why was he so angry all of a sudden?

They moved in and out of spots cast by overhead street lights, deserted summerhouses passing by on either side.

Oh yeah.

That little stab about his body keeping up with the fantasies.

Well, no man can really keep up with his fantasies.

They came to a stop at a T-intersection. A grass strip separated the street from a seawall on the other side, water reflecting off the headlights.

"Take a right here," Dodee said. "I think."

"You think?" He took the corner.

"I'm pretty sure. It looks different at night."

He continued on for three blocks.

"I don't think it was this way—no, there!"

He jammed on his brakes.

"Go on, go on," she said.

He sped on. "I thought you said it was—"

"It is, but we better case the place for the cops."

He glanced over to her. "This is not breaking and entering, you know."

She swung towards him. "You heard what Okawa said. We can get arrested for digging up trees along the side of the road without permission."

"Then why don't we just ask for permission?"

She shook her head. "We only have until Friday. Besides, I've always found it's easier to apologize than to get permission."

"But these are not trees." He saw her point to a side street and he turned down it. "I mean like planted trees. Aren't these some scruffy, half grown—"

"Yes, but the law is still the law."

"I think you're making a mountain out of a mole hill."

"Yeah, well, suppose they decided to confiscate your car?"

"They can't confiscate my car." He took another corner, heading back the way they had come.

She shrugged in the glow of the dash. "They do for drug busts. Anyway, it doesn't hurt to check."

They circled back past the spot. She seemed to be taking it light-heartedly. Like it was a big adventure. Why not? It wasn't her Lincoln.

"We can stop now," she said.

"No, I'm moving around the corner. I don't want anyone to see my car."

"Right." She nodded. "Good thinking. If the cops see a car they'll be suspicious right off."

"No, well, yeah, that too," he pulled over to a dark spot at the curb, "but if we're caught, we walked down here from the motel."

"What do you mean?" she half turned towards him.

"I don't want my car confiscated."

"For this," she held out a hand. "I don't think—"

"You want to get these trees?"

"Hello? Isn't that why we came?"

"Then I'm not taking any chances with my car. If the police come, we walked down here."

She shrugged. "Okay, we walked." She pulled the two ski masks out of her pocket, handing one over. "Put it on."

"Oh yeah, the police will get suspicious of a car at the curb, but we'll blend right in with these over our faces."

"That's not the point. If a casual pair of headlights come by, we freeze. Without anything to reflect the light, they drive right on by."

"Where do you come up with this stuff?"

"God, don't you ever watch the movies?" She slipped the mask over her head. "How's that?"

"It's crooked." He straightened it out so it centered over her eyes. Then he slipped his on. "Okay?"

"Wait." She straightened his out, then tweaked his nose. "We make a hell of a pair of cat burglars."

She grabbed the plastic bags and he grabbed the shovel. "What about our jackets?"

"We won't be that long," she shook her head, "and we'll be digging."

He locked the car and they stole down to Bay Side Drive, slipping across and creeping along the concrete sea wall.

"If anyone comes," he whispered, "we'll just jump over the side."

"Take a look."

He glanced down into the darkness. "I can't see anything."

She pulled a penlight out of her pocket and shined it on the other side of the wall.

Water.

Looked deep.

And cold.

They should have brought the jackets.

She led the way to a spot in the middle of the ten-foot grassy strip separating the curb and the seawall. Trouble was, the trees, about five feet apart, were centered in an overhead lamp's circle of light.

He recognized them as junipers, what most people called red cedars. Not only had they been repeatedly run over by lawn mowers, as she said, but there were also bicycle ruts on the curb side, limiting the growth of the two-inch trunks to branches snaking along the lawn surface towards the bay.

"You see," enthusiasm in her voice. "Look at the trunks. Isn't that what Okawa said to look for?"

He nodded. "They look wind-swept, like at the beach."

"Right, that's what I thought."

But digging in the glow of the streetlight left them sitting ducks for anyone who happened by.

"Well, we taking them?"

He checked the neighborhood, saw no signs of life, then jammed the shovel into the ground.

Sonofabitch.

Like concrete.

Great, just great.

They could be here until morning.

Morning turned out to be an exaggeration, but it was midnight, cold and freezing, he digging with the shovel, she fine-tuning around the roots with a spoon, exchanging a few choice words in the process, before they had both plants lifted out of the ground. He hurriedly filled the holes with some soil that had built up around the seawall while she wrapped the roots in plastic bags.

"Look," she held one of them up to the light for him, using the dark bay for a back drop. "Now wasn't it all worth it?" she asked, blue lips quivering from the cold. "In a pot, won't this look a like a wind-swept tree? Like on a California coast."

"Right now I'm too cold and tired to care. I just want to go home and go to bed."

He saw her face drop and regretted not showing more enthusiasm, but then he became aware of a new light source.

As if being spotlighted on a stage.

And watched Dodee's eyes, looking over his shoulder, grow wide.

"Police! Hold it!" a voice barked in the wind.

Oh great, just great.

SEVEN

THEY WERE IN the second of two rooms that made up the police station on 130th Street, one behind the other, with rest rooms in a connecting hallway to two, side-by-side jail cells out back.

Jim wondered if they ever had the need for more than two cells in Bolder Harbor where, "despite our name, the only boldness is in our vision and violence is unknown." Then he remembered the now semi-ghost town was probably hopping in the summer. They might even have an occasion to call the state police to cart off an overload of teenagers. And there was also the unsolved murder of the computer nerd, Bixby Boyd, that the desk clerk told him had happened four months ago.

But as for right now, only two major criminals had been apprehended, and the arresting officer, Sonny Raines by a plastic name tag, a six-foot-three, big-chested shit-for-brains, acted like nothing less than the electric chair would suffice as punishment to fit the crime. The boyish face and crew-cut made him look fifteen, but he had to be at least twenty-one to be carrying the cannon strapped to his waist.

Jim glanced at the other criminal. She sat in a metal chair, one hand cuffed to its back, beside a metal desk on which rested one of the junipers they had dug up, roots in a plastic bag. Dodee's cornflower eyes hung at half mast, wheaten hair mussed up from pulling off the ski mask.

Did he look any better? He combed his silver-gray hair with the fingers of his free hand, the other cuffed to his chair, beside another desk, the second tree on top.

Cork bulletin boards hung on white painted walls, smothered with papers, too far away to read. A calendar hung next to one, a picture on it of colorful April flowers; the real thing would be frozen stiff outside. A digital desk clock told him it was twelve-forty-five.

The front door swung open with a bang and an African-American woman with no makeup and a wild mop of curly black hair, came striding in, straight through the front room to stop in the doorway of the second.

She was wearing jeans, blue shirt under a short jean jacket, and a hand bag slung over one shoulder. About five-seven, narrow waist, comfortable hips and ample breasts, she had dark eyes in a milk chocolate face which fixed immediately on Jim, as if she could peer into his skull and fry his brains, before shifting onto Dodee.

"Okay, Sonny, what we got here?"

Her voice was high pitched, like that of a little girl. It was hard to figure her age, but Jim put it at mid-thirties.

"Two burglars," said the crew-cut shit-for-brains, bouncing to his feet and straightening his tan uniform. "I caught them casing some houses down on Bay Side Drive."

Jim shook his head. "We weren't casing—"

"Hey," the woman pointed a finger at him like a gun, "I'll get to you later, thank you very much."

"Yup," Sonny continued, "they were dressed up in black ski masks, didn't think I could see them, but I threw on my spot and had them fixed in my sights." He crouched and threw both his hands straight out, clamping them together. "Had they gone for a gun they'd be dead meat now."

"They had guns?"

The lips turned down in the boyish face, the hands

dropped to his side. "Well, he didn't. And not her either, far as I could see."

"Uh-huh." She walked around the desk beside Dodee, *Detective Belinda Smith* on a nameplate, and blinked at the dug-up juniper. "What's this?"

"Evidence."

"Of what?"

"Of them out there casing the houses."

Dodee twisted in her chair. "Could I explain—"

Belinda Smith held up the palm of her hand, glanced over to Jim, and then back to the cop. "This is evidence of their intent to burglarize a house?"

"Right. Mr. Diggs saw them from his bedroom window."

The woman's eyes rolled towards the ceiling. "Diggs."

"Right. They were trying to smooth out the holes when I got there, but you can see exactly where they came from."

"Holes?" She looked across to the second juniper. "Did they have any tools?"

"Yup, you bet."

"Well," she asked, teeth clenched, "what did they have?"

"He had a shovel and she had two spoons." The crew-cut baby-face nodded. "Probably going to use it to pry open a door. That's what Mr. Diggs said."

The woman rolled her eyes to the ceiling again. "Diggs."

"Yup, he came out after I had them cuffed."

"Did they say what they were doing?"

"Yup."

She waited a long moment, then the eyes rolled up one more time. "Well," the agitation in her little girl voice increasing exponentially, "how about sharing that with me, Sonny?"

"Oh, they said they were digging up these bushes."

She scratched her head through the mop of curly black hair and sat down behind the desk. "Okay, let me get their statements. Any coffee?"

"I'll make some, Belinda," Sonny said, heading into the front room.

She turned to Dodee, pursed her lips, pressing them tightly together so it dimpled her chin, then shifted to Jim.

"Okay," she said, "your turn."

"We weren't casing any houses," he said.

"We were just digging up some trees for bonsai," added Dodee.

"You mean banzai trees?"

"No," he shook his head, "it's pronounced...well, I guess you could call them banzai trees if you want."

Belinda picked up the ski mask and twirled it around her finger. "Why these? And why in the middle of the night?"

Jim peeked across at Dodee.

"I suppose it's my fault," she sighed, raising her free hand and letting it drop. "I got into town early—"

"What do you mean, early?"

"For the Elderhostel," she said.

"We're staying at the Windswept Dunes Motel," Jim added.

"We're taking the bonsai course."

Belinda shook her head. "Just tell me what you were doing out on the side of the road, in the middle of the night, dressed in black and wearing ski masks."

Dodee leaned forward, putting a hand on the desk. "The bonsai master, Mr. Okawa, said it was unlawful to take trees from the side of the road without getting permission. But we're here only until Friday—"

"The Elderhostel class ends then," Jim said.

"So I figured we would just slip over—"

"And dig up these two plants," Belinda pointed a finger at one and thumb at the other, "and no one would be the wiser?"

Dodee smiled and held up her hand.

"And we smoothed out the holes to keep the grass strip neat and clean," Jim said. "So as not to damage a lawn mower," he added as an afterthought.

"But you didn't figure on Mr. Diggs looking out the window. Now look at all the trouble you caused."

"She said," Jim nodded at Dodee, "it's easier to apologize than get permission. I told her—"

"Is he your husband?"

Dodee blinked. "No, of course not. We only met today."

Now Belinda blinked, and studied him anew. "And you just went along with this lady, ski mask and all, and broke the law? Someone you only met today?"

He could feel his face flushing and shrugged.

Belinda swung around in her chair to face him squarely. "You know," she whispered, making a big show of looking out to the next room, "I got this great investment you might be interested in. It's a bridge for sale, in Brooklyn." She called out to the other room. "Sonny, get me the number of the Windswept Dunes Motel." She swung back to Dodee. "I'm Detective Smith, and you are?"

"Dodee Swisher."

She wrote it down on a yellow pad. "And he is?"

"He's Jim Dandy," Dodee said.

Belinda's eyes went round as she stared at him.

"James P. Dandy is my name."

Belinda paused for a moment before writing it down, and then glanced back up at him. "This is no shit? Your name is Jim Dandy?"

He grit his teeth. "James P."

She smiled.

"I got the number," Sonny said from the doorway, holding an open phone book.

"Hey, Sonny, does this guy look Jim Dandy to you?"

"No, he looks rotten. He looks like a dirty rotten burglar that needs—"

"Okay, okay. It was a joke." She picked up the phone. "Give me the number." She punched it in as he read it out and listened for a bit. "Hi, this is Detective Belinda Smith with the Bolder Harbor police. You want to see if you have a Dodee Swisher and a Jim Dandy registered there?" She listened again. "A James P. Dandy? And you say they're with the Elderhostel group? Uh-huh. Are they taking the banzai class? Uh-huh. Well, could you tell me if there even is a banzai class? Knowhatamean?" She put her hand over the receiver, black eyes shifting to him. "No Jim Dandy registered, just a James P."

"Is that what you meant?" Sonny asked, eyes squinting towards him. "Is your name really—"

"James P. Dandy," he snapped.

"Hello," Belinda spoke into the phone. "One of the classes is banzai. Thank you, you helped clear up the crime of the year." She hung up. "Take the cuffs off them, Sonny. They weren't casing anything. They were just digging up these dumb trees." She nodded to Dodee. "I hope this taught you a lesson."

"Yes, it did," Dodee rubbed her freed wrist. "Maybe it is easier to get permission than to apologize."

"I should charge both of you, but—you're leaving Friday?" Jim nodded. Belinda Smith nodded in return. "I figure Sonny put you through enough stuff already. Go on."

"Can we take the trees?" Dodee asked.

"Yeah, yeah, get 'em outta here."

"And can we get a ride back?"

Belinda lowered her head and looked at Dodee through her eyebrows.

"That's okay," Jim held up his hand. "We can walk. It's not far. Nice night for it, really."

"Hey," the detective stopped them as they reached the door, her dark eyes glaring out of her chocolate face. "I'm going back home to bed. I don't want to hear about you guys again. Don't want to be woken up anymore and dragged out in the middle of the night. Knowhatamean?"

EIGHT

"OH, WE CAN WALK." Dodee's voice dripped with sarcasm.

A stiff wind blew off the beach, riffling her wheaten hair, looking darker in the street light.

"Nice night for it, really." Her lips quivered.

They lumbered along Ocean Drive, she laden with one of the trees, the sleeves of her sweater pulled down to cover her hands. He struggled with the second in one arm and the shovel in the other, resting it on his shoulder like a rifle. He felt like tossing the shovel rather then carrying it back to the conference room, still riled over being conned out of an extra five bucks, but he didn't want to be responsible for Billy losing his job over it, either.

"We don't have that far to go," he said.

"Do you know what street this is?"

He looked up at the signpost as they crossed it.

"One hundred and twenty fifth."

"And we have to go to—"

"Whose idea was it to go dig up the trees? Who didn't want to bring our jackets? Who was it who said it's easier to apologize than to get—"

"All right, all right. I'm sorry. I'm just cold and tired and my back and shoulders hurt."

"Here, let me take the other tree and you can carry the shovel." He made the exchange. "You should have told me it was too heavy for you." But after lugging them both a few steps he wasn't so sure he had made the right move.

"It wasn't too heavy, I just have a back that gives me problems, especially when it's cold."

"I'll massage it for you when we get back."

She turned and gave him a acid look.

He shook his head. "Strictly professional."

"Professional?"

"I told you, I'm a physical therapist. Only part-time now. I'm also a licensed personal weight trainer."

"That explains it."

He glanced sideways at her. "Explain's what?"

"You're in great shape. You must work out a lot. You into sports?"

"Not much now. Played some varsity football in high school, and some in the army. I bowl once a week."

She gave a little shiver. "I wish I'd kept quiet when you wanted to bring the coats."

He opened his mouth to agree, thought better of it, and brought the words back in.

They crossed another street, a dandelion, against all odds, growing in the shelter of the curb.

"I'm getting a week's worth of daily exercise-walking all in one evening." She gazed up at him. "So how come you're here alone? You are alone?"

"Yeah. My uncle was supposed to come with me, in fact I was supposed to bring him, but he canceled out."

"You're not married?"

"My wife died two years ago."

"Oh, I'm sorry to hear that."

He shrugged.

"Was it a long illness?"

"Yeah."

He shifted the weight of the trees in his hands.

For him it was long, but for Penny the year must have

been an eternity. Not only the pain, but the uncertainty, and in the end, just wanting to get it over.

Tough year.

Relief when it was over. Then guilt at the relief.

Yeah, he would say it was long.

"You brought your aunt. Family at home?"

"You don't bring Aunt Alice anywhere. She brought me. I have two daughters, if you're asking. Wendy, who's married to a pediatrician—"

"Ah, my daughter the doctor's wife."

"Uh-huh. And Alison, named after Aunt Alice, who is still single, has her own apartment. She works with me at the gallery. Allows me to get away."

"And what about your..." he hesitated, wondering if he had stepped into something if she wasn't married.

"My husband abandoned us twenty years ago." She looked up at him. "He was an alcoholic."

"I thought once you're an alcoholic you're always an alcoholic?"

"He's dead. About six years ago, now." She moved closer to him. "I know this is insensitive of me, but could I walk on the other side and let you block the wind for a bit?"

"Yeah, go ahead. You're not blocking a whole lot down there anyway."

"I'm not that short." She moved into his lee. "I supposed I loved him at first. Been so long now I can't remember. I know I was sad to hear he died."

"So you brought the girls up alone."

"Um. A struggle at times, but we managed. You have children?"

"Three. Paul, still single at thirty-five, owns a bowling alley. Cecily—we call her Ceecee, thirty, a computer programmer married to another programmer. And David, twenty-eight, a concrete contractor, married to a lovely woman, Liz, one child, Courtney my granddaughter, and another on the way.''

''I'm waiting for a grandchild. It must be nice.''

''Yeah, she's kind of fun to be around, and then she goes home.''

''How come your uncle canceled out?''

''Well, he died. Massive heart attack. Boom, he was gone.''

''Wow.''

''Nice way to go, but hard on those you leave behind.''

They walked on in silence for a block, the damn trees getting heavier by the step. He wished the hell he had stayed home and gone to bed.

''So you're into bonsai?'' she said.

''You sure ask a lot of questions,'' he smiled.

''I'm trying to get my mind off the cold.''

''Mainly I came because I let Ceecee goad me into it, and she got my boys in on the act. Get out and meet people they said. I'd have a really good time, they said. Yeah, right.''

''At least you got to meet some people.''

''Uh-huh. You mean, Officer Sonny and Detective Belinda Smith. Oh yeah.'' He looked at her. ''Of course, then there's you.''

''Then there's me.''

''Taking me out in the middle of the night, getting us arrested, and having to walk home in the freezing cold.'' He grinned down at her. ''Man, I'm having so much fun I could just shit.''

Dodee laughed. ''Me, too.''

When they finally got back to the Windswept Dunes Motel a dark-complexioned woman, vacuuming the rug in the lobby, jumped at the sight of them, like she had been shot.

"What's wrong?" Dodee asked.

The woman shook her head. "A man has been bothering me." She was thin, no more than five feet, with wide eyes reminiscent of the "little waif" pictures popular in the seventies or eighties.

Dodee must have seen something in them because she immediately leaned the shovel against a couch and went to her. "Do you want us to call the police?"

She shook her head again. "He works at the motel. It will be very bad if I call the police."

"Look, my name is Dodee Swisher, and your name?"

"Consuelo. I work mostly nights."

"Well, Consuelo, you can't let this man harass you just because you're working here. We have laws against that."

Jim rested the trees on the back of the couch and scanned the tomb-like lobby. "What about the night manager?"

"Ramon, he is eating. I have already told him."

"And he did nothing?" Dodee asked.

"Are you married?" Jim said. "How about your husband?"

"*No,*" Consuelo's dark eyes opened wide. "My husband would kill him. And me, too."

"You want us to talk to the day manager?" Dodee asked.

"No, it will be all right. I was just frightened when you came. With the cleaner running I didn't hear you. Please, I must get back to work."

Dodee held the woman's arm for a moment. "Okay, Consuelo, but if you have any problems, come and get me, okay? I'm in room two-twelve. Promise you'll call if he bothers you?"

She nodded, and added a wan smile that went with her big waif-like eyes before she turned away.

Jim picked up the trees and Dodee the shovel, and in the

silence of late night, they headed down the glassed-in walk-way toward the conference room.

"I'm worried about her," she whispered.

"I gathered."

"You shouldn't have mentioned her husband."

He blinked at her. "Why not?"

"Because you don't bring your husband into your business. He could get her fired. You saw how frightened she got."

"She was frightened because she thought the guy would charge in here and kill someone. Maybe he has a violent temper."

"Think we should call the police?"

"Not if she doesn't want you to," he answered, wondering what would happen if they hauled Detective Belinda Smith out of her bed again. "I'm sure the night manager is not going to let anything happen to her."

"Well, apparently he didn't do anything when she told him." Dodee tried the conference room door. "It's locked."

"Just lean the shovel against it," he said.

"But we promised to put it inside."

"We didn't promise."

"Let me get the key from Consuelo."

He propped the plants up against the wall, only to have her come back a few seconds later. "I can't find her."

"Leave the damn thing against the door."

"All right. Here, let me take one of the trees."

He did not resist; by this time each one weighed twenty tons. They took the elevator and carried them to his room, sticking them on the floor by the sliding glass door, a moon smile visible over the balcony railing, a muffled roar of the surf coming through as background music.

She stared at the plants. "I wonder if it would be better to put them out on the balcony."

"Screw it. We can think about that in the morning."

Suddenly she started rummaging through her pockets. "Oh shit. I mean, damn."

"What's the matter?"

The cornflower eyes leveled with his. "I left the key to my room in my purse."

He blinked. "Which is back—"

"In your car."

He shrugged. "You'll have to wake up your aunt."

"She'll never hear me knock."

"Call on the phone."

"Without her hearing aid she wouldn't hear a bomb."

Jim took a deep breath and let it out, then spread out his hands. "Well, there are two beds."

She frowned and folded her arms, shook her head, then sighed. "I need a hot shower. I promised myself twenty blocks ago, if I could just hang on, I'd take a hot shower."

"Take one here. Go ahead. I'll wait and take mine when you're finished."

She stared at him, mind churning away behind the blue eyes. "Do you happen to have an extra pair of PJs?"

"As a matter of fact, I do. Summer and winter. You can have the winter ones, but they're going to wrap around you a couple of times."

"It's better than the alternative, isn't it?"

NINE

HE HOPPED IN for a quick shower, Dodee leaving him a steamy bathroom, and came out in his summer pajamas to see her standing between the beds in his winter ones, one hand holding up the bottoms, the other stretching high over her head, a grimace on her face.

"Want me to massage that?"

"No, you're tired—"

"Lie down. Over here." He patted the nearest bed as he walked around the foot of it.

"I don't want to make you—"

"Lie down."

She stretched out on the bed. He patted the side of her butt. "Move over a bit." She scooted over. He sat beside her and started working on the infraspinous and trapezius muscles of her back, softly at first, until he felt them yielding, then more deeply.

"Ohh, that feels good," she moaned. "You have strong fingers."

"The better to see you with my dear, said the bad old wolf." Her muscles felt well-toned under his hands. "You do any other exercises beside teaching aerobics?"

"I'm in a Heartwell program."

"Ah, that explains it. Aerobics will burn off fat, but to firm up the muscles you need strength training, like you get in Heartwell."

"Do I take that as a compliment?"

"Well, you heard the cliché, use it or lose it."

He labored on the deltoids of her shoulders, then moved on to massage the back of her neck.

"Ohh," she groaned again, "I'd kill for this."

He worked his thumbs deep into the muscles, accompanied by her grunts and groans, then gave her a pat on the rump. "Flop over."

She did and he moved to the other side of the bed, taking her arm and stretching it out. The pajama top skooched up, showing her midriff from below her navel up to the round curve of her breasts. He worked the front of the deltoid and the pectoral muscles, the upper part of her shoulder and chest, letting her arm rest in his lap.

What he hadn't counted on was the smoothness of her hand against the bare skin of his leg, giving him a hell of an erection. And it didn't help when she started moving it back and forth, like sending molten hot bullets shooting up to explode in his brain.

Sonofabitch!

His pajamas were probably popping out a mile and a half.

Oh yeah, talk about bragging.

He worked down the pectoral muscle to feel the soft beginnings of her breast under his hand, and wondered if there was sweat on his brow.

How the hell was he going to stand when he finished?

What he needed was to think of something cool.

Like a waterfall.

Or the muted rumble of the waves drifting up from the beach.

Trouble was, the smooth hand caressing his thigh was like a pulsating volcano that kept throbbing through his mental images.

She reached up with her free hand to smooth back his hair.

"Jim."

He looked into her deep blue eyes and swallowed hard.

"I think..." she hesitated, voice husky. "Have we gone beyond physical therapy?"

"I'm sorry—"

"Don't be sorry."

She looped her arm around his neck, pulled him to her, and he kissed her.

A sweet taste, like toothpaste, added to the soft lips and warm tongue, intermingling with the clean smell of soap to send blood boiling to his groin. But now the niggling dark fear that lurked deep down in a musty corner of his psyche exploded full-blown in his brain.

Here he was, with Dodee, against all the odds, but would his body follow through on the contract? Or leave him in embarrassed defeat?

He broke the kiss.

"Maybe we shouldn't be doing this."

She stiffened, her lips tightening. "Well, now I guess I'm sorry. I didn't mean to—"

"No, no!" He took a deep breath and let it out. How could he explain when he wouldn't even tell his own doctor? But if he didn't, it would be like slapping her in the face. But he didn't know her well enough—

"Dodee, I'm worried about me."

"Oh?"

"It's been over three years since..."

"Oh."

He took another deep breath.

The cornflower eyes softened, the lips relaxed, then the hand caressing his leg moved up to linger under the shorts of his PJs.

"Did you ever ride a bike, James?"

"But it's been over—"

"Did you ever ride a bike, James P?"

"Yeah, but—"

"Turn off the light."

He hesitated, then did as he was told.

"Here," her voice hardly louder than the tumbling surf outside, and in the semi-darkness handed him back his winter PJs. He dropped them on the second bed, along with his summer ones, and slipped in beside her, the sheets smooth and crisp, but like sandpaper compared to the silkiness of her body.

And they went bike riding.

Over hills and dales, racing through the flowers, kicking up multicolored leaves in their path, and charging, wind-in-the-hair, down a steep hill, shrieking with pleasure to collapse like giggling children, exhausted and gasping, in a shady grove.

He felt her breath in his ear, the tip of her tongue caressing the rim.

"I had a premonition about this," she whispered, her hands curling around his shoulders. "I get these feelings sometimes. When I first saw you I felt like we were two dive bombers on a collision course, but I didn't know if we would be fighting like enemies or—what would you call this?"

"Friendly fire?"

"Uh-huh," she laughed, "very friendly fire. I couldn't figure any diversionary tactics."

"I'm sorry."

"No, don't be sorry. I don't think I tried all that hard." She pushed his head up and gave him a kiss. "It might sound wanton, but it's been a long time. This was the best thing that's happened to me in a long, long, long-long time. Thank you."

"Nope," he kissed her back. "Thank you. You lifted a

ten-ton fear off my back. You showed me, well, I could still ride a bike.''

"And very well, I might add." She pulled his head down next to hers. "Of course," she walked her hands down his back to make circles on his rear, "we might want to practice some more. What did you say? Use it or lose it? We might want to practice just so you're sure you have the hang of it."

"Practice would be nice."

SHE LEFT AS the first thin sliver of light showed on the horizon.

"Where are you going?"

"I don't want the world to know I slept over." She slipped out of bed and climbed into her clothes. "I figured out I could get an extra room key at the desk."

He watched with the interest of an unrepentant voyeur. "Glad you didn't figure that out last night."

Then she kissed him and was gone, the door clicking behind her.

They hadn't practiced like she said.

Pissed him off.

Then he laughed.

Last night he was afraid to do it, now he was afraid he wouldn't get to do it again.

He got up and went to the bathroom, coming out as someone banged on the door. He grabbed his pants, jerking them on, and peeked outside.

"Come with me," Dodee whispered. "Something terrible's happened."

"Let me get dressed—"

"No, come now."

But he pulled on a T-shirt and snatched a pair of loafers, slipping them on one at a time as he followed her down

the hall. They ran into Winifred Harmony coming around
the corner from the cross wing.

"Oh, you scared me," she said.

"Everything okay?" Jim asked.

"Insomnia. I didn't want to keep Clarence up."

"Excuse us, Winnie," Dodee said, "Come on," and
pulled Jim towards the stairs, double-timing them one flight
down and along the hall to the exhibition room, stopping
at the door and looking back at him.

"I was heading for the front desk and as I came by I
saw the shovel was still here and the door was like,
cracked." She gasped for breath like she had just run a
twenty-mile marathon. "I thought I'd put it inside, you
know, like Billy told us."

"So?"

"So take a look."

She swung opened the door and he stepped in.

The lights were on.

Billy was there.

Prone on the floor.

His pig eyes stared into eternity, mouth agape as if cut
off in mid-surprise. A rough circle of rust stained the carpet
underneath him.

And, oh yes, sticking in his chest, like an arrow shot into
a bull's-eye, dirt scattered all about, clay pot off to the side,
was the spear point of Okawa's bare wood bonsai, rammed
up to the hilt of the first wired branch.

Wow, just because the guy hadn't returned a shovel?

He looked over to Dodee, hanging back by the door, both
hands covering her mouth.

"You okay?"

She nodded, but her face had lost all color, and he realized he wasn't feeling so spiffy himself. The shovel
leaned against the wall beside her.

"What should we do?" she asked.

"We call the police."

"But what about the shovel?"

"What about it?"

"Won't that implicate us?"

"I don't know. But we're calling the police."

"Maybe we should think about it."

"We're calling the police."

"But the shovel—"

"Screw the shovel," he took her by the hand, wondering if she were in a state of shock, and led her out of the room, shutting the light and closing the door.

"Maybe we should get rid of the shovel?"

"No. We don't tamper with anything. We call the police. Fooling around could get us in deep shit."

He glanced down to the pay phone by the elevator, but hustled her on to the front desk and banged on it. Nothing.

Dodee glanced around the tomb-silent lobby. "Where is everyone?"

A shadow slipped across the office behind the desk.

"Hello, back there." Still nothing, so he ran around the counter, yanking open the office door.

"Aaah," Tiffany Crew jumped back. "I was looking for a room key." Her twenty-something body was encased in a Spandex running suit. "I forgot mine when I went jogging and I didn't want to wake up the world to get in."

Jim reached past her, finger-tipped a hold on the phone, and punched in 911.

THE FIRST RAYS of sunlight sent a horizonal beam through the patio doors, across the lobby, and out the front doors onto the parking lot, where a police car pulled in. An unmarked car followed. Tiffany Crew had long departed for her room, apparently deciding to wake up the world after all. Jim had managed to add a shirt and socks to his apparel. Dodee had put on a new face. She stood next to him now as they watched the tall, blond Sonny Raines, in a tan police uniform, get out of the tan police car. The detective, Belinda Smith, climbed out of the other. She was dressed in the same jeans and jean jacket as the night before, but had swapped the blue shirt for a yellow one. She slung her handbag over her shoulder as she came through the door. She did not look happy.

"You two." Her little girl voice did not quite pull off the exclamation. "I thought I told you I didn't want to be dragged out of bed in the middle of the night again?"

Jim motioned towards the sun. "It's light out."

"It's still the middle of my night."

As if hearing the conversation, the swarthy-complexioned night manager, Ramon Reed, came out of the back door of the restaurant and strode up to them. "Is there something wrong?"

"We got a call about a homicide here," Sonny said, adjusting the belt holding his gun and handcuffs.

"Where did you hear that?" Ramon asked.

"I called them," Jim answered. "There's a dead man in the conference room. We think he's been murdered."

"You didn't tell me," said the Juan Valdez look-alike.

"I couldn't find you."

"I was making coffee."

"I could use some coffee," Dodee said.

"It is not ready yet."

"Hey, I hate to interrupt this chitchat," Belinda held out her hands, "but I'd like to see the body, knowwhatamean?"

"It's down here," Jim led the way down the glassed-in corridor.

"You say you think he's been murdered?" Ramon asked.

Jim entered the conference room, turned on the light, and stepped aside. Dodee followed, standing next to him, then the tall Sonny, and Ramon, and finally Belinda, squeezed between them and advanced a couple of steps.

"Well, hooolyyy shit." She turned her chocolate face to Jim. "And you say you *think* he's been murdered?" Belinda nodded. "Right off I'd say that's a pretty damn good guess."

"That's Billy," Ramon said.

"You know him?" asked the detective.

"Billy Dack, he works here. Afternoon and evenings. I don't know why he'd still be here."

"Maybe because he can't get up and go home? Kinda hard to do that when you're pinned to the floor with a—what is that?"

"A bonsai tree," Dodee answered.

"A banzai tree? Say, weren't you two—"

"Yes," Jim nodded, "but we had nothing to do with this. Our trees are upstairs."

"Mr. Okawa owns this tree," Dodee added. "He's the bonsai master."

"We told you about him last night—"

"Wait a minute, wait just a damn minute." Belinda strode over to stand directly above the body, gazing down on it. "Wow, I bet this is the first time someone's been banzaied to death." She leaned over and looked more closely. "Somebody really wanted to put a hurt on this guy." She straightened up and turned towards them, putting her hands on her hips, pressing her lips tightly together, dimpling her chin, then nodded towards Dodee. "Is that your shovel?"

Jim turned to see it lying on the floor beside Dodee.

"Yeah, the hotel's, but we left it leaning outside the door last night."

"It was locked and we couldn't get in," Dodee added.

"Uh-huh." Belinda pressed her lips together again and nodded. "And who found the body?"

"I did," Dodee answered.

"And what were you doing down here so early in the morning?"

Dodee glanced at Jim before going back to the detective. Jim wanted to jump in with something helpful, but Dodee went on before he had a chance.

"I came down here to see if I could get an extra key to my room at the desk. I was locked out and my aunt is completely deaf without her hearing aid."

"What happened to your key?"

"We left it in my car," Jim said, "back where we were digging."

"Uh-huh."

"And when I came by here, I saw the door was cracked, so I decided to put the shovel inside."

"Why?"

"Because we had promised Billy to leave it inside."

"Uh-huh," Belinda folded her arms under her ample breasts. "And if you couldn't get into your room, where did you spend the night?"

Dodee turned to him.

"I have two beds in my room," Jim said.

"Uh-huh. How come you just didn't get a spare last night?"

"There was no one at the front desk."

"Uh-huh." Belinda turned to the night manager. "And where were you?"

"Me?" The Juan Valdez look-alike shrugged. "I was making coffee."

"All night long?"

"No, no, just this morning. Last night," the ends of Ramon's lips turned down, dragging the thick mustache with them, "I must have been in the bathroom. Or eating dinner."

"How long you been here?"

"Since eight last night. I work four ten-hour days. I'm due to get off."

Belinda pursed her lips and glared down at the body. "Sonny, what about getting on the horn and seeing if we can get the state crime lab in here."

"I think that's a good idea," Sonny answered.

"No, Sonny, I don't want your opinion, thank you very much, I want you to do it. And when you get back put a guard on this door."

"Oh, right. You got it," he said and hurried out.

She turned to the night manager. "You got a key?"

"Yes," Ramon answered. "You want me to lock it?"

Belinda nodded. "I'm gonna need the use of some space. You say you made coffee?"

"It should be ready by now."

She turned to Jim and Dodee. "How about it? You two want some coffee?"

Jim glanced towards the ceiling. "I really want to go clean up—"

"No," Detective Belinda Smith waved a flat hand back and forth, "you wanna come and have some coffee, or you wanna come and not have some coffee?"

"Coffee's good."

"Me, too," Dodee put the inflection midway between statement and question.

"Good, let's go get some coffee."

Ramon led them through the lobby to the back entrance of the restaurant, by the windows to the patio.

"It is almost done," Ramon said. "You can probably still— Ah, there is the light," he smiled. "It is ready."

Jim waited till the detective poured herself a cup, then he poured one for Dodee, handing it to her. "I don't know how you take it."

"Cream and Equal. I'll fix it."

The detective took a sip. "I'm gonna take over a couple of those tables by the window, you don't mind?"

"No," Ramon shook his head, lips and mustache turning down. "The motel and the staff will cooperate all we can."

"You get your coffee, Mr., ah, oh yeah, Jim Dandy. Get yourself a cuppa Jim Dandy coffee and sit over there," she nodded to a three-person table in the corner by the window. "I'll talk to you after I'm finished with Ms...Swisher?"

"Dodee Swisher," Dodee said.

"Wait a minute," Jim leaned towards the detective. "Are we suspects?"

"No," Belinda waved Dodee towards another three-person table, two over, and turned back to him, raising her eyebrows, "at least, not yet."

TEN

JIM SAT AT the corner table Belinda had indicated, took a sip of coffee, and watched them over the rim of his cup.

They sat one empty table over, both by the window, Dodee with her back towards him. The detective pulled out a notebook and placed her handbag on the vacant chair between them, saying something he couldn't hear, but saw Dodee shake her wheaten head.

So, what had Belinda asked?

Did you kill Billy?

Hell no, shake of the head, Jim Dandy did it, I was just along for the ride.

He stared into his cup.

Who would want to kill the sneaky little busboy enough to jam the pointed end of a helpless bonsai into his chest?

The wind chime clanged outside and he turned to see it dancing from the patio bar's imitation-palm roof. The pool, filled with leaves and rippled water, seemed cold enough to freeze his ass even from here. Beyond, the sun, marching along in full stride, turned wind-sheared waves into glittering diamonds, crashing and bouncing along the surf.

So what was going to happen to Okawa's bonsai?

No one seemed to care that most of the dirt had fallen onto Billy's chest and the roots were drying up.

Sonofabitch.

Here he was about to have his backside slapped in the slammer and he was worried about Okawa's damn bonsai.

He stared at the back of Dodee's head.

What could he read there?

Nothing.

How was she faring under the detective's bluntness?

Maybe they really should get lawyers.

Could she afford one?

Well, maybe he could get one for both of them, if they needed it, and if the case didn't drag out forever.

The thing was, she had a perfect alibi.

Except for about five minutes, she had been with him all last night. And he had been with her. But if they were both suspects, could they alibi for one another?

"Hi, Jim." Clarence Harmony came in and poured himself a cup of coffee. The grossly overweight man added cream and sugar and started toward him. "How come you're sitting in a corner?"

Jim motioned to Belinda. "I have to answer some questions."

Clarence's eyebrows rose as he glanced at the woman detective, and then back. "Who's she?"

"A detective."

"She is? What's happened?"

"Someone killed the busboy."

"Sir," Belinda held up her shield. "Bolder Harbor police. We have an investigation going on here."

Clarence turned back to Jim. "Did she say you can have a lawyer present?" He gave the woman another look. "I know something about the law. Did you tell him he can have a lawyer?"

Belinda's chest rose in a heavy sigh. "An attorney, yes, sir," Belinda nodded politely through a tight smile, "but we're only asking a few questions here."

Clarence held his ground for a few moments, showing more guts than the gross body would have led Jim to suspect, but then the two younger women from the bonsai class showed up and Clarence, now the expert on the scene, hurried to them. Kelly Massey, streaked blond hair neatly in place, appeared only half awake. Not so her roommate, Sana Powell, her black eyes, alert in the Indian face, scanning the room. They huddled up with coffee at a far table.

So what was the fat man telling them?

Oh yeah, Clarence would nod, the busboy's been croaked. Probably drugs. Jim's a suspect.

Jim turned toward Dodee. From the back of her head he could tell nothing. Maybe he ought to get up, walk over, and just damn well tell Belinda to stop browbeating her or he's calling in a mouthpiece.

He remembered that from an old movie.

James Cagney?

I ain't talkin' wit' out me mouthpiece, copper!

Yep, that's what he should do, walk right up to the woman copper and say—

Belinda stood up, Dodee following, and they shook hands.

Shook hands?

What had she told him?

Yeah, copper, I'll sell Jim Dandy right down the river, all you have to do is let me go.

Dodee turned to give him a little wave and a smile.

He liked the way it lit up her face—but was it a Judas grin?

Belinda motioned him over.

He picked up his cup, surprised to see it was still full, and took the seat Dodee had just vacated, folding his arms and crossing his legs.

"You want to warm up your coffee?" she asked.

He shook his head. "I like it cold."

Now why the hell did he say that? He could drink it cold; he didn't like it cold.

"You mind if I get another cup?" She held up the empty.

He shrugged. "It's your show."

That sounded better.

Made him sound like a tough private eye.

Or a jerk.

She left for the coffee urn.

Shove it, copper, I ain't talkin' wit' out me mouthpiece.

The trouble with using *mouthpiece* today was that everyone thought it was something football players shoved between their teeth.

He looked across to see Dodee talking to the other Elderhostelers, her Aunt Alice among them now, and the Miettlinens, the female of which appeared robust and ready to take on the world; the male seemed in need of a transfusion.

Belinda re-seated her attractive figure in the chair opposite him. "Okay," she adjusted her pad and picked up her pen, "you want to tell me your side of the story?"

"What do you mean, my side? You mean like her side and my side?"

The woman blinked. "Your side. Your version. There's no conflict here." She tapped the pad. "I have Ms. Swisher's story. If you had been here together, you might have interrupted to say something you saw. Ms. Swisher might then convince herself that's what she saw, too. The facts would have been contaminated. Now it's your turn and then maybe we can piece the picture together, knowwhatamean?"

"I don't need to have a mouth—a lawyer present?"

She put her pen down. "You can have one if you want. I'm just collecting facts here."

He took a breath and let it out through puffed cheeks. "Okay, I guess not." He took a sip of cold coffee. "You want me to tell you what I saw in the room?"

"Why don't you start from the beginning."

He nodded. "Yesterday, Dodee told me about the two trees she saw—"

"We don't have to go back that far. How about after I talked to you last night and you left the station? Tell me how the shovel fits into this."

"Okay." He sipped some more coffee, wishing now he had gotten a fresh cup instead of being a stubborn ass. "We came in the front door, I was carrying both plants and Dodee had the shovel. We had agreed with Billy—"

"The dead man?"

"Yeah. He got us the shovel. Cost me fifteen bucks to borrow it. Dodee didn't tell you?"

"Just tell me your story. The dead man got you the shovel."

"Right. And we promised to leave it in the exhibition room—conference room—so he could put it back without getting in trouble. Personally, I think it was all an act just to milk us of whatever money he could get."

"The shovel?"

"Right. When we came by the conference room, Dodee tried the door. It was locked, so we leaned the shovel against it and continued on up to my room."

"And this morning?"

"This morning Dodee told me—"

"No, Mr. Dandy, not what you heard, what you saw yourself."

He rubbed his jaw. "I saw Dodee leave, the door shut, and I went to the bathroom. Just as I was coming out, she banged on the door and told me to hurry up, someone was murdered in—no," he stared across the room, "no, she just said to hurry up. Something terrible happened. So we rushed down to conference room and she opened the door. And there was Billy, the pointed end of the bonsai sticking in his chest." He leaned back in his seat. "You think they could spray those roots with water so they don't dry out?"

Her mouth dropped open.

"Yeah," he nodded. "Someone's been killed and probably I shouldn't be worried about a damn tree."

Now she nodded. "After the crime lab is finished, I'll see what I can do for the plant. Now what else did you see?"

He held out a wondering hand. "That's it. The tree sticking in his chest. Wasn't that enough? Blood staining the carpet like a big round bull's-eye under his chest."

"See, there was the blood. What else?"

"Nothing. Except the shovel. That was leaning up against the wall. I guess. I'm not sure I remember."

"Then what?"

"That's it. We got the hell out of there and ran down to the front desk, but no one was there."

"You didn't see Ramon?"

"No one. Well, Tiffany Crew was looking for a spare key."

"Who's Tiffany Crew?"

"She's here with the Elderhostel. She went out jogging and forgot her key."

"Then what?"

"I called the police. Called you guys."

"That's it?"

"Yeah."

"And was it Dodee's idea to call or yours?"

"Mine. Dodee was reluctant—" he caught himself and shrugged. "Well, not reluctant. Concerned. About the shovel. That's all. But we didn't touch anything."

"Uh-huh. And you didn't notice anything else about the room?"

"Like what?"

"Like you tell me."

"Like... Look! There was a dead man on the floor. What was I supposed to notice after that?"

Belinda nodded, glanced at her pad, pressed her lips tightly together, dimple on the chin, and nodded again, closing the pad. "Okay, Mr. Dandy. I have a lot more people to get statements from. You'll be around until Friday? Would there be a problem if we needed you to stay after that?"

He shrugged.

Why would she want him to stay after that?

Unless she figured the state would be supplying the accommodations by then.

Oh, happy thought.

ELEVEN

HE TRUDGED PAST waiters setting up trays for a buffet
breakfast, to the table where Dodee was sitting with the
others, and plopped into a seat.

"How did it go?" she asked.

He shrugged. "I don't know how it was supposed to go.
I've never been questioned by the police before."

"Well, I mean, did she seem satisfied?"

"I guess. I told her everything I knew."

"Dodee told us about the nice trees you collected," Clarence said, "but with all the trouble they caused you, I'll
bet you wish you'd stayed home in bed."

Jim nodded, then turned to him. "I appreciate you trying
to look out for my interests earlier."

"You mean about the right to have a lawyer?" A big
grin split Clarence's round, ruddy face. "Nah, no problem.
Just that I have to deal with inspectors and lawyers all the
time, everyone wanting to know how I'm disposing of
waste material. I'll tell you, the trash business has gotten a
lot more complicated than when I first—Winnie," he interrupted himself, waving towards the door where he wife
had just come in. "Over here." Clarence pulled over another chair and placed it next to him. "Jim and Dodee here
have just been questioned by the police."

She stared wide-eyed and opened-mouthed. The eyes
were red, reminding Jim of Penny's eyes during her last
few months, when, like Winnie with her insomnia, she had
little sleep. But he had seen something else in Penny's eyes

as well, toward the end, anxiety perhaps, like a rabbit trapped in a cage frantically searching for a way out.

That's how Winnie's eyes looked now.

"What happened?" she asked in her mousey voice.

"There's been a murder," her husband blurted out.

"Well," Aunt Alice spoke up, "we don't know it was a murder."

"What?" Clarence's eyes popped open. "Like that bald cypress flew up in the air and stabbed the busboy by itself?"

Aunt Alice looked down her nose at the fat man. "It could have been an accident. Not as you say, but..." She turned to Dodee. "Couldn't it? Did the detective actually say it was a murder?"

"She sure seemed to think so, Aunt Alice."

"Oh my. I hate to think of a light going out that way. Even such a dim one as Billy Dack."

Jim turned to Winnie. "You didn't happen to see or hear anyone last night?"

"Me? No." Her brows knitted. "Was it bad?"

Dodee closed her eyes and shook her head. "It was pretty gruesome. I thought I was going to throw up."

"Thought you were going to throw up?" came the booming voice of Barney Sopwaite as the tall retired general came marching up to the table, and they had to go into the gory story all over again.

"Get a lawyer," Barney said gruffly.

"I told him he could have one," Clarence said.

"No sir," Barney gave a nod, once again a general commanding his troops, "don't talk to the police without one."

Dodee shook her head. "I don't think—"

"Act tough, show no emotion," Barney continued, still in his military mode. "Get a lawyer."

They broke up to go through the breakfast line, Jim wondering, now that Barney had joined in Clarence's opinion, that maybe he should get a lawyer. He reached for some pancakes, but hesitated as he spotted, only half believing it, Eggs Benedict down the line, and passed up everything to scoop three of them onto his plate. Dodee watched from the other side of the buffet table. Two lonely pieces of melon rested on her plate.

He shrugged. "I want to make sure I'm getting my daily requirements of cholesterol."

She smiled. "I'd say you're giving it a pretty good shot."

Aunt Alice, limping along behind Dodee, had an egg, two sausages, and three slices of bacon. "At my age I say, screw the cholesterol. I'd just as soon have my ticker go pop than have something dragging me out a dime at a time."

Jim picked up two orange juices.

That at least would be good for him.

Probably not going to counteract the Eggs Benedict, but, what the hell.

He followed Dodee to a table, set down his tray, and hurried back to take the one Aunt Alice was trying to carry in one arm, her cane in the other.

"I can manage by myself," she said, handing it over, "but it's nice to have a gallant young man take it for me."

He looked at her. "Young?"

"Compared to me, everybody is young."

"Three Eggs Benedict?" asked the female half of the Miettlinens in her European accent, sitting straight-backed at the table like she was rehearsing for Queen Victoria's court.

"He's getting his daily cholesterol requirements out of the way," said Dodee.

"I believe in a good breakfast," he added, "it sets you right up for a good lunch."

Neither Miettlinen cracked a smile.

A new woman, gray hair, watery blue eyes, and name tag of Mary, sat at the table next to Sana Powell. "Did you hear someone was murdered last night?"

And so they had to go into it yet again.

"Brrr," an ironic smile played on the woman's face, "nice you didn't tell me before I ate. I'm glad I'm in the Ecology class. I wouldn't want to go in that room."

"So," said the male Miettlinen, coffee transfusion bringing him wide awake, "what is going to happen to your class?"

Jim shrugged and looked at Dodee, who shrugged back.

"Well," the man went on, "I cannot take you in my Aquatic Ecology class. I have maximum now. Any more, even one, would adversely effect the knowledge I intend to impart to my students."

"Gee," Jim shook his head, "Aquatic Ecology, that really breaks my heart."

By the time he finished breakfast and came back with another cup of coffee, only Aunt Alice and Dodee remained at the table.

"I have to get my car sometime."

"I'll drive you," Dodee said.

"Sure, with your keys in my car."

"I have a set," Aunt Alice said, digging in her purse and producing the keys. She set them on the table and reached for her cane. Jim helped her to her feet. "Thank you. It's nice to have a man about." She glanced down at Dodee. "I knew something more serious than collecting trees had to have happened to keep you out all night. Like murder."

Dodee kept a straight face and sipped on her orange juice.

"I'm going to freshen up before class time," Aunt Alice said, taking two steps towards the door, but then turned as if she had an afterthought. "Yes, murder would keep you out all night." She glanced from Dodee to Jim and back again. "Either that or, how do the kids say it? You got lucky," and she hobbled away.

"Damn," Dodee nodded, staring after her, "she knows."

"She's guessing."

"She knows. You don't put anything over on Aunt Alice. She was just setting us up with the murder business." She turned to him. "Do I look like a woman who got," she imitated her aunt's voice, "as the kids say, got lucky last night?"

"I don't know. Do I look like a man who got lucky last night?"

She cocked her head, studying him. "Yeah. You were acting uptight yesterday. Now you seem," she wagged her head, "loosey-goosey."

"With this murder business I don't feel loosey-goosey."

She stood up. "Yep, I'd say you look like you got lucky last night."

"I'd prefer to think I look like a man who's going to get lucky tonight."

She gave him a half smile, lips turned down at the end. "Tonight is a long way off."

BELINDA SMITH, aided by state troopers, was still questioning people in the lobby when Jim returned from picking up the Lincoln. He went up to his room, shaved, showered, and brushed his teeth, put on a fresh cotton shirt, thick and warm, climbed into clean cords and headed downstairs for the nine-thirty class.

Barney stopped him in the glassed-in hall. "Our room has been reassigned, Jim."

"Our room?"

"The bonsai room," he barked, clearing up the question. "Crime lab is mopping up the place down here." The square jaw set in his chiseled face for a moment. "I wonder what will happen to Okawa's bonsai. Shame for it to go to waste."

"To say nothing of Billy."

"Billy? That the man's name?" He led the way back up the stairs. "We're having it in the hospitality room." Barney turned his mostly bald head to him as they reached the second floor. "Say, Jim, who do you think killed him?"

He shrugged. "Why might be a better question."

"I mean you didn't— No sir, of course not." Barney rubbed his square jaw. "But that detective might have thought it strange, you arguing with the man about a shovel last night and it ends up at the crime scene."

Jim glared at him. "I didn't argue with him about it."

"You didn't?" The general gave a little wag to his head, lips forming an upside down U. "Could of fooled me."

"What makes you think we had an argument?"

"He didn't try to get money out of you?"

"Oh, that." They turned right at the top of the stairs, and left at the street wing of the motel. "Just a misunderstanding. Dodee gave him the extra five dollars."

"See. That sounds like an argument."

"For five dollars?" Jim stopped in his tracks. "That wasn't an argument." The sonofabitch had probably blown the whole thing out of proportion, like they were going to start punching one another. "You don't kill somebody over five dollars."

He expected Barney to tell him to get a lawyer again, but the man kept on marching for the hospitality room. Trouble was, after all Barney's blabbing he'd probably need one.

Dodee and Aunt Alice had saved a seat for him. He saw the four women who had driven in together, and Kelly Massey, and Sana Powell, her waist-long black hair braided and piled on top of her head. The Harmonys, Clarence and Winnie, came in off the balcony, shutting the door against the cold wind blowing in off the sea.

The Crews followed Jim in, Tiffany's teenage body encased in a blue Spandex exercise suit, different from the jogging suit she'd been wearing that morning. Meanwhile Simon, playing the elder squire with his silver mane and full beard, dressed nattily in a yellow shirt and pale blue tie, made ready to grovel into bonsai soil by the protection of a white lab coat that reached to his knees.

Jim was betting Sana was right, about Simon owning the red Mercedes roadster.

"Ah see that everyone is here," said Okawa, Georgian accent rolling up from deep inside his powerfully built body, "in spite of last night's distraction."

Small junipers in quart cans had been placed about on tables, one per student, and some bonsai tools, wire cutters, and sharpened chopsticks to share. Rolls of copper wire in different gauges were attached to a board set on the front table.

"Today you start on your own bonsai. Let's hope yours doesn't run into the same trouble as mine."

"What's going to happen to the tree?" asked one of the four ladies.

Okawa shrugged. "By the time they're finished using it for evidence, I doubt there will be much left, don't you know. Most of the soil has been knocked off the roots so..." He shrugged again. "If I had the tree in my room where I could spray the needles eight or ten times a day, it would have a fighting chance."

"Spray them?" asked Tiffany Crew.

"When you re-pot something, or transplant a tree from the wild, it's a good idea to keep it sprayed. The tree picks up moisture from the foliage and gives the roots time to recover."

Dodee turned around and looked at him, raising her eyebrows.

Yeah, buddy.

They would have to go out and find a sprayer.

If they weren't booked for a five-dollar murder first.

And he wondered about the argument he had witnessed between the bonsai master and Billy the night before. Was that another five-dollar misunderstanding?

TWELVE

CLIPPINGS LAY all about him on the table. Small stuff. The fuzzy stuff that clung to the main trunk of the little juniper. Any fool could take it off. Deciding the front of the tree took a little more intelligence, but the roots and the shape of the trunk dictated that. It was the actual clipping of branches that terrified him.

Cut off the wrong one and—

Whoops.

Where's the Crazy Glue?

But there was really no way of putting it back.

No one questioned the placing of branches on a real tree because God put them there, but a bonsai—

"How are you coming?" Dodee asked at his side.

Lee Sullivan breezed in. "I have a present for you," said the Elderhostel hostess, handing out sheets of paper as she flitted from table to table.

"What's this?" Dodee asked.

"An address list of everyone in the class," she answered with a white-toothed smile. "In case you'd like to keep in touch." Then she breezed out again.

Jim glanced at it, alphabetical now, Alice Atwater at the top, the Crews next, his own name third, and Dodee's down near the bottom.

"So, how are you doing?" Dodee pointed to the plant.

"Huh," he set the list aside. "Okay, I guess."

"I think you need to trim out some of the branches."

"I know that. You have to see the trunk. I've worked on some bonsai before."

"Oh, okay. Yeah, it looks like you got a good start."

He turned to her.

Was she being sarcastic?

But sincerity radiated from her face, warm, guileless.

"To tell the truth, I'm always worried I'll cut off the wrong branch. Especially the bottom ones."

"Well, how about—" her hands, already reaching for the juniper, stopped midway. She looked at him. "I could give it a quick sketch and we could decide together how it would look. Want to try?"

He shrugged. "Why not?"

She got her pad and in minutes had a good representation of the tree without foliage. Then they went through it, comparing tree to sketch, re-drawing each choice with the missing branches until they had it the way they wanted, trial and error, Dodee agreeing with him only after he determined what should go and what should remain.

"Okay," he said taking the final drawing, "thanks."

Armed with the sketch he got busy, clipping off the branches and cleaning the fuzz off the ones that remained. He wired all the branches, careful not to break the bark, as Okawa had said, then he bent them into position, twisting them slightly to flatten them out, and before his very eyes— a shrub turned into a miniature tree.

Shazam.

"You going to lunch?"

He looked at Dodee, and the nearly empty room, and then at his watch.

Sonofabitch.

What happened to the morning?

"Yeah, I guess so." He held up the tree. "How does it look?"

"Ah, nice. Maybe the tips of the branches should come up a little bit? What do you think?"

"Like what?"

"Like," she reached out and then stopped, "but maybe—"

"No, go ahead."

She took the tree and gently made a few twists and tugs, bringing the branches down a tiny bit more, the tips up, minute adjustments it could easily have done without, but made it look so much better.

"Have you worked with bonsai before?"

She shook her head. "It's just," she shrugged. "I've spent so much time studying design, and spent years observing substance and space, I guess I've developed a feel for what looks natural."

"I wish I had a little bit of that feel."

"You've got another kind of feel," she said, raising and lowering her arm where he had massaged it. "See."

"It isn't stiff?"

"Uh-uh. C'mon. I want to clean up."

He followed her. "I think I'll run out and see if I can find a sprayer, give our plants a shot. I don't want them to croak after all the work we went through to get 'em."

"I'll save you a place at lunch."

"Great."

He dropped off the address list, picked up his coat, and skipped downstairs, passing the conference room, doors closed, yellow police tape shutting it off from accidental traffic. Out in the parking lot his blue Lincoln was parked next to the red Mercedes 450 SL, and unless Tiffany was Simon's daughter, or granddaughter, he was betting the car belonged to the Crews.

Maybe he should buy a red Mercedes roadster.

Yeah, buddy, like he could ever afford one. Besides, only in his wildest fantasies would he be able to keep up with a woman like Tiffany.

He saw Winifred Harmony heading for the street and called out to her. "Can I give you a ride somewhere?" The mousey woman spun around like she had been shot. He patted the car roof. "I'm going to the store if you want a ride."

She smiled and pointed to a side entrance leading back into the street wing of the motel.

He waved back, climbed behind the wheel of the Lincoln and started the engine. *"Give me that old time rock and roll!"* blasted out from a golden oldies radio station. Trouble was, their golden oldies were a lot newer than his golden oldies. He took a music cassette, "Carousel," from a wooden console he had built to fit over the floor hump between the seats, and snapped it into the tape player. *"When you walk through a storm,"* filled the cabin interior.

He stared at a tree rattling in the cold wind at the edge of the sunny parking lot.

It could have been their theme song for the last year of Penny's life. Hard to hold your head up high when you can't even get it off the pillow.

He took a breath and blew it out through puffed cheeks.

When you walk through a storm you need to carry an umbrella.

What a priest friend had told him.

The only way you can get through the dark is to carry an umbrella of faith, and if that faith is strong enough, the Son light will come through no matter how dark the storm.

Easy words for him to say.

Hard words that Penny lived by.

He blinked as the wind bounced sunlight off the tree's new spring leaves.

Then he jammed his finger against the eject button, popping out the tape, slipped the car into gear and wheeled out to the edge of Ocean Boulevard, checking for traffic in the deserted resort town, and saw Barney leaning against the end wall of the motel wing, puffing away on a cigarette like the world was coming to an end.

The general, USA retired, gave him a salute.

He waved back, pulled onto the street, made a U-turn around a concrete island, and headed for downtown Bolder Harbor with the soothing notes of "Give me that old time rock and roll!" bashing his ears again.

He found the local hardware next to the Bolder theater, where *Stupid and Stupider* was still playing. The store had a rustic smell to it, like linseed oil had been used to preserve the floor's narrow boards. Electronics, tape recorders, radios, lamps and light bulbs occupied one side. Shovels and rakes and garden tools stood in a prominent place near the door, ready for spring, seeds and potting plants behind them, and a bin full of plastic spray bottles after that. He picked one out and took it to a counter midway in the back of the store where a young man with black curly hair, the name *Jim* on his shirt, rang it up.

"Need a bag?" the hardware Jim asked.

"Take it as it is," he answered.

On the other side of the Bolder Theater he found a liquor store attached to a café bar. Be nice to have a beer before dinner. He went in and bought a six-pack of Samuel Adams, and wondered about picking up some wine coolers in case Dodee might want a drink, then gave it a pass. If her dead husband had been an alcoholic, maybe she didn't drink.

He backed out the Lincoln and made another U around the statue in the middle of the intersection of Bolder and 130th Street, heading back towards Ocean Boulevard and the Windswept Dunes Motel.

When he got back he filled the plastic sprayer and started squirting the red cedars, only to have the sprayer clog up.

He opened the top and cleared the tube and got it sort of working, needing a lot of trigger pressure to get an anemic spray on the foliage. Then he shoved the beer in the mini-fridge, and skipped down to the noon buffet.

One thing he could say so far about the Elderhostel: they had plenty to eat. Fried chicken, broccoli, peas and carrots, mashed potatoes, green salad, corn chowder, and ginger-bread squares with white icing.

Like a pig, he tried it all, carrying it to the table.

"Hello, Jim," the black-haired Sana greeted in her India English. "We were wondering if you were going to make it in time for tea."

"Made a quick trip into Bolder Harbor for a spray bottle," he said, spreading lunch booty around his place setting. "I want to keep the foliage moist on the plants we dug up last night."

"I see you're eating a light lunch," Dodee smiled as he sat next to her.

"I believe in eating a good lunch, it sets you right up for a good dinner." Smiles around the table and giggling from Tiffany Crew, who with Simon, joined them at their table for the first time. "Fact is," he went on, "living alone and cooking just for myself everyday, I tend to go a little wild when I get a chance like this. I'll exercise an extra hour for a couple of days to take it off."

"How about a week?" said Dodee.

"How about a month?" added Kelly Massey.

"How about a year?" said the female half of the Miet-tlinens, showing the first sign of humor he had been able to discern, with a pursed-lipped smile that seemed a stranger to her tanned, robust face.

"Now, you all let Jim alone," Aunt Alice came to his defense. "He looks in pretty solid shape to me. Besides," she continued with a straight face, "he probably already worked it off with all energy he expended last night."

Jim glanced at Dodee, but she had her head bent to her salad.

"I'm in garbage," Clarence Harmoney said, turning to Simon Crew, "that is, I own the company. So, you retired?"

The two were a study in contrasts: Clarence, crew-cut and ruddy faced, heavy arms sticking out of a short-sleeve sport shirt pulled tight over his huge belly; Simon, silver-gray hair and beard, trim in a pale blue shirt, muted yellow tie, and navy blazer.

"Semi-retired." Simon dabbed his lips with a napkin. "I'm a stockbroker. I don't have any clients anymore, but I'm always working on my own portfolio."

"Uh-huh. That how you met your wife, she a client of yours?"

Jim put down his fork.

Had Clarence just blundered into it, or had he deftly turned out the question that had been on everyone's mind?

"No, actually," Simon adjusted his hexagonal glasses and glanced at Tiffany, patting her hand, "I was a client of hers."

That sort of settled the wife question, but opened a brand new one about what kind of service the redheaded Tiffany had provided, one which no one seemed to have the guts to ask, and which the Crews didn't volunteer.

After lunch, Jim joining the clean plate club, he accompanied Dodee and Aunt Alice out to the glassed-in hallway.

"I don't know about you young people, but it's nap time for me."

"I was just thinking the same thing," he said.

"I think I'll go for a walk on the beach," said Dodee.

They fell silent as they strolled by the cordoned-off conference room, yellow tape still barring the door, and rode up to the second floor. He held the elevator until they were off. "Maybe I'll walk on the beach with you."

"No, go ahead and take your nap," Dodee said.

"I'll take it later. I don't mind a walk."

"No take your—I'd rather walk alone," her cornflower eyes bored into him.

"That's not very nice, Dodee," Aunt Alice said.

"It's just that…" she gave a small wave, and stared at him with wide-open eyes, "I need some time alone."

"Sure," he stopped at his room, "no problem. I'll see you later."

He closed the door and leaned against it.

Where the hell had that come from?

Was he wrong in thinking they had been getting along?

Shrugging, he went over and started squirting their trees, only to have the sprayer shut down all together.

Great, just great.

First Dodee, now the damn sprayer.

Well, screw you.

He grabbed the damn thing and yanked on the handle to the balcony door, intending to sling it over the side, but the sliding glass hesitated, the lock catching in the clasp, then it gave way and slid open.

Sonofabitch.

He locked the door and tried it again, the lock catching before slipping open under pressure.

Great room security.

No wonder they were bringing men in to work on the locks.

He shut the door and tossed the sprayer onto a chair. Take the damn thing back, is what he should do. He crossed to the bathroom and brushed his teeth, staring at himself in the mirror.

If Dodee wanted time alone, well, what was wrong with that?

Why should it bother him?

But, dammit, it did.

Maybe because of the abruptness.

He rinsed out, came back into the room, and tried the sprayer again, unscrewing the cap and cleaning the bottom, but the thing was dead.

Sonofabitch.

What else?

What the hell else?

What the hell else was a light knock on the door.

He opened it and Dodee slipped in.

"God, I didn't think you would ever get the hint," she said, peeling off her overcoat.

"The hint?"

"You did invite me?" she asked, with a question in her blue eyes.

"Yes, of course I did," he nodded, wondering what the hell she was talking about.

"Well, I didn't want the whole world to know about it." She put her arms on his shoulders. "You know, about our practicing. Bike riding. If you're up to it."

He tried to keep what he knew had to be a stupid grin off his face, and knew he was failing utterly. "I'm getting up to it even as we speak."

It was warm and tender, and a little mad at the end as they raced in a wild ride towards the finish line, and arrived in a dead heat.

THIRTEEN

HE SNAPPED OPEN his eyes as he felt someone stir at his side. He had been down so far into the bowels of a deep pit, and come out with such a rush, the bright afternoon flooding through the balcony window, that it took him a couple of blinks to realize where he was.

Dodee's head rested on his shoulder, cradled by his arm, as her smooth hand played across his belly. He yawned and her head popped up, blue eyes pushing sleep aside.

"Have a nice nap?" he asked.

"Ummm," she stretched like a cat and then laid her head back on his chest. "Delicious. How about you?"

"I was out. Goodbye world, I think I'm dead."

"Our trees seem to be doing okay," her voice resonated on his ribs as well as his ears.

"The damn sprayer's broken. I'm gonna take it back and get a new one. Want to come?"

"Not just now," she kissed him on the nipple, sending a tingle down to his crotch, but it was an invitation he knew his body could never keep. "About Billy's murder," she gave up on the nipple, "you don't suppose the cops think we had anything to do with it?"

"I was afraid of that when we were being questioned, but I don't know if it was fear or real."

"Only that we didn't do it. Or at least I didn't. Maybe after you had your way with me last night, you snuck out—"

"I had my way with you! Ha, I like that."

"You seemed to."

"It was the last thing on my mind until you attacked—"

"I suppose I should keep myself to myself from now on?"

He stared up at the ceiling. "So, as you were saying, after I had my way with you?"

He heard her giggle, feeling it through his body. "Afterwards, while I slept, you might have snuck on down—"

"Sneaked down."

"You might have snuck sneaked on down and stabbed Billy with the bonsai in a fit of rage."

"Yeah buddy. In a rage of why?"

"Rage of what."

He studied the ceiling some more. "But you're right about the rage. Someone would have to be half out of his mind to stab him with a tree, slam it into him with enough force to penetrate his rib cage."

"Right," she lifted her head. "So that means the police should realize we didn't do it."

"Except that they probably believe I'm one of the ones big enough to have done it, thanks to Barney Shithead Sopwaite...sorry, Barney Sopwaite."

"Why is he a Barney Shithead Sopwaite?"

"He told Belinda—"

"Shithead Smith?"

"You really get into this, don't you?"

"I try to help."

"Anyway, Barney Shithead Sopwaite told Belinda Shithead Smith that we got into a knock-down argument with Billy in the parking lot."

"It was only over five dollars."

"That's what I said. Besides, if you really wanted to pin it on an argument, I saw Billy and Okawa get into it hot and heavy the night before he was killed. Now there's someone who was powerful enough to ram a tree into Billy's heart.''

"Could be a woman, too. Kelly Massey could probably do it." She patted his stomach. "You think she's gay?"

"You mean because she's with Sana Powell? I don't think that proves anything."

"No, I suppose. Maybe it's just the difference in size that gives them the appearance of being a couple." She laid her head back down. "So what do we do now?"

As if in answer, the phone rang.

"Mr. Dandy, this is Belinda Smith," came the little girl voice of the detective. "I wonder if I could see you. I'm in the lobby."

"I'll be right down."

"Would Ms. Swisher happen to be with you?"

"Dodee? With me?" he asked, and saw her shake her head. "No," he said, looking into her eyes, "what makes you think she is?"

"Just on the off chance."

Dodee mouthed *the beach* and walked her fingers across his chest.

"I think she went for a stroll on the beach."

"Well, we kind of checked the beach. There's no one out there. We'd really like to talk to her as well."

"If I see her, I'll let her know."

"You do that."

He hung up.

Her eyebrows arched. "Belinda Shithead Smith?"

"Uh-huh. I don't think she believed the beach business."

"She wants to see us both?"

He nodded, swinging back the covers. They dressed and he stood waiting while she put on lipstick and combed her hair.

"You're beautiful."

"I'm hurrying."

"No, you are beautiful."

She looked at him, frowning. "You already had your way with me, Jim." She went back to combing and patting her hair. "Or are you laying the groundwork for future conquests?"

"You really are beautiful. Of course, that groundwork thing isn't bad, either."

She grabbed her coat and they hurried out, Dodee continuing on past the elevator.

"Where are you going?"

She stopped at the cross hall leading down the street wing. "Outside," she whispered, pulling on her coat. "I'll take the back stairs to the parking lot. You go on down and I'll come in like I've been out walking."

Belinda Smith waited in the lobby, sitting in one of the easy chairs that combined with two settees and a wall to make up a conversational alcove. Big, quick-on-the-draw Sonny Raines sat in the second easy chair. They stood up as he came in and Jim's stomach did a flip-flop as he wondered if they were going to arrest him.

He looked past them to the patio, wondering if Dodee would keep to the strolling-on-the-beach charade, then glanced over his shoulder to see her come through the front entrance.

"Here's Dodee Swisher now," he said, playing the game.

"Yes, I'd like to see you both," Belinda said.

Dodee's eyes open wide with innocence. "Me, too?"

If she hadn't been an artist, she could have made it as an actress.

"Yes," Belinda yawned, distorting her pretty milk-chocolate face, "both of you."

She led them into the restaurant. "You know this morn-

ing, when I asked you if it would be a problem to stay on
for a few days after your banzai course is over?''

"Uh-huh," Jim nodded.

"Well, now I'm going to turn it around.''

"What do you mean?''

She continued back to the same three-person table by the
window they had occupied that morning, big Sonny bringing up the rear. "Don't leave town without notifying us.''

Jim gaped at her. "You're telling us we're suspects?''

She motioned to the chairs, but no one sat. "I'm not
reading you your rights, Mr. Dandy, or you Ms. Swisher,
but I do want you to understand that what you say will be
on record. And you don't have to answer, and you can have
an attorney.''

He felt goose bumps rise on his arms.

It sure sounded like she was reading him his rights.

She motioned to the chairs again. He dropped into one
by the window, Dodee, ashen-faced, took the one next to
him, and Belinda the other one by the window, across from
Jim. Big Sonny grabbed a chair from another table, swung
it around and straddled its back, sitting to the side of Belinda, like he was ready to drop them should they make a
break for the door.

"But we're not under arrest?'' Jim asked, his mouth
sucked dry of saliva.

She pressed her lips tightly together, forming a dimple
on her chin, and shook her head. "I just want to make sure
you're aware that what you say from now on is on the
record and can be used in court, knowwhatamean?''

Hell yeah, he knew what she meant.

He could feel the cell door already slamming him in the
face. What would his kids say? He would have to call them,
probably Ceecee, to come bail him out.

How could an Elderhostel bonsai course turn into shit so fast?

He leaned on the table. "Listen, we did not have an argument. Billy promised to get us that damn shovel. He said it would get him into a lot of trouble if they caught him taking it and wanted a ten-dollar tip. We agreed, but when we got to the parking lot he wanted more money."

"It was only five dollars," Dodee blurted out. "You don't kill someone over five dollars."

"I was about to tell him what he could do with the shovel when Dodee gave him the other five. That's it. There was no argument. I don't care what Barney says."

"Barney?"

"Barney Sopwaite. Didn't he tell you?" He blinked. "You didn't even know about it, did you?"

She smiled. "I do now."

He took a breath and let it out. "Then what are we talking about?"

Belinda flipped back the pages of her pad, studied it a moment, then fixed her dark eyes on him. "When Ms. Swisher brought you down to the conference room, you didn't notice anything unusual?"

"Unusual?" He sat back and held out his hands. "You got a dead man with a tree sticking out of his chest and you ask me if I saw anything—"

"I mean aside from the body?"

He tried to visualize the room in his mind, but then shook his head. "Once I saw Billy, that was it. There could have been a herd of elephants marching through for all I knew. Except for the shovel, and Dodee pointed that out. I don't see that many dead people. Outside of a funeral home, I've never seen one."

"And yet," the detective shifted to Dodee, "you saw a

set of bonsai tools on the table," she checked her notes, "and a small rectangular object?"

"It looked like a miniature tape recorder."

"Was there a tape in it?"

"I don't even know if it was a recorder."

Jim rested an elbow on the table. "Was it?"

Belinda shifted her dark eyes to him for a moment before going back to Dodee. "And you say there was a wallet?"

"Right. It was flopped open, you know, unfolded, but face down. About two feet away from him."

The detective scratched off a few more notes and glanced at Jim. "You didn't see any of this?"

He shook his head.

She turned to Dodee. "How long was it, when you found the body, that you'd been away from Mr. Dandy?"

Dodee glanced at him and shrugged. "Just long enough to walk down and run back up."

"Five minutes," Jim said. "Maybe less. I went to the bathroom and by the time I came out Dodee was there."

Belinda pursed her lips for a moment. "How long does it take you to go to the bathroom?" Her little girl voice almost made the question laughable.

"Long enough to lift the toilet seat and dump a pint of water. If you want the gory details, I had my prostate reamed out a while back so the thing flows like a faucet."

She nodded, a slight smile playing about her lips. "Did you do anything else? Before she got back?"

"Not that I can remember. Washed my hands—no. Not even that. Why all the big deal—"

"What I can't figure, you didn't see anything lying about, and you," she pointed to Dodee, "you saw all this other stuff. How do you figure that?"

She shrugged. "I'm observant?"

"With a dead body there?"

"Wait a minute," Jim cut in, feeling like the detective was trying to back Dodee into a corner. "She's an artist. She notices details. That's her job. Or art or whatever. And she also had a second look."

"So did you, when you showed me the body."

"But the second time I never moved from the doorway." He rubbed his nose. "Look, I'm a physical therapist. I notice bodies. You want me to tell you which ribs the bonsai probably pierced and which muscles it probably tore? And about—"

Belinda held up the pale palm of her hand, a stop traffic gesture. "See, the thing is…" The dark eyes darted between them. "Did either of you touch the body? Touch anything?"

"No," he shook his head, "I told you, we came right out to the desk and called nine-one-one."

The dark eyes shifted to Dodee.

She shook her head. "Nothing."

"You're sure about the bonsai tools?"

Dodee shrugged, glared out the window for a long minute, and shook her head. "I know I saw them in the afternoon, Mr. Okawa's tools, so maybe they just stuck in my memory from then."

Belinda clicked her pen shut and used the end to scratch her head, then shot Dodee a glance. "How about when you showed me the body? Everything the same?"

Dodee held out a wondering hand. "Jim was standing in front of me, and, ah," she motioned towards Sonny straddling the chair, "him too, so I didn't really see anything. To tell you the truth I had seen enough already."

"See, the thing is," Belinda clicked her pen in and out, "we didn't find any tools, and we didn't find a tape, but

we did find the miniature recorder, and we did find the
wallet, when the crime lab arrived, but they were both in
Mr. Dack's—in the body's pockets. So my question is, how
did you know they were there?''

FOURTEEN

A CUTTING WIND slanted off the water, smelling of sea salt, tasting of it, too, as occasional drops of spray landed on Jim's lips.

"Why didn't you tell me about the tape recorder and wallet?"

Dodee kicked up Lilliputian sand storms five feet up the slope from him as they dawdled along the beach.

"Because I thought you saw it." She spoke above the roar of waves pounding on the shore, foaming white in a spring sun that promised warmth, but delivered nothing, even at mid-afternoon max intensity. "I saw them," she took a hand out of her navy corduroy jacket to wave in the cold, "I assumed you did, too."

That didn't really bother him so much as what Belinda Smith had implied. That they had tampered with the tape recorder and wallet. Or Dodee had, before she came to get him, then stumbled and trapped herself.

At best it made him an accomplice.

Well, he knew she wasn't involved.

He chewed on the inside of his cheek.

But did he really know she wasn't involved?

Look at all the strange shit they'd gotten into in only one day. And how many women had made love to him before? How did he know it wasn't some grand calculated plan?

That's what had been playing in the background of his mind.

But now that the thought was out in the open?

He shook his head and wiped wind-tears from his eyes.

That kind of thinking was bullshit. Dodee wouldn't hurt anyone. He was ready to go to the wall on that.

"Are you angry at me?"

"Huh?" He raised his eyebrows. "No. What makes you think that?"

"You're walking way over there. Like Detective Smith thinks I'm the prime suspect and you don't want to be contaminated."

He closed ranks and put his arm around her.

"Better."

Small shrug and banging of hips as they strolled.

"I didn't realize we were apart, just that we were thinking. As far as I'm concerned, we're in this together."

She stopped and turned to him, putting her arms around his neck. And he kissed her. Warm, innocent kiss.

"Feeling better?"

Her lips spread, but the worry in her eyes made it into a sad smile. "Tell you one thing, Jim Dandy," she blinked, and then the smile came full on, "as a Jim Dandy, your a Jim Dandy—"

"Don't start that shit."

She gave a slight nod, yellow-brown hair whipping about her face. "It's nice having you here to support me."

"And you to support me."

He swung her around and started back, arm on her shoulder, their shadow a four-legged beast stretching towards the waves, the breeze out of their faces now. She put her arm around his waist, reaching up under his camel hair jacket to rub his back.

He hadn't done something like this since...

He was a teenager?

Penny, of course, they had loved walking together.

But the hand up the back thing?

A long long time ago.

"What I can't figure," her cornflower eyes glanced up at him, "is how the miniature recorder got from the floor into Billy's pocket."

"Somebody put it there."

"Oh duhhh, why didn't I think of that?"

"Okay, okay, stupid remark. Thank you for subtly pointing that out."

Her hand slipped to his hip, hooking onto his belt. "What I meant is, *why* would they put it back in the pocket?"

He stopped, swinging her towards him. "You know, if you saw the tape recorder and the wallet—did you see them both times?"

She shrugged. "I'm not sure."

"Somebody was probably in there when you discovered the body."

"I didn't see—"

"Did you look behind the door?"

"The first time I didn't even go in. I just opened the door and flicked on the light."

He started walking again.

"What are you saying?" she said, keeping up.

"Maybe I didn't see the tape recorder and wallet because they had already been slipped into Billy's pocket. In which case you might have saved your life by running to get me."

"You mean he was behind the door?"

"No, duhhh, he was in the middle of the room."

"Okay, I deserved that." She grinned up. "Thank you for subtly pointing it out."

"The killer could have been planting the wallet and tape recorder for some reason."

"Suppose it wasn't even the killer." She held out her free hand, thumb and forefinger together. "Suppose somebody came along, saw the dead busboy, decided to rob him of the money we gave him, and put the wallet back to cover up.''

Jim turned his lips down. ''That doesn't account for the tape recorder. Besides, if you don't kill somebody for five bucks, fifteen isn't going to make it a whole lot better.''

They took a quick couple of steps as a gust of wind skooched them in the rear. She scrunched closer, using him as a shelter from the breeze.

''You okay down there?''

''Just freezing.''

''I can think of something to warm you up.'' The blue eyes glared up at him. ''I'm kidding, I'm kidding,'' he added.

What the hell, did she think he was a fifteen-year-old?

On the other hand, yesterday morning he wouldn't have thought about it. Now he had done it twice. Maybe some latent sex drive had welled up in him—

''But suppose it was the killer,'' she said.

''The killer?'' he asked, trying to switch gears.

''Maybe the killer wasn't planting something, maybe he was taking incriminating evidence out?'' She waved her hand. ''Suppose there was something on the tape? Billy had something on this guy so he kills him and gets the tape from the recorder.''

He swung her around and they both said it together.

''Blackmail!''

''He was blackmailing somebody,'' she rushed on, ''and when the guy killed Billy he took the tape out of the recorder.''

''But why the wallet?''

''I don't know.'' She gave a dismissing shrug and they started off again. ''Maybe he was feeling around and thought it was the tape recorder before he took it out. Anyway, all we have to do is find out who Billy was blackmailing and we're off the hook."

"Yeah, buddy. We'll take a poll of the hotel. Hello everybody, if Billy was blackmailing you, raise your hand." He shook his head. "No, we'll just tell Belinda Smith and let her handle it."

"I'm sure she'll appreciate us telling her how to do her job. Besides, don't you think she would have figured it out herself?"

They reached the motel and turned in, and she broke away from him. "I have the feeling we're already getting to be thought of as an item." She walked on a couple of steps, then pointed towards the corner of the motel. "I wonder if that's the potting shed Billy was talking about."

He glanced over to where a privacy wall on the left separated 111th Street from the patio and a door into the motel marked STORAGE. "Don't know." He raised his eyes to the Hospitality Room above, scanning the deserted balconies that stretched from there, down past his room, to the far end of the building on the right.

If she was worried about being an item, no one else was.

They skirted the pool and she turned as they neared the lobby. "Well, we have to do something."

"Yeah, hire a couple of lawyers." He went to open the door for her, and hesitated. "I don't know how to put this, but I could help you out with a lawyer if you need it."

She cocked her head and smiled. "That's nice of you, and I mean really nice because I'd be hard-pressed if we really have to get into it, but I think Aunt Alice would help me out. But more than the money, I'm worried about what it would do to my children."

He grimaced. "God, I know what you mean."

He pulled open the door and followed her into the lobby, crossing paths with the night manager.

"You're in early," Jim said.

Ramon smiled, stretching the black mustache. "Yes, I have some things...some files I have to clear up."

"Have we had any messages?" Dodee asked.

"I don't know, I am not working. Excuse me," he said, rushing off.

"Should we ask?" Dodee turned to him. "Maybe Belinda Smith has called for us."

"Let sleeping dogs and policemen, or policepersons, lie."

She pointed towards the front doors. "How about the sprayer? You going to exchange it?"

"You changed that topic fast."

"It's this murder. It's got me crazy. I have to do something."

"Okay, give me a few minutes to get it."

He rushed up to his room, retrieved the broken sprayer, and they strode out to the parking lot. The sun had slipped towards the horizon, giving up even the pretense of warmth. The red Mercedes 450 SL pulled in off Ocean Boulevard, a masculine guttural to the roadster's engine, and screeched to a stop. The thirtyish Tiffany Crew sat behind the wheel. Simon, wearing a leather jacket over his shirt and tie, sat in the passenger seat.

"Ah," Jim nodded, "I knew it."

"Knew what? Who owned that car?"

"Hi," Tiffany called, getting out, knockout body still dressed in the Spandex workout suit, "we got some fixings for gin and tonics. Can we offer you some?"

"That's nice," Dodee smiled, "but we're on our way to the store."

"Ah, too bad," Simon smiled, holding a bag in his gloved hand. "A rain check then?"

"Yes, a rain check," added his wife, tossing her red hair.

"Maybe when you get back. You guys are celebrities. I never knew a murder suspect before."

"They probably want to pump us for dirt," Jim said under his breath, holding the door of the Lincoln for Dodee. "I wonder if they'd treat us the same way if we had leprosy?"

"How did they find out we're suspects?" Dodee asked when he slipped behind the wheel. "Are we suspects?"

He took a deep breath, blew it out, and shrugged.

"What was the other thing you were talking about?" She swung her knees toward him. "Making smart remarks about the red car?"

"Nothing smart. I just made a bet with myself about who owned it and I was right."

"Because of Tiffany? You see a good-looking woman going out with an average man—"

"Good looking *young* woman and average *old* man."

"—and right away you think she's after him for money."

"You got a better reason?" He pulled out onto Ocean Boulevard.

"It could be love."

"Yeah," he answered, swinging around the concrete island and heading back towards Bolder Harbor. "It could."

"No, darn it," she insisted, "it really could. It doesn't have to be about money." She stared at him a moment, then laughed out loud. "It could be because he's big as an elephant."

Long shadows stretched across their path, trees with new spring leaves aglow on one side, somber on the other. Jim turned right on 130th Street, catching the sun full in his eyes, and pulled into a parking space half a block down, in front of the Bolder Theater. They entered the hardware emporium next door and, leaving her to wander, he strode to the cash register midway in the back.

"Get ya somethin'?" asked a bald old man with a nasal voice, sniffing like he had post-nasal drip.

"I want to exchange this sprayer."

The man sniffed a couple of times, taking the sprayer and looking at it. "Ya get it here?"

"Yeah, why else would I—"

"These things not made to last forever, ya know."

"I just got it this morning," he said, a little anger creeping into his voice. "It didn't work right even—"

"Hey Jim," the man called and sniffed again. "Guy buy a sprayer this morning?"

The same young man who had waited on him stuck his head around the door to the back room. "Yeah, Dad. He bought it this morning."

"Okay, then. See, ya bought it this morning, ya deserve a new sprayer." Sniff, sniff. "Thing should last more'n a day, right?" He led the way to the bin of sprayers. "Quality. Ain't got it no more." He picked one out and handed it to Jim. "Trouble with the world." Sniff, sniff. "No one gives a damn about quality."

"How much is this tape recorder?" Dodee called from across the store.

"Which one a those?"

Jim followed the sniffing man over to her.

"This miniature one."

"Forty-nine fifty. Ya want it?"

She looked to Jim and back to the man. "I don't know."

"Last one we got." Sniff, sniff. "Gotta order more. Everybody's been comin' in an' buyin' 'em. Mustta sold four the last two days. One to the police even."

"I'll take it." She turned to Jim. "I don't have my pocketbook. Can you loan me some money?"

"I'll get it," he said, pulling out his wallet as they followed the man back to the cash register.

"Yeah, the police even." He rang it up. "Ya want any tapes? Ain't got too many a them left."

"Do we want tapes?" he asked her.

Dodee shook her head.

"Who can figure?" Sniff, sniff. "Maybe it's got something to do— You heard about that murder?"

"Murder?" Jim handed over the money.

"Yeah, up the way. The Windswept Dunes Motel. I knew the guy."

"The murdered man?" Dodee's eyes opened wide.

"Yeah, came in here alla time. Always buyin' tapes for these things," he held up the miniature recorder before putting it in a plastic bag, added the receipt, and pushed it across the counter with the change. "A creepy kinda guy, ya know. Hung out in the library, but the librarian—comes in here, buys a lotta glue she didn't like him. I think he was tryin' ta, ya know," he flopped his hand back and forth. "She didn't want anything ta do with him. Anything else I can get ya?"

They left the store.

"Why did you want to buy—no," he shook his head, "I don't think I want to know."

She wrapped both her arms around one of his. "Let's go by the library."

He looked into her vivid blues and she batted her lashes at him. "You want to go to the library? I don't want to know about that, either." He opened the car door. "But why?"

"I want to know why Billy went there all the time."

"The guy told us. He had a thing for the librarian."

"Maybe."

He walked around and climbed behind the wheel, staring out the windshield.

"All right. Why did we buy the tape recorder?"

"Well," she swung her knees towards him, "I got to thinking, if Billy had one tape, maybe he had more."

"Uh-huh." He waited for her to go on, but she just smiled. "So?"

"So," her voice almost cooing, "I was thinking that maybe we could snoop around and find them?"

"Now you see, that's what I didn't want to hear."

FIFTEEN

THE LIBRARY WAS half a block away. Hardly worth getting in the car. The post office occupied the corner across from it on 130th, and a gift shop on the other corner across Bolder Street. And out in the middle of the intersection, so cars had to go around it, was a statue of the man resting his hand on a sword and holding a wide-brimmed hat.

Inside, the library was larger then he expected for the size of Bolder Harbor, with a selection of periodicals worthy of a big city, a lot on wildlife and fishing, eight racks of books, double-sided, and a small second-floor loft with more books. A computer system with three monitors sat forward of the book racks for patrons to use, and another on the librarian's desk behind the check-out counter.

"Nice place you have here," Dodee smiled when a woman came forward from stacking books in the back.

"Thank you," she said in a southern accent, coming around to stand behind the counter. "The town is proud of it." She was a skosh past the line into chubby with dark hair and eyes, and bright teeth showing through an easy smile. "We have a trust that allows us to be generous." The nameplate on her desk read HARRIET BLEACHER. "What can I do for you folks?"

"Harriet…" Dodee's eyebrows rose. "Is it Harriet?"

"I use Harry. It might be more a man's name, but Harriet sounds like an old woman."

"You don't talk like you're from around here, Harry," Jim said. He figured her as late twenties, early thirties.

"I'm from North Carolina," the easy smile slipped back onto her face. "I didn't know it still showed."

"We were wondering—" Dodee nodded towards the street "—the owner of the hardware store said there was a man who came in here a lot." Harry's brow knitted and she cocked her head. "The man who was killed last night, did you hear about that?"

The lips thinned on the round face, the dark eyes hardened. "I heard."

"He used to come in here a lot. I think his name was Billy Dack."

The name acted like the snap of a bowstring, jerking Harry's plump body up tight. "I had nothing to do with that man. Anything you want to find out, go to the police."

"I'm sorry," Dodee said, "I didn't mean to..." She shrugged.

Jim leaned on the counter. "Can I tell you one thing?" There was no warmth in the eyes that turned towards him, her arms folded under her breasts. Jim put on what he hoped was a desperate face. "The police think we did it. We didn't. So what we're doing is trying to clutch at anything we can that might prove our innocence." Harry's eyes didn't change, but she dropped her hands to the counter and folded them. "If there is anything you could tell us—" her knuckles went white, and Jim turned, waving a hand to take in the room "—like what books or magazines he read, or—"

"Didn't read anything."

He glanced at Dodee and back to the woman's taut face, her arms refolded now. "That's the only thing he ever used" —Harry jutted her chin towards the computer monitors— "he just used the computers."

Jim nodded. "You don't know what for—"

"No, I tried to stay as far away from him as possible."

"Can we..." Dodee waved at the computers.

"They're for public use."

"Thank you," Jim said, putting his sad face back on, "you've been a lot of help."

They went across and stared at the monitor.

"You know anything about these things?" Dodee whispered.

Jim put on his reading glasses. "I know when it says 'hit enter for menu' that it's probably a good move."

He tapped it and a list came up, numbers beside items, not only of things like subject, author, title, but networks, utilities, games, and business.

"Now what?" she asked.

He shrugged. "Games?"

"Utilities," called a voice behind them. Harry unfolded her arms and leaned on the counter. "He never played the games, as far I know. At least—" She shrugged. "He seldom cleared the monitor when he was finished. It goes back automatically on a timer, but whenever I checked it was either left on utilities or networks."

"Networks?" Jim nodded to the set. "Can you get to the Internet on here?"

"Yes, sir." She came around the counter. "But if he had anything there, like e-mail, you would have to know his password and logon ID to get to it."

"What do you mean, e-mail?" Dodee asked. "Like someone might leave him a message? How would he get it?"

"He has an electronic mailbox and when he signs on— Here, I'll show you." Her practiced hands clattered on the keyboard and she signed on to Prodigy. "This is the network I use." The Highlights screen came on and she pointed at a white envelope icon in the lower right corner. "This tells me I have mail waiting." She moved the curser to the mail icon on the tool bar and clicked it. The screen changed to show a list of messages. "This one," she pointed to the top, "is from my sister in Beaufort, my Mom, too," she smiled, "because she tells my sister what to say. The next is from a librarian friend in New York who I only know through the computer. And so on. The mailbox is waiting for me when I sign on."

"Umm," Dodee stared into the air, "maybe he was setting up payments through a network."

"Payments?" Harry asked.

Jim shook his head. "That would be big-time stuff. This guy was—what did your Aunt Alice call him, a weasel?"

"That's what I'd call him," Harry nodded.

Dodee put a hand on Harry's arm. "I have the impression that he, ah, came onto you?"

Harry's dark eyes shifted from him to Dodee. "Coming on to me wasn't half of it. But I never went out with him." She nodded towards the intersection. "There's a woman in the Ben Franklin who I know hated him, but every once in a while I saw him pick her up in his car. I often wondered what he had on her. Well, dead or not, I'm not sorry he won't be around. The last four months have been hell."

"Four months?" Dodee cocked her head. "Why—"

"That's when he started coming in here."

"What about the utilities?" Jim asked, tapping the monitor. "What's in there?"

Harry did some more clacking on the keyboard, getting back to the main menu and then off onto the utilities menu. "We have a lot of things we can access—"

"Telephone," Dodee's finger homed in on the entry. "Local telephone?"

"Yes, and any other."

"Any other?"

"The whole country. They're on CD-ROM. Even un-

Get
FREE BOOKS
and a wonderful
FREE GIFT!

Try Your
Luck At
Our Casino,
Where All
The Games
Are On
The
House!

PLAY ROULETTE!

PLAY TWENTY-ONE

Turn the page and deal yourself in!

WELCOME TO THE CASINO

Try your luck at the Roulette Wheel ...
Play a hand of Twenty-One!

How to play:

1. Play the Roulette and Twenty-One scratch-off games, as instructed on the opposite page, to see that you are eligible for FREE BOOKS and a FREE GIFT!

2. Send back the card and you'll get hot-off-the-press Mystery Library books, never before published! These books, have a cover price of $4.99 each, but they are yours to keep absolutely free.

3. There's no catch. You're under no obligation to buy anything. We charge nothing — ZERO — for your first shipment. And you don't have to make any minimum number of purchases — not even one!

4. The fact is, thousands of readers enjoy receiving books by mail from the Mystery Library Reader Service™ before they're available in stores. They like the convenience of home delivery, and they love our discount prices!

5. We hope that after receiving your free books you'll want to remain a subscriber. But the choice is yours — to continue or cancel, any time at all!

So why not take us up on our invitation, with no risk of any kind. You'll be glad you did!

Play Twenty-One For This Exquisite Free Gift!

THIS SURPRISE MYSTERY GIFT WILL BE YOURS FREE WHEN YOU PLAY TWENTY-ONE

It's fun, and we're giving away *FREE GIFTS* to all players!

PLAY ROULETTE!

Scratch the silver to see that the ball has landed on 7 RED, making you eligible for TWO FREE romance novels!

PLAY TWENTY-ONE!

Scratch the silver to reveal a winning hand! Congratulations, you have Twenty-One. Return this card promptly and you'll receive a fabulous free mystery gift, along with your free books!

YES!

Please send me all the free books and the gift for which I qualify! I understand that I am under no obligation to purchase any books, as explained on the back of this card.

Name: _____
(PLEASE PRINT)

Address: _____ Apt.#: _____

City: _____ State: _____ Zip: _____

The Mystery Library Reader Service™ — Here's how it works:

If offer card is missing write to: Mystery Library Reader Service, 3010 Walden Ave., P.O. Box 1867, Buffalo, NY 14240-995

BUSINESS REPLY MAIL
FIRST-CLASS MAIL   PERMIT NO 717   BUFFALO NY

POSTAGE WILL BE PAID BY ADDRESSEE

MYSTERY LIBRARY READER SERVICE
3010 WALDEN AVE
PO BOX 1867
BUFFALO NY 14240-9952

NO POSTAGE
NECESSARY
IF MAILED
IN THE
UNITED STATES

listed numbers. And if you know the number, you can cross-reference to get the name and address.''

Dodee gave Jim a smug I-told-you-so face and turned to the librarian with a look of concern, like that of an older sister, "I'm sorry that guy was such a creep, but you've really helped us out a lot.''

"You won't tell anyone about the woman across the street? I shouldn't have said anything.''

"No,'' Jim shook his head. "Besides, we're leaving in a couple of days. If the police don't arrest us first.''

They headed towards the door, but Dodee swung back, pointing toward the intersection. "Who's the statue?''

Harry gave her easy smile. "Martin J. Bolder, a Colonel in George Washington's army. The town's only claim to fame, but I did some research and Washington almost had him hung for cowardice. The only bold thing about him was his name. Everyone around here calls him 'Stony.'''

Outside in the gathering evening, Dodee turned to him. "I started to ask why she put up with Billy instead of going to the police. If he had been going in there for four months—''

"If he was into blackmailing, he could have had something on her.''

She pursed her lips, then looked across the street to the Ben Franklin store. "Wish I could talk to that woman.''

"C'mon,'' he took her by the arm and lugged her towards the car. "We don't know her name and we promised we wouldn't say anything about it.''

"You promised.''

They got in the car and rounded the statue of old Stony. "I have some beer back in my room...but with your dead husband having been an alcoholic, you probably don't—''

"I'm not an alcoholic. I enjoy a drink now and then.''

"I could pick up some wine coolers if you like. Have a drink before dinner."

"No, beer will be fine. I have eclectic tastes."

"And a fifty-cent vocabulary."

"Nice to walk among the commoners occasionally. Makes one appreciate real class."

"Screw you."

"Again?"

EVENING HAD PASSED into darkness by the time they made it back to the Windswept Dunes Motel, too late for that pre-dinner drink, and entered The Whispering Sands dining room. On the upside, there was no line of hungry Elder-hostelers at the buffet. He moved along one side piling on potatoes with gravy, two chicken thighs, green beans, a roll with butter, and a desert of tapioca. Dodee had pretty much the same, only half-sized portions, and no roll or pudding.

Aunt Alice had saved them seats. "Where have you two been?"

"We had to get a sprayer for the plants we dug up last night," Dodee said.

"Like to see them, Dodee," Barney gruffed. "For all the repercussions you and Jim went through, I certainly hope they were worth it."

"Yes," Aunt Alice nodded towards the windows, "you should ask Mr. Okawa what he thinks."

Jim turned to see Okawa sitting with Lee Sullivan at what he was beginning to think of as the interrogation table. The bonsai master must have given one of his funny lines because the Elderhostel coordinator broke out laughing.

Clarence turned to his wife. "How about the bonsai you saw in Japan?" the garbage executive asked, thick arms sticking out of a multicolored short-sleeve shirt. "Some of those were pretty big in the pictures. They collect 'em?"

Winnie raised a finger while she swallowed. "I think they've been in the families for hundreds of years. Almost like an old relative."

"They do out west." Tiffany turned her fair-skinned face to her husband. "Don't they? Collect them?"

Simon Crew, in a fresh tie, shirt, and jacket, put down his fork and nodded. "From the mountaintops and high desert. We've seen trees out there that are hundreds of years old, maybe even older than those in Japan, but it's tricky collecting them. And you have to get permission. Then it takes years of styling to really bring out the artistry." He turned to Jim. "How old are your trees?"

He shrugged. "Their trunks are about two inches in diameter."

"I guess if I'm going to get into this," said Simon, "I'm going to have to break down and lay out the big bucks for some tools."

Jim stabbed some green beans with his fork.

Big bucks?

For someone driving a Mercedes 450 SL?

"Mr. Okawa is supposed to have tools for sale tomorrow," Aunt Alice said, "along with some books."

"I bought my tools when I was in Japan, Alice," Barney barked, "at the bonsai nurseries in Omiya. At the time they were more reasonable than you can buy them here."

"Anything more on the murder?" Clarence asked, and then Winnie must have kicked him for he turned to her. "What? I'm just asking what everyone wants to know."

"It's not something for the dinner table," Winnie said.

"Now that it is out in the open," came Sana Powell's India-accented English, "would it be too impolite to ask if there are new developments?"

Jim grimaced. "I guess we're suspects, if that's what you mean."

"Nothing new," Dodee said.

"They asked us not to talk about it," Jim added.

There were nods and vacant looks around.

"Just the same," Barney leaned forward, speaking in his general's voice, "I recommend you two get a lawyer. You could be completely blameless, but make an innocent statement that can be twisted around and you're plunked right in the stockade."

Jim took a sip of coffee and looked into the man's hard brown eyes.

For the first time he thought old Barney might be right.

SIXTEEN

AT ELEVEN, by his watch, he heard a soft knocking on his door.

Good thing he wasn't hard of hearing like Aunt Alice.

He had gone to an impromptu sale mart Okawa had set up after dinner, looked at the tools, but at their price decided to think it over for a night or two, and instead bought a book which he had been reading—well, actually just looking at pictures of bonsai trees.

He opened the door to see Dodee standing there, dressed in dark clothing, the same she had worn the night before. Warm face and bright blue eyes, wheaten hair fluffed up on her head, he could think of a lot of things he'd rather be doing than heading into another grave adventure. He had to be out of his frigging mind.

She crossed her eyes and made a face. "Are you ready?"

He let out a big sigh. "Okay," he whispered, "but I want to go on record that I'm against it."

"So noted."

Yeah great, just great. That would carry a lot of weight if they were hauled before a judge.

They passed the elevator, stopping by the open stairs next to it, listening for lobby sounds that might be drifting up from the glassed-in walkway, and hearing nothing. Maybe she had been correct in picking the time. They hung a right at the street-wing hallway, following along until they came to a back staircase and took it down to the parking lot, the frigid night a reminder, in spades, of the long walk back from the police station, one he'd just as soon not repeat.

They crossed to her Ford Taurus and she rummaged in her glove compartment, coming up with a second penlight, one already in her jacket pocket, then she took his hand and they headed for Ocean Boulevard, swinging their arms, two lovers out for a stroll.

Yeah, buddy, but at their age, on a frigging freezing night, who were they fooling?

They rounded the wing of the motel and cut up 111th Street, wind full in the face, a good excuse to bundle close. They had to go out on the beach to circumvent the privacy wall—pounding surf filling his ears, sand filling his shoes— sonofabitch!—to skulk back in by the pool patio, keeping out of sight of the lobby and the restaurant windows on the right, to the potting shed on the left.

Even the name sounded ominous, like a paraphrase from the Bible.

Come down to the potter's shed, where I will remold your clay head into the mask of the dead.

"Why do you think there's something here?" he whispered.

"Billy said he had to steal a key to get the shovel."

"So?"

"Why would he need a key unless there was more inside than just a shovel?"

"But if he had to steal a key, why would he keep his own stuff inside?"

"Because that way no one could get to it. See if you can get the door open."

He stared into the night.

There was no logic to what she said. But did he want to get into a big-time discussion about it? Standing outside in the cold night? By a potting shed he was about to—

Break into?

He shuddered, but ran his hand down between the door and the jamb until he reached a lock latch.

"Shine your light," he whispered.

She switched on a penlight and centered it over the latch. It was open. From the clasp hung an insubstantial lock, unlatched, with gouges scratched into it, reflecting the light.

He glanced at her shadowy face. "It's unlocked."

"Uh-huh."

"So maybe there's someone in there."

"No, they probably keep it unlocked. They just hang it there to discourage burglars."

That had as much logic as Billy keeping his stuff there.

He cracked open the door and heard something scurry inside.

Rats?

Sonofabitch, he hadn't counted on rats.

He held his breath, listening, but heard only Dodee breathing in his ear.

"What are we waiting for?"

"I thought I heard something."

"Squirrels."

Squirrels?

Yeah, right.

He swung the door wide and entered the shed, scraping his feet along the dark floor in case there was a step. He had expected a musty odor; it smelled of furniture wax. Dodee followed him in and shut the door, plunging them into complete darkness. It was warm, probably plugged into the building's heating system, dark and warm, like they were in a womb. Which is where he'd rather be. Then the shaft of a penlight cut through the darkness and she handed it to him, cutting on one of her own.

In one corner there was a shovel, a companion to the

one the police confiscated, and a rake, a trowel, and some empty plant pots, but that was it for the garden department. The rest was plastic barrels of furniture and floor cleaner, two rolling racks of folding chairs, spare hardware parts, roll-away beds, and a double door at the far end, locked, leading inside to the motel, another open doorway to the right leading to a darkened room or closet.

"This is just storage," he said. "Anyone working for the motel can get in here."

"Which means that Billy could get in to hide some things."

"What things?"

"Tapes," came her exasperated voice. "Isn't that what we're looking for?"

The words were right there, in transit from brain to tongue—why would he hide them in here?—when his foot came down on something that cracked under his weight. He bent down and picked up a miniature recording cassette.

"See," Dodee's triumphant voice floated through the darkness.

Five others were scatted on the floor leading to the darkened room. He picked them up and slipped them into his jacket pocket.

"Let me have one."

She knelt on the floor. He squatted beside her to see she had their miniature tape recorder. He pulled one out and set it in the open cassette receptacle. She closed it and pressed a button.

He shined the penlight in the tiny window and saw the cassette revolving, but there was no sound.

"These are unused tapes. No wonder they're here."

"Let's try it the middle."

She pressed the Fast Forward button and the thing

spun into a blur for a few moments, then she stopped and played it again.

Nothing.

"I told you—"

She hit the Fast Forward once more, letting it really spin this time, finally stopping halfway through the tape.

Still nothing.

She shrugged. "I guess you're right."

He took it from her and turned the volume knob on the side.

...right, like a French kiss, no, don't stop.

A man's voice first, answered by a woman's with a southern accent.

You better not do it in my mouth. You promise?

At least you won't get pregnant.

No, I'm not—

Just kidding, Harry, I promise, I promise. Just do it and I'll do you.

Jim stared into Dodee's eyes, shining in the glare of the penlight.

Silence from the tape recorder.

Then groans.

Oh god, ahhh ah oh God.

Then some spitting noises.

You sonofabitch.

I couldn't help it.

You didn't have to hold my head, you forced me—

I couldn't help—

I'm getting some mouthwash, you lying bastard.

Dodee clicked off the tape, then gave a nervous giggle. "Well, that was different."

"At least it confirms the blackmail theory. If we take these to Detective Smith, it shows Billy was blackmailing people and it gets us off the hook."

"Except he could also have been blackmailing..."

But he let it trail off as a new thought came to him.

How come the tapes had been scattered on the floor?

By the door to another darkened room?

Wasn't that rather convenient?

"Could have been blackmailing who?" she asked.

And the gouges on the lock had been reflected in the penlight.

Why weren't they rusted from the salt air?

And the scurrying sound when he opened the door?

Maybe it really was a rat, a two-legged one.

He swung towards the open doorway, trying to get up, swinging the penlight, and caught a blur charging out of the darkness.

A knee smashed him under the chin.

And the world became a tumbling barrel.

The penlight flew from his hand, lost among a bazillion other whirling stars. Something concrete slapped him in the back. And the head. And an un-embodied scream pounded against his eardrums and faded into a far off nothingness—

Dodee!

He grabbed on and fought his way back, opening his eyes to a shaft of light that hugged the floor and gave long shadows to candy wrappers and furniture casters and the abandoned tape recorder. He picked up the penlight and flashed it around.

Dodee lay five feet away, one knee raised, arms spread-eagle. He crawled to her as the slamming of a door raced through his head, but he couldn't tell if it was real-time or the echo of a previous event. Her face was white; her eyes were closed. She had a strong and steady pulse, but, out cold, she could be suffering from a concussion.

He staggered to his feet and stumbled out into the starry

night. The cold air helped to clear his head as he raced for the lobby.

Ramon looked up from behind the check-in desk as Jim crashed through the door.

"Quick," Jim yelled, "dial nine-one-one. Dodee's just been knocked out."

"Who?"

"Dodee, she's—just goddamn do it! Get an ambulance here!"

He rushed back out to the potting shed, found a switch on the wall and snapped it on.

Dodee started to sit up.

"Stay there," he ordered, pulling off his coat and rolling it into a pillow. "Just stay there."

"I'm okay."

He pushed her down. "You could have a concussion."

"Just because you're a physical therapist—"

"You're not moving."

"But I wasn't hit. I don't think."

"Tell it to the doctor."

"All right, all right," she held a hand up to him. "Do you have the tape recorder?"

"I'll get it," he said, retrieving it and slipping it into his pants pocket.

"What *are* we going to say when they ask us what we were doing here?"

"What are you doing in here?" Ramon's voice, harsh and demanding, carried across from the outside doorway.

"Did you call the ambulance?"

"Yes, and the police."

"The police. I didn't tell you to call the police."

"No, I did that on my own. I am the night manager, if you please. When someone is killed in my motel, and then another guest is knocked out in the storage room, I take it upon myself to call the police. Did you see who did it?''

"Somebody big."

"Which still doesn't answer the question." The night manager came to stand over them.

"What question?"

"What were you doing here in the first place?"

"We heard someone rummaging around," Dodee said.

"Right," Jim added. "I saw the door lock broken and decided to investigate."

"Oh," Ramon's lips turned down, dragging the ends of his Juan Valdez mustache with it, sounds of sirens in the distance. "You decided to investigate?"

"When someone is murdered at a motel I'm staying in—''

"And we're under suspicion for it," Dodee cut in.

"Right, and we're under suspicion, I take it upon myself to investigate."

"How did you know it was not me?" Ramon patted himself on the chest.

"Because it was dark in here. What would you be doing in the dark?"

"And if it was dark in here," Ramon said, as the sirens got louder, "was not it also dark outside?"

"So?" Jim held his hands out.

"So how did you know the lock was broken?"

Good question.

Too bad he didn't have a good answer.

His mind raced through the gears, but nothing was coming down the pike, not helped by the screaming sirens that were pulling up outside.

SEVENTEEN

HE SAT ON AN oak bench, jacket folded beside him, in a white hallway, white vinyl tiles on the floor, registration desk down by the entrance, and waited for the door beside him to open.

More of a clinic than a hospital, but if anything serious happened he'd bet the real thing would not be far away. A too-young doctor, looking none too happy about being called out in the middle of the night, had arrived at the same time as the ambulance people had rolled Dodee in on a gurney.

One of the ambulance people had come out with the gurney.

Dodee, the doctor, and one attendant, a woman, were still in there.

Before jumping in the Lincoln he debated waking Aunt Alice, but when he remembered she would be in a deaf sleep he chased off after the ambulance.

He shifted on the wooden bench, felt the tape recorder in his pocket and pulled it out, turning the volume low, rewound the tape a second, and hit play.

At least you won't get pregnant.

No, I'm not—

Just kidding, Harry, I promise, I promise.

He cut it off.

Harry.

How many Harry's did he know with a woman's voice?

The librarian. Harriet, she said to call her Harry. First time he'd heard of a woman called Harry. But then he didn't know any Harry men either, except for Harry S. Truman, whom he really didn't know anyway.

How many other Harry women were out there?

Bet not many.

At least he had an explanation of why she had put up with him for four months without going to the police.

He popped the cassette out of the tape recorder and slipped it in his pants pocket. He rummaged among the four cassettes in his jacket and fished out a new one, snapping it into the recorder, pressing the Fast Forward until it was about midway through, then hit play.

It was almost a duplication of Harry's tape, only this time between two men, both different from Harry's man from the sound of the voices. Oral sex must be big on Billy's blackmail list, but with the openness of today's society, would it be grounds for blackmail? Unless one of the parties was married to someone else. Or living with someone else in the case of the two men.

The door opened and he slipped the recorder into his jacket.

Dodee came out looking scuffed up, but otherwise okay. The woman ambulance attendant, young and good-looking, came behind her, then the doctor, a kid with a bi-level haircut looking like he'd just stepped out of high school, brought up the rear.

"Should she be standing?" Jim asked, getting up.

"I'm okay," Dodee said, "I told you I was."

The doctor didn't answer while he slapped a professional eye on the good-looking female attendant walking down the hall, but when she left he turned to Jim. "You her husband?"

"No," they both said in unison.

"I'm just…" Jim started, and wondered just what he was, lover, accomplice— "A good friend," Dodee finished.

"Yeah, well, she's fine."

"I was afraid she might have a concussion."

"I don't remember getting hit. I think I fainted."

"Yeah, probably fainted." The doctor motioned down the hallway to the entrance past the registration desk. "I hope she's coming to see you."

Belinda Smith opened the door, pulled up short at the sight of them, put her hands on her hips, bowed her curly black head and shook it. "Why did I know it was going to be you two?" The detective looked from one to the other. "When are you two leaving again?"

"Friday," Dodee said.

"If you let us," Jim added.

"Oh, I'll let you. Fact, I'm ready to help you pack right now, thank you very much."

"I take it you're not here to see me," the Doctor said.

"Not unless there's anything you think I should know."

"Nope, she's okay." He headed back to his office. "I am out of here."

Jim stared into Belinda's dark eyes. "Help us pack? That means we're no longer suspects?"

She waved them to the oak bench and he sat down, Dodee beside him, the detective beside her.

"You wanna tell me what happened tonight?" They looked at each other, but Belinda cut them short. "Don't tell me," she pointed to Dodee, "it was your fault?"

She nodded sheepishly.

"And you," she pointed to him, "didn't your mother ever tell you the one about: if a friend told you to jump off the Empire State Building, would you do it?" Belinda took a pad out of her pocketbook. "All I gotta say is I hope you're getting fantastic sex to make this all worth while," which brought a blush to Dodee's face. "Okay," she flipped open the pad, "tell me what happened."

He held out a hand. "We're trying to figure out some way to prove our innocence. You say we're no longer suspects?"

"No, you're no longer suspects, not that you were ever strong ones. You gonna tell me what happened tonight?"

Dodee's brow wrinkled. "How come we're not suspects?"

"Because the coroner put the time of death between ten and midnight last night. At that time you were either under surveillance by Diggs, or Sonny, or were in the office talking to me. That kinda lets you off the hook as murderers. Now," Belinda took a deep breath, "are you going to tell me what happened tonight?"

"Billy was blackmailing people." There was a note of triumph in Dodee's voice. "That's why he was killed."

"Uh-huh."

"You don't seem surprised." Dodee's triumph deflated.

"When you find a tape recorder in a dead man's pocket with the tape missing, it's not a big jump to put blackmail on the motive list."

"Then why were we suspects?" Jim asked.

"Because Billy must have kept that tape recorder on all the time. We found a tape with your voices on it."

"But," he shrugged, peeking to Dodee and back, "we have nothing to hide."

"And there was nothing on the tape to incriminate you, unless we want to press charges for digging up those plants. But without making an extensive investigation, how do we know there weren't tapes of previous visits?"

"We've never been here before." Dodee glanced at him. "At least I haven't."

"Wait a minute." Belinda held up a pale stop-the-traffic palm. "I'm the one who's supposed to be asking the questions around here, knowwhatamean? What were you two doing tonight?"

"Well," Dodee pointed, thumb and forefinger together, "when we figured out that Billy was blackmailing people, we figured that's why someone—"

"Offed him," Jim volunteered.

Belinda's eyes burned into his. "You've been watching too many television shows, Dude."

"So I thought, if he—" Dodee pointed again "—Billy, was making a big thing out of getting the shovel from the potting shed—"

"Which is really a storage room," Jim added.

"—that perhaps he had kept his blackmail tapes there. Like handy, so he could use them to make some fast bucks."

"You've also been watching too much television."

They went on to tell her of finding the tapes, Jim getting kicked in the chin and Dodee knocked down, and calling the ambulance.

"Did you see what the guy looked like?" Belinda asked.

"A dark shadow moving at great speed," Jim said.

"Oh, that will help a lot."

"He looked tall, but from my perspective on the floor, Dodee would look tall. I'm not even sure it was a him."

"You couldn't prove it by me either way," Dodee said.

"I guess I should have chased him, but I was more concerned with Dodee."

"Which probably saved your life. Next time leave the police business to us." Belinda skimmed her notes. "You have how many tapes?"

"Five tapes," Dodee said.

"Four tapes," he said, trying to gloss over the one of Harry.

"I thought there were five?"

"Only four." He dug in his jacket and handed them over, including the cassette in the tape recorder, but keeping quiet about the one in his pants. "Oral sex on the one we listened to. At least that's what it sounded like."

Belinda wrote it down. "That's not a big deal."

"Unless they were married," Dodee said.

"They were both men." He watched Dodee's eyes open as she turned to him. "Yep," he said forcefully, glaring back, "they were both men."

"Even that's not a big deal. Okay, I'll take it from here. Go back to your motel and go to bed. And for God's sake, stay out of trouble for the rest of the night."

He helped Dodee to her feet. "You know," he said, "Ramon was there. Didn't he report it?"

"The night manager?" Belinda closed her note pad and stood. "Why would he?"

"He was upset we were in the storage room. He said he was going to report it."

Belinda touched a hand to her cheek. "Yeah, I wonder why he didn't. Unless Sonny took the call." She shouldered her handbag. "Maybe I'll ask him. In the morning. Right now I'm going home to bed." She looked from Dodee to him. "Am I going to be able to sleep the rest of the night?"

"Ask Dodee," he said, as they all started for the door.

"I've learned my lesson. I'm going to bed—we can go home?"

"Yes," Belinda nodded, "go home and never come back."

"Anyway," Jim said, as he held the door for them, "it's nice to know we're not suspects. I never thought I'd be glad to be brought into a police station."

Dodee stopped in the middle of the doorway. "Something is screwy here." They both turned to face her. "If he was murdered when we were with you last night, then how come the killer waited five or six hours, until after I saw the tape recorder on the floor, to put it back in Billy's pocket?''

"That's right." He glanced at Belinda. "Why did he wait until we discovered—"

"I don't know." She raised her hand in the stop signal. "At this moment I don't care." She started for her car, then turned back. "And now that you got me thinking about it, thank you very much, I probably won't sleep when I do get to bed."

Dodee turned to him when they were in the car. "Why did you tell her we only found four tapes?"

"One of the people on that fifth tape was a woman named Harry."

"Ah, okay. So where did the tape of the two men come from?"

He turned onto Ocean Boulevard. "I listened to it while you were in with the doctor."

"But why didn't you tell her about Harry's tape?"

"I figured Billy had given her enough problems without it continuing after the grave." He yanked the miniature cassette out of his pocket and mixed it with the larger music cassettes kept in the console he had built between the seats. "I thought we'd give it to her."

"That's very noble, sweetie, but isn't that withholding evidence?"

EIGHTEEN

CONSUELO WAITED IN THE doorway of the Windswept Dunes Motel as they walked across the parking lot, her arms folded across her blue cleaning uniform, staring at them with her wide waif-eyes.

"You have found the tape," she blurted out, even before they were in the lobby.

He nodded. "The police have them."

"The police," her eyes filled with tears. "I am lost."

Dodee went to her, putting an arm around her shoulder. "I'm sorry. There was nothing else we could do."

"Now they will believe I killed him."

"No they won't," Jim said. "You wouldn't have had the strength to lift the bonsai, much less jam it into his chest."

Yet, after a glance at her wiry arms, he wasn't so sure.

"But they have the tape." The big, waif-eyes looked up at him. "When my husband hears it, he will kill us."

Jim blinked.

Right, her husband.

"I don't think the police will release what's on the tapes," Dodee said.

Who's to say he hadn't already done it?

"Tapes?" Consuelo glanced at her. "More than one?"

"There were five—four," Jim said. "And that's only what we found on the floor."

She buried her face in her hands. "Four. He had four tapes of us?"

"I don't know if any were of you," Dodee tried to comfort her. "At least, not what we heard."

She looked up, eyes shifting between them, trying to work it out. "He was doing this to other people?"

He nodded. "Quite a lot, I think."

She rubbed her chin. "Then maybe," hope came into her face as she stood there, vulnerable in her blue uniform, "maybe they do not have the tape of us?"

Jim wanted to ask who "us" was, but said instead, "What I don't understand is, how much money could he hope to get out of you?"

"It was not money that *cabrone* was after," she spit out, folding her arms. "He was a pig. Ramon..." She bit her lip and lowered her head.

"Ramon was your lover?" Dodee blurted. "Then why didn't he put a stop to Billy?"

She shrugged. "I think Billy had a tape of Ramon, too."

They left her in the lobby and started down the glass walkway toward the elevator.

"Sounds like Billy was a real sweetie," Dodee said.

"Oh thanks," he said, feigning huffiness. "In the car you called me 'sweetie,' so that means Billy and I—"

"Wrong word." She took his hand. "You are a sweetie. Billy was a sonofabitch."

"Ah, that's better—"

She jerked him to a stop outside the conference room. "The door," she whispered. It was ajar; no light came from around the crack. "Maybe someone's in there."

He whispered back. "Good enough reason to pass it by."

"Do you think there could be any tapes?"

"The police lab already went through it. If there were any tapes—"

"No, they could have been stashed after the lab left."

"Huh? Why in the world would—"

"Think about it. Where would be the safest place to hide them? Let's take a look—"

"And suppose there's someone in there?"

"But suppose the tapes are in there? Wouldn't you like to help Consuelo?"

He shook his head. "No, Dodee, no. We've gotten into enough trouble—"

"One fast look." She raised her chin, full face to him, taking both his hands now. "Sweetie."

"Oh shi—oh damn. I know I'm going to regret—"

"A quick peek," she said, already moving to the door. "Two minutes and we're on our way."

He raised his head towards the ceiling, holding out his hands, but found no divine guidance and followed after.

"Be careful," he whispered. "Let me go in first." He took her by the shoulders, nudging her out of the way. "If there's someone in there you run like hell for help."

He kicked open the door, listened, then reached in and snapped on the lights. He heard Dodee suck in her breath and he spun around.

Someone *was* in there.

Lying face up on the table Okawa had used to style the cypress tree, arms and legs spread-eagle, neck crooked at a funny angle, glazed eyes staring into the bright overhead lights, was Winifred Harmony.

THE DETECTIVE STOOD in the lobby doorway, dark eyes rolled back so that only the whites were visible, giving her the momentary appearance of a zombie. The pupils came down to fix them in a smoldering stare. "I feel like a recorder, the same thing over and over. When the phone rang, why did I know it would be you two?"

Jim turned to Dodee, then realized it was almost like

blaming her and swung back to Belinda. "What were we supposed to do, wait until morning?"

"We were going to have Ramon call it in," Dodee added, "but—"

"You mean like for variety?" Belinda asked

"—but we couldn't find him."

Belinda looked to Consuelo. "Where is your boss?"

"I'm sorry, he is supposed to be here."

Belinda's dark eyes shifted towards the desk, as if he would suddenly appear, then came back. "You've searched for him?"

"Everywhere," she said, her waif-eyes wide. "I cannot find him."

The detective's lips turned down, and her eyes shifted once more, locking onto Jim. "Where's this new body?"

"The same place as the other one." He led the way to the conference room.

Belinda Smith whistled and shook her head. "You wouldn't happen to know who she is?"

"Winifred Harmony," he said.

"Part of your group?" He nodded and she nodded back. "Anybody been in here since you found her?" He shook his head. "How do you know?"

"Because I stood guard while Dodee made the call. We kept our eyes on it until you showed up."

Belinda motioned towards the body. "Is she here alone?"

Jim glanced around, then held out his hands. "It's the only body I see—"

"No," her little-girl voice exuded patience. "Did she come here alone?"

"With her husband," Dodee said.

"No one notified him?"

"We were hoping you would."

"Want me to get him?" Jim asked.

"No, don't go near him. I'll take care of it when backup—Sonny or the lab guys get here."

"You can't suspect Clarence?" Dodee asked.

Belinda waved her off and advanced on the body. Jim followed. "Don't touch anything."

"I won't."

There was a bruise on Winifred's cheek and her head rested at an unnatural angle to the body.

Why would anyone want to hurt her?

Much less kill her.

She seemed completely unobtrusive, following along in the shadows.

Maybe Belinda was right, that Clarence had done it. The fat man had been attentive to her at meal times, but in private, who knew?

Jim jumped as something touched his hand.

Dodee stood beside him, staring down at the body.

Belinda turned and scanned the vinyl-tile floor, her mouth open, eyes spacy, then she hastily motioned to them. "Everybody out of here. I want the door locked." She nodded to Consuelo. "You got a key?"

The cleaning lady shook her head.

"Then I need someone to guard the door until I get back."

"But the phone, if it should ring?"

"I'll watch it," Jim said.

"No, now that I'm here, I think I want you to show me that storeroom."

Dodee held up a hand like a kid in school. "I'll stay by the door. Consuelo can watch the phone."

He waited in the lobby while Belinda put in another call to the state police. "Yeah, right," she said over the phone, "we got another one. Same place. Probably connected, but that's what I'm hoping you'll tell me."

When she hung up, Jim led her through the patio to the potting shed, shining the penlight on the broken lock and reaching out to touch it until she knocked his hand away.

"I told you, don't touch anything."

She went in and flipped on the lights. He followed her, smelling the furniture cleaner stacked in plastic barrels. Folding chairs, spare hardware parts, and roll-away beds, all displayed in the full glare of fluorescent lights.

"Where did you find the cassettes?"

He led her to the back of the room, by the locked double doors and the open door to the next room, and pointed to the floor. "They were scattered along here."

She entered the next room, clicking on the lights.

Mattresses and dressers, plumbing supplies, four televisions off to the right, and five boxes containing the two-cup coffeemakers like the one in his room.

"Don't touch anything. In fact, stay in the doorway."

He backed away and watched as she pulled out a pencil, bent over, and picked up another cassette by slipping the point through the sprocket hole.

"If he kept dropping these things all over the place," she said, "he must have had an armful."

"Are you holding it like that in case of fingerprints?" He watched her nod. "You didn't do it with the tapes we found."

She cocked her head to him. "With the way you handled them?" She stared at the tape a moment, twisting the pencil, and the cassette with it. "You know anything you're not telling me?"

He held out his hands in a shrug, ready to protest his innocence when he thought of stashing Harry's tape among his music cassettes. But all he meant to do was keep the librarian out of it.

"We found out he was using a computer," he said. "Down at the library."

"Billy? How did you find that out?"

"The guy in the hardware store said Billy used to hang out in the library a lot, and the librarian—"

"Bleacher?"

He blinked. "Bleacher?"

"Bleacher, Harry Bleacher, the librarian. That's her name."

"I guess. She said everybody called her Harry. She told us he used the computer a lot. We came to the conclusion he was using the telephone directory they have on CD-ROM."

She pressed her lips together, dimpling the chin on her chocolate face. "Why not just pick up a phone book?"

"Because the computer has all the phone numbers in the United States. You can also get addresses from it."

She nodded and studied the cassette perched on the pencil point. "Initials on here and a number."

"Could be a phone number?"

She glanced around one more time, then motioned him ahead of her. "Let's get out of here. I want to keep this place clean for the lab guys."

They headed for the door.

"Somehow I can't picture Dack handling a heavy black-mail operation like this," she said. "But then I would never have suspected him of visiting the library either, much less using their computer."

"Uh-huh. For the last four months, Harry said."

He led the way back through the main storage room.

Why four months?

"Hey, wait a minute." He spun around, feeling like a

little light had popped on in the dark recesses of his brain. "Did Billy know Bixby Boyd?"

"Where did you hear about Bixby Boyd?"

"The desk clerk told me. Said he was a computer nerd who was murdered here four months ago."

Her dark eyes studied him for a moment, then she motioned for the door again. They headed out into the gelid night, bright stars in a moonless sky.

"How about you," he said, putting the question to her, "you know anything you're not telling me?"

"Hey," she held out her arms, her face hidden in the shadow of the patio lights, "I'm the police. I'm the one who's supposed to be asking the questions, knowwhatamean? You don't need to know anything."

"I was just wondering. It seemed to fit, Boyd getting killed and Billy starting to use the library's computer around the time." They skirted the pool. "And if Winnie was killed in the same room as Billy—"

"I don't know that she was. Wait, scratch that." Belinda turned to him, hand on the lobby door. "Were you ever in the military?"

"Korea. Wasn't everybody my age?"

"I wouldn't know, but I don't want you to repeat that. Like it's a military secret."

"Repeat what? You didn't tell me anything."

"That. Don't repeat anything. Not about the body or the tapes or the blackmail or Bixby Boyd. And that goes for Ms. Swisher, too. I could still run you both in for poaching plants on city property."

NINETEEN

QUARRELING BIRDS jerked him wide-eyed awake, some sort of territorial dispute taking place out on the balcony.

He glanced at his watch.

Ten o'clock.

Sonofabitch, he'd miss the morning's bonsai session.

Not surprising, considering he didn't hit the sack until four a.m. He had sent Dodee off to her room at two-thirty, after telling her about Bixby Boyd, but hung on with Belinda until the lab people arrived from the state police.

He threw back the covers, climbed to his feet, and stared out the glass doors.

At the horizon a blue sky, streaked with mares-tails blended with a blue sea streaked with spindrift.

Ramon had never shown up.

So, did that mean the night manager was a suspect?

Who cares?

Just so long as it wasn't him and Dodee.

He plugged in the two-cup coffeemaker, sprayed the collected junipers, thought about shaving, decided he could hold off, showered, toweled off, and stood in the window in his shorts, drinking coffee, watching Barney come trudging into view along the deserted beach, just above wave reach, hands tucked deep in the pockets of his leather bomber jacket, collar pulled up around his neck, head hunched down against the cold.

What was he doing out there?

Why wasn't he in the bonsai class?

Unless, after visiting the nurseries in Japan, he considered the classes too elementary.

Elementary, my dear Watson.

He sprayed the junipers again, put on a pair of stone gray Square Riggers, a thermal-type waffle weave vanilla shirt, a pair of penny loafers and headed downstairs.

In the lobby he found a small knot of people: Barney, still in the bomber jacket; Dodee and Aunt Alice; and Kelly and Sana, all gazing out at the parking lot. Simon Crew stood to one side by the registration desk, dressed in slacks, shirt and tie, and gold-buttoned blazer.

The object of interest turned out to be Clarence Harmony, standing beside his car, a young woman hugging him, her head buried in his shoulder, a man standing next to them, awkwardly holding a suitcase and an overnight bag.

Dodee wrapped both her arms around one of Jim's. He motioned towards the parking lot. "Took it hard?"

She nodded. "From what I understand. That's his daughter, and I guess her husband. Clarence went to the airport and picked them up."

"Um. At least he has someone here to comfort him."

She sighed and shrugged. "The police are looking for him."

He turned to her. "For Clarence?"

"He was supposed to stay at the motel and give Belinda a statement."

"Well, then he's not wanted," he turned back to see them heading into the motel, "I mean like wanted wanted."

"Wanted for questioning. Belinda wants him to call as soon as he shows up."

They came in the door and Aunt Alice walked over to give Clarence a hug, and the rest of the group, as if that were a signal, circled around.

"I'm so sorry, Clarence," said Aunt Alice. "I know a real big light has gone out of your life. Is there any way I can help?"

"Ah," he looked at her and the others with dazed blue eyes, and raised his pudgy hands only to let them fall. He turned to the woman standing next to him. "This is my daughter, Linda."

"Hi," Linda said, big tears welling up and threatening to spill over a round, ruddy face she inherited from her father.

"I'll check in," said her husband, heading for the desk, "and we can go from there."

"The police have some questions for you," Dodee said to Clarence. "They've been here a couple of times already."

Clarence blinked at her, the words not sinking in.

Linda moved in protectively, the tears disappearing. "What kind of questions?"

"I don't know." Dodee's lips turned down. "Maybe like when he last saw your mother."

"Wouldn't tell them a damn thing," Barney growled, square chin jutting out. "Get a lawyer, Clarence. Make sure he's at your side when you report."

Linda's eyes turned hard as she put a hand on her father's shoulder. "I don't think it's that kind of questioning, Pop," she said, and wheeled on Barney. "You're getting him worried." Her husband came up with a room key. "Pop, why don't you wait here while Paul and I drop our things off and go to the bathroom? Then we'll drive to the police station and straighten it out."

Clarence watched, zombielike, as they headed down to the elevator.

"Come sit," Aunt Alice said, putting her hand on his shoulder and leading him to the first of two facing divans.

Jim sat across from Clarence, Dodee at his side. Barney took a chair at one end of the conversation enclosure. Sana squeezed in next to Dodee, and Kelly rested one leg on the arm of the divan next to her, one hand resting on the seat back, her larger stature giving the appearance of being in a protective mode to her smaller friend. Simon Crew moved in to stand nearby, joined by Tiffany in a green cable sweater and shorts, green stretch leggings underneath.

Kelly folded her large hands on her knee. "We're all sorry, Clarence," she said in her husky voice. "Would it help to talk about it?"

The fat man shrugged and gazed glassy-eyed at her. "They woke me at five o'clock and asked me to come downstairs. They said there was an accident." He scanned the group. "They wanted me to identify the body. Winnie—" His lips quivered.

Dodee shook her head. "You don't have to talk about it."

"No, maybe I should," Clarence said, regaining control. "Get it out like." He glanced back to Kelly. "She was bruised, and they said she had a broken neck. Probably never felt a thing, they said. Could have fallen down some stairs, they said, or been pushed." His eyes opened wide and he scanned them again. "Then they told me she might have been murdered." The fat man held out his pudgy hands, beseeching them. "Why would anyone want to kill Winnie? Never gave anyone a cross word. Why would anyone do that?" He buried his face in his hands.

Silence descended like a shroud as he fought to regain control, Aunt Alice giving him baby pats on the back.

Then Clarence abruptly glanced at Dodee. "What kind of questions they gonna ask?"

She shrugged. "Like: when did you see her last."

"When I went to bed. She was still up watching television. I woke up around eleven and the television was off and she was gone."

"If it would not seem too impolite to ask," came Sana's singsong voice, "why is it that you did not go looking for her?"

"I should have." Clarence hung his head and shook it. "I should have. She would be alive now. It's my fault."

"No," Aunt Alice patted his back again, "it's not your fault. You can't blame yourself for things you couldn't foresee."

"I don't know what I'm going to do." He shook his head and heaved a massive sigh. "At least Winnie got to travel, like she always wanted." He nodded. "I should have gone with her more, from the beginning rather than wait until now. Always worried about the business. How could it run without me? Somehow I forgot Winnie was the whole reason for making the money."

"Excuse me, but I still don't understand why you didn't look for her," Kelly said.

Clarence stared at his hands, opening them up as if they held the answer. "She'd been having trouble sleeping lately. The last two months or so. Even here, going out to get fresh air, she said. So I didn't think anything about it."

"See," Barney clapped his hands together, "that's why I'd advise getting a lawyer. Without proof they could twist that around and claim you were making it up."

Jim glared at the retired general, then noticed everyone doing the same thing, everyone silently shouting for the man to shut up.

"We can testify to her insomnia," Dodee said. "We saw her roaming the halls."

"Even so," Barney, oblivious, kept right on, "I've served on enough courts-martial boards to learn one thing: take a lawyer. Cover your ass."

Clarence was spared any more of Barney's advice as his daughter came around the corner, gathered him up, and headed him out the door.

Jim turned on Barney. "Why didn't you shut the hell up?"

He held out his hands. "What did I say?"

"You just made him a nervous wreck, that's all, with everything else he has to worry about."

"Just trying to protect him, Jim."

Dodee stood up. "It's not that kind of questioning."

"How do you know, Dodee?" Barney stood up with her.

"Because it's not," was her lame retort.

Jim put his arm around Dodee's waist, tempted to give a stronger defense—like the guy who killed Billy probably also killed Winnie. But he didn't know that. And Belinda had told him to shut the hell up, about the tapes and the blackmail and everything else.

"We heard you two also found Winnie's body," Tiffany said, stretch leggings showing off long legs.

"Yes," Simon smiled, "maybe we shouldn't be standing so close to you."

Tiffany's brow wrinkled. "And somebody knocked you out."

"Who told you that?" Jim asked.

The April-December couple turned to Alice Atwater.

"Maybe I did," she said from her place on the divan. "Wasn't I supposed to?"

"I don't see any secret to it," Dodee answered.

"How did you get hit on the head?" Tiffany asked again.

"I wasn't hit on the head," Jim said. "Someone kneed me in the chin."

"Really?" Barney's eyebrows raised. "How did he knee you in the chin, Jim?"

"I was sitting on the floor at the time." He didn't want

to get into this. It only led to the storeroom and the cassettes and the blackmail. "What did I miss this morning in bonsai class?"

Sana bounded off the couch. "We potted the plants we wired yesterday."

"We start on group plantings this afternoon," Kelly added.

"I wonder why they didn't cancel the session," Tiffany said, "with the murder of Winnie and all."

Dodee shrugged. "Maybe it's in the Elderhostel contract."

"Oh, maybe," Tiffany nodded, then glanced at Jim. "What were you doing sitting on the floor? You know, when you got kicked?"

Jim took a deep breath and let it out.

They kept coming back to the same damn subject.

But Dodee answered. "We were sneaking around where we didn't belong, in the storeroom, looking for a shovel."

"Digging up more plants?" asked Barney.

"We thought we'd go back and smooth out the hole," Jim said.

Tiffany's eyes widened. "So it didn't have anything to do with the tapes you found?"

Jim gaped at her.

"Tapes?" Sana pounced.

"Recording tapes?" Kelly snatched at it, too. "Where did you find them?"

"What was on them?" Barney said.

"How did you find out about the cassettes?" Jim asked.

Tiffany shrugged. "Somebody told me." She turned to her husband. "You remember?"

Simon shrugged as well. "I think it was at breakfast."

Sana put her hand on Tiffany's arm. "Please, could you tell me, please, what indeed it was these tapes contained?"

Tiffany motioned to Jim. "You'll have to ask him."

"I don't know," he said. "We found some cassettes on the floor and turned them over to the police."

They all thought about that for a moment before Tiffany tried again. "Are they linked to the murders?"

He shrugged.

"Yes, it must," Tiffany went on, tenacious as a prosecutor. "Why else would you turn them over? Are you suspects for this murder as well?"

Dodee shook her head. "We don't even know if there's a connection between the two."

"But they're not suspects anymore." Aunt Alice glanced up to Dodee from the divan. "Isn't that what you told me?"

Dodee nodded. "At the time the busboy was killed we were at the police station."

"Is it possible, please," Sana said, "for someone to tell us what indeed is on the tapes?"

"Something incriminating, I should imagine," Tiffany answered.

Jim shrugged again.

They were creeping along the edge of blackmail, and if Belinda suspected him of spreading it all over the motel, what delicate parts of his body would she cut off?

TWENTY

WINNIE'S UNTIMELY DEATH cast a pall over the afternoon class. Still, aside from Clarence, everyone showed up.

"Ah see our sleepyheads are with us again," Okawa grinned, deep Georgian accent rolling off his tongue as he gamely tried to capture their attention. "This afternoon we'll be working on a group planting, three or five trees, your choice, to a pot. Why not four, anyone?" His impish grin returned when no hands were raised. "The only even number of trees we use is two, because even numbers tend to look artificially planted, so we always use odd numbers."

"How about if it's a large number," Simon Crew asked, looking like a professor with his shirt and tie covered by a white lab coat. "Say if you have, oh, five hundred trees?"

Okawa grinned. "If you have five hundred trees you don't have a bonsai. You have a real forest." He looked down at the plants he had assembled on the table and backed up. "I suppose if you had a planting of so many trees that it would be hard to count, then maybe an even number would pass, but the idea of bonsai is to give an impression of nature using a minimum of materials—" he raised his muscular arm, but made a delicate motion with his fingers "—like an artist using just a few strokes of the brush." His voice dropped as he talked with deepening emotion. "Three, five, seven trees well-styled can give the illusion of a forest. That is the art of bonsai. That was the original purpose of bonsai, to create not a copy, but a remembrance of God's handiwork."

So inspired, everyone started choosing their trees, all junipers, seeming to be the tree of choice for bonsai classes. Probably because they were hardy. And maybe because they were cheap.

Dodee was doing five trees.

Screw it.

Jim was only doing three.

With Okawa's help he got the three trees placed, off the centerlines, and so no one tree hid another. Then he trimmed and wired the branches so that the outline of all three had a pleasing triangular look, and he was ready to add soil.

Dodee came over to stand beside him, examining his work.

"What do you think?" he asked.

"Good. You do that yourself?"

"Yeah, all by myself, without any help from Okawa." He watched her lips spread with ends turned down. "Well, maybe a little help."

"I didn't figure you did it alone. Even so, it looks good."

"How about yours?"

She walked back to her table and returned with the finished product. "I needed help, too."

He raised the pot to study it at eye level, like a person standing in a field, rather than gazing down on it like a god.

The trees were planted in two groups, three in one, two in the other, separated by a little swale in the soil, creating the impression of a dry stream bed. The thinner trees placed to the back gave it depth, like the forest continued in the distance.

"That's really great. I can almost see myself sitting down and resting my back against one of them."

"It will be better when I get some moss on it," she said.

"Um," he handed it back, "then I'll be able to lie down."

"We can bring a basket and have a picnic."

"Ah, then we can both lie down and—" he blinked at her.

"Dirty old man."

"I'm not that old," he whispered.

He worked down a dry, course soil mix between the hair roots of his trees with a pointed chopstick and turned at the smell of stale cigarette smoke.

Barney grinned beside him. "So, Jim, what do you think?" he asked, holding up his creation.

Barney had also used five trees.

"Not bad at all." Whatever else, it was better than his, but it wasn't as natural as Dodee's. Then again, he was no doubt prejudiced in her favor. "You did a good job."

Barney nodded, trying not to smile. "Yours is coming along too, Jim," he said and drifted off to share his masterpiece.

By the time Jim finished potting his trees, Dodee had her soil covered with moss. Okawa held it up to the class.

"This is an excellent start of a group planting," he said. "Notice how Miz Swisher put this chere nice layer of moss on it. Shazam. Looks like a small glen or dell, doesn't it?"

"Looks like a little lawn under some trees," Simon Crew said, his white lab coat still impeccably clean.

"Or a golf course," added Kelly.

"Indeed it is much like a place where a Bengal tiger lurks," Sana continued, "ready to jump out and eat you up."

Okawa brought the pot up close to his eyes, turned and smiled. "Nope, no tigers." Grins all around. "Moss on the bonsai shows well for display, and it holds the soil while everything settles for the first week or two, but after that, take most of it off. It holds too much moisture and prevents air from getting to the roots.''

At the end of the class all the group plantings were lined up on a table to be viewed.

Jim judged his own to be somewhere in the middle of the pack, with the low end being Simon Crew, who seemed to lack any artistic talent, and Kelly Massey, who was barely better. Dodee's was up at the top end, but one group of seven trees, prejudice or no, was clearly better, and understanding dawned when they found it to belong to Okawa.

"This was good, wasn't it?" Dodee asked, cleaning up her work station.

He nodded. "I learned a lot."

"We ought to show Okawa our collected trees and see what he suggests." She turned to the bonsai master. "We collected two trees that we think will make good bonsai. Would you like to come see them?"

"No, bring them here and we can show the whole class."

"I'll go," Jim said, running down the hallway and retrieving the trees from his bedroom, returning to plop them on the table.

"Very good," Okawa nodded. He pulled out a bonsai clipper and cleaned off some scruffy branchlets, leaving the stubs. Already they looked better. Then he cut a branch off each, leaving the remaining one as a twisted trunk, and carved bark off the rough stubs so they looked like nature had peeled them back. Okawa studied them a moment. "Winds coming over a cliff killed these stubs and stretched everything out in one direction. They are going to make nice wind-swept bonsai. Where did you find them?"

"Here in Bolder Harbor," Dodee said.

"The police caught us and we were almost thrown in jail," Jim added.

Okawa grinned and wagged a finger. "What did I tell you about getting permission?"

When the class ended Jim hefted the trees.

"Can you make it alone?" Dodee asked. "I want to help Aunt Alice. Are you caught up on your sleep from last night?"

He nodded. "Yeah, I think so."

"Oh. I thought you might still be tired." A fleeting smile crossed her face. "Like you could use a nap?"

"Hey, now that you mention it," he yawned, "I can hardly keep my eyes open."

"Let me take care of Aunt Alice and maybe I'll be by."

"I'll try to stay awake."

He took the trees back up to his room, setting them by the window and spraying them, then he rushed into the bathroom and ran his hand across his rough cheek.

Damn.

Should have shaved when he showered.

He spread gel on his face and did a hurry-up with the razor, splashing his face with a sexy-smelling Paul Sebastian aftershave that his daughter had given him for Christmas, and heard a knock on the door.

But when he yanked it open, instead of Dodee's blue eyes, he stared into two dusky ones set in a milk-chocolate face.

"Hello, Detective."

"Were you sleeping?" Belinda Smith asked.

"No, of course not."

"Too bad."

"Too bad?"

"Yeah, I'd like to get you out of bed for a change. May I come in?"

He held the door open and she entered, glancing around. "She's not here?"

"Dodee, no, but—"

"Her aunt said she was on her way."

"Is there something I can do for you?"

She took a seat at the table by the window. "Nice view," she motioned towards the ocean where late afternoon clouds were building.

Well, shit. If he and Dodee wanted to get in a nap before dinner, he would have to get rid of the detective, but instead found himself saying, "Would you like a beer?" and then mentally kicked himself for asking.

She looked at her watch. "Yeah, I guess I would."

Double shit.

Now she'd stay forever.

He popped opened two Samuel Adams and handed her one. "Glass?"

"This is fine." She tipped the bottle and swallowed a third of it. "I was on my way home and I wanted to check Ms. Swisher's—Dodee's—statement about the tape recorder on Billy's body." She took another sip, studied the label, and took another. "We didn't come up with any prints on the cassette we found, or down in the storeroom. Except for yours and hers."

He sat on the bed. "This mean we're suspects again?"

She shook her head. "Coroner puts Winifred Harmony's death at about the time," she flopped a hand back and forth, "roughly, when you two were in the clinic. How do you manage to do that? Have perfect alibis?"

He smiled. "By being perfectly innocent?"

"Yeah." She sipped from her beer. "Everybody is innocent." She drank some more.

He took a sip from his bottle. "Everybody? Who else do you suspect?"

She shrugged. "Of course nobody has alibis like you two, but then nobody keeps popping up like you two, thank you very much." She glanced at him. "You seen Ramon, the night manager?"

He shook his head. "You think he's involved in the blackmail?"

"Who don't I suspect?"

"Like who?"

The dark eyes locked onto him as she pressed her lips together, wrinkling her chin. "What do you know about your fellow classmates?"

He shrugged. "Not a lot. Barney Sopwaite is from Pittsburgh, I think, and—"

"No, he's from Chad's Ford."

He thought about that a moment, then turned and found the address list Lee Sullivan had passed out. "You're right."

"Of course I'm right."

"But it's near Pittsburgh."

"Philadelphia."

"Okay, Philadelphia. I had them mixed up."

"So if you got the list, where do the rest of them come from?"

"Kelly Massey comes from New Hope—that's near Philadelphia, right? And so does Sana, Vasantha Powell."

"That's good. Now what about the Crews?"

He looked up to the top of the list. "Philadelphia."

"Ahh. And what else do you know about the Crews?"

He looked down at the list, running through it again. "They have the same zip code as Clarence Harmony?"

She nodded. "Furthermore, Billy Dack was arrested for breaking and entering up in New Hope, and served time before showing up down here. These guys are all from roughly the same geographic area."

"So you think—"

"I don't know. I'm just dumping the facts like a computer." She motioned across the room. "Is Ms. Swisher coming?"

He shrugged. "She mentioned she might." He watched as she drained her beer. "What about Billy and New Hope?"

"Just what I told you. We're running background checks on everybody now." She stood up. "Something else, Ramon was a suspect in a murder case in Pennsylvania, but they couldn't make it stick. Case is still open."

"How about Bixby Boyd? That case still open?"

She nodded. "Boyd was a hacker. Worked odd jobs. Tax records show he had a computer business on the side. Had income, but no clients." She shrugged. "Could have been Billy. Then maybe Billy learns how to handle the computer himself and decides Boyd's dispensable. Who knows?" She examined the bottle. "Samuel Adams, eh? First time I ever had one. Not bad. Gotta go. Have Dodee call me tomorrow."

He saw Belinda out, finished off his beer while watching the sea and clouds, and lay down on the bed, folding his hands behind his head.

So everyone was from the same area.

What did that mean?

He stretched and rested his eyes for a moment, and when he opened them, the room had shifted from daylight to shadows. He popped off the bed and rushed to the window. A slate gray sea, under a slate gray sky, rolled onto the beach, the waves humping out of it like prehistoric monsters.

Where the hell was Dodee?

Had she knocked on the door when he was asleep?

He changed his shirt, put on a jacket, and headed down to the dining room.

Aunt Alice, two empty chairs beside her, like she was saving them, sat with the Crews and Sana, but he could see Dodee nowhere. A sharp knot of apprehension twisted his stomach and he hurried towards the table.

It was silly, he knew. She could still be in her room, putting on makeup, or not feeling well, or at the desk getting information or something, but the two empty seats sucked him in like a malevolent tornado.

"Where's Dodee?"

Aunt Alice's mouth dropped open and the watery blue eyes widened. "Why, I was going to ask you the same thing."

TWENTY-ONE

HE RUSHED OUT to the registration desk.

"Any messages for me? James P. Dandy, room—"

"Yes, as a matter of fact," interrupted the redheaded desk clerk who had checked Jim in the first day. He looked in the key box on the wall and then around the counter. "I just had it—ah," he picked up a piece of paper and handed it over. "We rang your room, but you must—"

"Thanks," he grabbed it out of the man's hand.

I'm onto something. Please call ASAP. Dodee.

There was a phone number with it.

He let out a sigh of relief.

"Is this a local call?" He showed the note to the clerk and watched him nod. "Thanks," he said, and headed for the dining room.

Now what the hell was she up to?

"I got a phone call from Dodee." He waved the message at Aunt Alice. "She wants me to call."

"Where is she?"

He shrugged. "You know Dodee." He bent over and whispered in her ear. "She says she's onto something. I hope we're not digging up another damn tree."

He called from the public phone by the elevator.

She answered on the third ring. "Hello?"

"Dodee, what's up?"

"Oh, Jim, I—"

Tussling noises came through from the other end, and a loud bang like the receiver falling and hitting something, and a whistling, like the wind across the mouthpiece, then a new voice.

"Okay, I gotcha girlfriend here." It was guttural and gravelly and obviously disguised, and it raised chill bumps on his skin. "Ya wanna see her again? Alive?"

The thought ran through Jim's head that maybe it was a joke. But even though Dodee might kid around, he couldn't believe she would do this. And how could she pull it off in a strange city?

"Ya hear me?" demanded the voice, muffled roar of the surf as background. "Or you wanna hear yer girlfriend scream a little bit so you know I'm serious?"

"No!" Definitely not a joke. "What do you want?"

"What was that cop doing in yer room this afternoon?"

The guy was doing a poor job disguising his voice, an inconsistent pitch, but then Jim hadn't a clue to who it was so maybe it was effective after all.

"Ya hear me?"

"Yes. She wanted to tell me they didn't find any fingerprints in the storage room."

"That's all? She spent fifteen minutes in yer room and that's it?"

"No. We had a beer and she told me Dodee and I were in the clear." He debated telling him about going over the list and decided against it. "We talked about Samuel Adams, uh, that's the beer we were drinking." If the guy knew Belinda had come to his room, he had to be staying at the hotel. "And about Billy Dack having a criminal record." If it even was a he. "That's all."

Silence on the other end, only the soft whistle of wind, and the far off crash of a wave, and just as he thought the guy had cut out, the voice came again.

"I want the tapes."

"I don't have the tapes."

"The man who hit ya in the storeroom has the tapes."

"Okay, who is it?"

"You find out. Get the tapes."

"Hey, wait a minute—" Jim held out his free hand "—how do you expect me—"

"Find the tapes and ya get ya girlfriend back. Ya don't, kiss her goodbye. The same if ya call the police. I'll call ya in two hours."

"Wait a minute, wait a minute!" He listened to see if the man was still there, hearing wind and waves, but no dial tone. "I'll do what you want, okay, but how am I supposed to find—"

"Search the rooms. Someone in that class should have 'em. You have two hours."

"But, wait…"

Now he did hear the dial tone.

He put down the receiver, holding his hand on it.

He should call Belinda.

Get the state police in and when the guy phones back, trace the call and nail him. Over. Finished. Complete.

He picked up the receiver and waited for the dial tone.

"Hi, Jim." He jerked around to see Kelly coming from the dining room, looking rugged in her trail clothes. "We're going to the movies. You and Dodee want to come?"

"No, I don't think so."

"Picture's changed. They're playing *Ping Pong*. We're meeting in the parking lot at seven if you want a ride."

"Uh-huh." He watched her hit the elevator button. "Who's going?"

"Everybody's talking about it. I don't know if everyone is going, but we're all supposed to meet afterwards at the bar next door for a drink."

"Maybe we'll meet you there." He watched the elevator close on her.

Suppose it had been Kelly on the other end?

Probably not, but suppose?

The number he had called could be in the motel. Well, not in the motel, but, say, out on the pool patio where he could hear the wind and surf. And then Kelly could have raced across the lobby to see how he was reacting.

Oh, so, making a call to the police, eh, Jim? Well, Dodee's toast, buddy.

Whoever it was knew Belinda had spent fifteen minutes in his room, and maybe knew what he was doing right now. He would certainly know if the police suddenly showed up all over the place.

He looked at his watch.

Six-thirty. Probably six-twenty when the guy hung up. Ten minutes already gone.

Search the rooms, the guy had said.

How the hell was he supposed to do that?

It's not like he had a key—but maybe.

He marched down to the lobby.

"Hi," said the redheaded clerk.

"Is Ramon here?"

"No, I don't know where Ramon is. Can I help you?"

He wondered what the chance was of getting a master key from him. Probably slim to none. "Actually I wanted to see Consuelo."

"Consuelo?" The clerk pulled a paper from a desk drawer, running his finger along it. "Consuelo doesn't come on until eight. Would you want her to contact you?"

"I'll contact her. I asked her to look for something I lost. Just wondering if she found it."

He headed for his room.

Eight o'clock. Sonofabitch. If he waited for her he'd

have only twenty minutes to search. And suppose she was late?

Maybe he could get an extension.

He entered his room, picked up the phone, and re-dialed the number on the message slip.

No answer.

No surprise.

Probably a pay phone somewhere.

He swung to the balcony doors.

If the phone call was made from the motel, the guy could be out on the beach right now, watching him.

He turned off the light, crossed the room, unlatched the sliding glass door and slipped outside, letting his eyes adjust as the darkness sucked the heat from his body. Heavy clouds had moved in since the afternoon, blocking what little light the stars provided, so even if there was someone lurking on the beach, or on the pool patio below, or down the row of balconies stretching across the length of the motel, he would never be able to see him. Shivering, he bundled back inside, slid the door shut, locked it, and stood staring at it in the dark. If the motel was bringing in a crew to work on the balcony doors…

He snatched the handle and yanked it sideways.

The lock caught in the clasp, held a moment, then gave way under tension.

Were all the balcony doors the same way?

Why not find out?

He pulled off his shirt and pants, put on his dark clothes from the night before, found Dodee's penlight in his car coat, made sure it was working, then stepped into the cold.

Only a low wall separated the balconies, each abutting the next. Most of the Elderhostelers were staying on the ocean side. That's what Lee Sullivan had said. Problem was, who belonged to which?

Then again, what did it matter?

He peeked over the railing to the room next door.

Lights out, curtain closed.

He peered down the row of balconies, and to those above, to the heavy black clouds threatening rain, and to the beach below, seeing no one, smelling no one either, like a smoker out for a cigarette, and scampered over the wall. The lock caught on the clasp, than gave way under pressure, and he slipped in behind the closed drapery and shut the door.

What would he say if someone were in the room?

Hi, I got locked out on my balcony and I'm just passing through.

Well, actually, that wasn't bad, if he had knocked on the door to begin with.

He pulled back the curtain and flicked on his penlight, giving the room a quick scan. The beds were made. The dresser drawers shut. No light came from the bathroom.

He rushed across and listened at the hall door.

Nothing.

But somebody could be on the other side, key in hand.

He carefully set the night chain.

Sure, they might be suspicious if they couldn't get in, but in the meantime he'd be long gone.

God, he wished Dodee could see how slick he was.

He flashed the penlight into the closet, opened the dresser drawers, checked the suitcase rack. Empty, empty, empty. Folded towels in the bathroom. Sanitary paper wound around the toilet seat.

Sonofabitch.

The room was unoccupied.

He unlatched the night chain, hurried outside, and scampered over to the next balcony. Light seeped out from the edges of the closed drapery. Trouble was, most people left a motel light on when they went out. He knocked softly on the glass door.

"Hi," he rehearsed, "I got locked out on my balcony. Could I pass through to the hallway?"

He knocked again, harder this time, still no answer. He forced the lock and hurried inside, peeking around the curtains.

A taste of perfume hung in the air. It went with a pair of high heeled shoes lumped atop one of the beds, the made up one; the other with two white pillows exposed at the top. One sheer stocking hung over the edge of an open dresser drawer. A closed bag sat on the suitcase rack. Two glasses rested on the bartop of the small fridge, one a quarter full of an amber fluid, like ice had melted in a sip of scotch.

He pushed the drapery aside and stepped into the room.

"Honey, is that you?" a female voice called from bathroom.

At the same time someone shoved a key into the hall door.

kitchen light on when they went out. He knocked softly on
the door.

"I'll be right out," she answered him on the hi-tone
Could....

TWENTY-TWO

JIM SCRAMBLED behind the curtain as the hall door flung
open.

"Are you ready yet?" came Simon Crew's voice.

He heard a small squeak—the bathroom door opening?

"What's the matter?" Simon's voice again.

A silence taut as a rubber band.

"I thought I heard someone out here," Tiffany answered.

Jim sensed the redhead's round eyes searching the room.
Was the drapery moving? And his shoes, suddenly feeling
big as clown's feet, were they sticking out underneath?

"No," Simon again, ending the silence, "you heard me
at the door. Come on, if we're going to do this thing, I
want to get it over and done with."

"Okay, let me get my flashlight and jacket." The sound
of coat hangers clacking against one another on the rack.
"You got money?"

"Yes, let's go, let's go."

Jim heard the door close and let out a quiet breath.

Sonofabitch, he wasn't made for this.

How do criminals do it?

He waited for an eternity, just in case; with the lights
still on, they could have only played at leaving while se-
cretly waiting for him to step out and expose himself. Well,
not expose himself, but be exposed. He peeked around the
curtain at the empty room, hurried across and put the night
chain on the door, then wiped it clean of his fingerprints.

Damn, he should have worn gloves.

He found a gender division on the bathroom sink: man's

underarm deodorant and aftershave—Eternity for Men by Calvin Klein—and Schick razor on the left; medicated hand lotion, fingernail polish, Passion perfume spray by Elizabeth Taylor, and a battery-operated Panasonic Smooth Operator on the right. Toothbrushes in cases occupied the middle ground.

But no tape cassettes.

On the countertop of the waist-high fridge, along with the two glasses and the hotel coffeemaker, he found a stethoscope.

Was Simon a doctor?

No, he was a stock broker.

Maybe Tiffany was the doctor. Simon had said he was a client of hers.

Next he tried the closet, an open alcove with closed looped hangers on a plastic bar. He patted the pockets of the dresses and suits, feeling something in the side pocket of one, a woman's dress jacket, and pulled out a small wallet fold. He opened it up to find a private detective's license issued in the state of Pennsylvania to Tiffany Corbett Crew, her picture identification on the opposite side.

Well, how do you like that?

He closed it, then opened it again.

Was she down here on a case? Using the Elderhostel business as a cover? It would explain a lot of things, like what was a young woman doing here with a man old enough to be her grandfather.

And maybe really was!

He pictured the statuesque redhead in his mind and tried to figure if she was tall enough to be the one who kneed him in the storeroom. When you're kneeling on the floor things can get out of perspective. And now all those karate kicks and hand chops he had seen Tiffany practicing that first afternoon on the balcony made sense.

If we're going to do this, let's get it over with.

Get what over with?

He replaced the leather ID folder and started through the drawers, patting down shirts and blouses and looking under socks and stockings. In the bottom drawer, under dirty underwear, he came upon a number ten business envelope. Inside he found a photocopy of a letter from the law firm of Solomon, Levey, Berkman, Garzerelli, Mukherjee, Thomas, and White, commissioning the Tiffany Corbett Detective Agency to represent them in the recovery of information, printed and otherwise, pertinent to the pending divorce cases of Robert M. Powell and Raymond Massey, and authorized her to spend up to fifty thousand dollars in the recovery of same.

Fifty thousand dollars!

Sonofabitch.

He refolded the letter and peered down at the open drawer.

Suppose, if Tiffany was a detective, suppose she had placed some hairs on the drawers to check if someone had searched the room while she was out. Like in the James Bond movies. He bent over and carefully repositioned the envelope as he had found it, covering it with the dirty underwear, then inspected the area, finally giving it up. There could be a hundred screwed-up telltales by this time.

He straightened up and felt a zing of protest from his back, old bones and old muscles reminding him of his age. Stretching and bending, he carefully worked out the kink, thanking God he kept up with strength exercises or he'd be flat on the floor. He was glad he wasn't young anymore, with all the problems and worries and uncertainties of youth, but he damn sure wouldn't mind having a young body again.

He continued the search, beneath the bed, under the pillows, feeling between mattresses and the pockets of suit-cases.

No tapes.

Stands to reason.

If Tiffany had found what she wanted, wouldn't she have returned to Philadelphia and collected her fifty thousand?

He gave a last look around, slipped onto the balcony, and rushed back in to unlatch the night chain.

The next room contained no men's aftershave, but double everything for a woman. He found a half full bottle of Scotch on the fridge's countertop, and a name tag on one of the suitcases: Vasantha Powell.

He patted down clothes in the closet, dresses and slacks, felt something in a jacket that turned out to be a piece of folded paper with nothing on it, but a Land's End label on the inside had a name stitched to it—Kelly Massey.

He checked dressers—bras, panties, and hose. Both beds were messed up and he searched between the mattress and under the pillows.

No cassettes.

But something nipped at the edge of his mind as he scanned the room—yeah, buddy.

Tiffany was suppose to recover documents in the divorce cases of Robert M. Powell and Raymond Massey.

Names a coincidence?

Not very damn likely. Not with a stethoscope in the Crew's room and an adjoining wall in between.

Assume Billy was blackmailing the husbands, say like they had been down here screwing around. So here comes Sana and Kelly, trying to buy the evidence to use in divorce court. And Tiffany trying to keep it out.

That works.

And say Billy carried on a bidding war between the two,

and the loser, showing a definite streak of bad sportsman-
ship, got pissed enough to bump him off.

Bump him off?

Ha, he was sounding like a two-bit detective novel.

But did any of them have the strength to jam a bonsai
into Billy's chest? Kelly Massey, definitely. And Tiffany,
probably. And Simon, maybe.

But what about Winnie?

Nothing fit with that.

Unless, roaming the halls at night, she had seen one of
them do it. Or the murderer thought she had seen him. Or
murderess. Either way, Winnie gets it.

Or unless it was Clarence. Now there was someone with
the strength to ram home the bonsai. If Billy had caught
Sana and Kelly's husbands in an affair, why not Clarence?
Except he couldn't see Clarence having an affair, and the
way the man had acted so broken up over Winnie's death—
unless it was just that, an act.

Maybe there was no link between the murders, just a
copycat to make it look like there was.

He wished Dodee were here to bounce off ideas.

Which brought back the urgency of the search.

He undid the night chain and rushed onto the next balcony, then flattened against the wall as he saw a woman
through the half-open draperies, his breath billowing like a
smoke stack in the cold night air. She lay on one of the
beds, book in her hand; he eased forward to see Aunt Alice's face and let out a sigh.

He darted across to the next balcony, Aunt Alice never
looking up, and repeated what was becoming a routine:
night chain, bathroom, closet, dresser, beds, night chain and
back on the balcony, only this room was dark and he had
to use the penlight rather than run the risk of being seen
by the occupants, the Miettlinens it turned out, probably

taking a brisk constitutional along the beach. Now you want somebody who could ram a bonsai into Billy's chest? Either Miettlinen could do it with one hand.

So could the man who occupied the next room, along with some bonsai plants and rocks and specimens. The bed was mussed up, like it had been used for a wrestling match. The usual stuff in the bathroom and clothes rack, but on the dresser top he found two name-tag string-ties. Printed on the first, *John Okawa,* and on the second, *Lee Sullivan.*

The bonsai master and the Elderhostel coordinator?

He turned to the tumbled bed.

Yeah, buddy.

So, the married Okawa did have something Billy Dack could put the squeeze on him for.

By the time Jim set the night chain in the last room in the row, he was pushing eight-twenty, and still no tapes. He zipped through the bathroom and closet and had opened a dresser drawer when he heard someone out in the hall.

Then a key in the lock.

Steeling himself against panic, he eased the drawer shut as the door swung opened and caught on the chain.

"What the shit?" cried a man's voice.

But by that time Jim was flying in the starless night, racing across balconies, hopping walls, cracking his knee against an iron chair outside Aunt Alice's room—sonofabitch!—sending it crashing to the concrete floor, the old lady never looking up, and stumbled on, knee hurting like hell, chest pains from sucking frigid air, until, finally—finally finally—he charged into the sanctuary of his own room, slamming the door behind, collapsing in a chair, and gasping for breath as adrenaline pumped blood through his pounding brain.

He wasn't made for this shit.

When the chest pains eased, he realized his throat was

dry, and wondered if he could make it across the room for a Samuel Adams. Then his shoulders slumped and he hung his head.

The fridge.

Sonofabitch, the fridge.

He hadn't looked in a single one.

He did a finger examination of his knee, feeling nothing out of place. An X ray might show otherwise. He stood and walked back and forth to keep it from stiffening up, and decided, as his mother always said, he would live.

He glanced at his watch.

Ten minutes late.

Had the guy already called?

Would he call back?

What the hell was he going to tell him if he did?

Then it rang and he jumped to it.

"Hello?"

"Ya got the tapes?" came the guttural, disguised voice.

"No, I couldn't find any."

"Did ya even look—"

"Goddamn it! I've been racing up and down balconies all over the place. Nobody has the damn tapes."

"Ya looked in all the rooms?"

"Yes, yes, I searched them all," he said, and wondered about Aunt Alice's room, and those on the other side of the hall, and that last room where he'd almost been caught. And the fridges. Sonofabitch, he should have checked the fridges! "I'm telling you there's nothing here." But if there was, bet your sweet ass he wasn't going back. "Look, I did as you asked, now let Dodee go."

Silence on the other end, no screeching of wind, or crash of surf.

Probably no longer on the street.

"There's one more place," came the disguised voice.

"Get yer car and meet me at Bay Side Drive and Eighty-sixth Street."

"Meet you?" He didn't know what he had expected, but it wasn't that.

"Don't you hear well? Meet me. Bay Side Drive and Eighty-sixth. Ten minutes. Ya bring the cops and ya can kiss yer girlfriend goodbye."

The line went dead.

TWENTY-THREE

HE SCOOTED the blue Lincoln along 86th, heater purring, and realized the kidnapper had made a good choice. Dark houses. No cars at the curb. The resort town's deserted street straight-arrow for ten blocks. If he came with the police they would stick out like a flasher in a convent.

The guy was no dope.

If it was a guy.

Could just as easily be a woman, like Tiffany Crew.

If we're going to do this, let's get it over with.

Get what over with?

Bay Side Drive made a T-intersection with 86th. This stretch of road was also straight-arrow, with dark houses lining his side, seawall and dark bay on the other.

What if an innocent car happened along?

Would the kidnapper panic, or hang in there until it passed?

He parked on the seawall side, under a street lamp, cutting his lights as a new thought hit him, one he tried to dismiss, but it kept floating in front of him.

Suppose there wasn't a kidnapper?

Suppose it was Dodee, disguising her voice and pretending she had been kidnapped? Easy to do. Say a few words in her own voice, and then put on the hoarse disguise.

The question became moot as he saw, in the rearview mirror, two huddled figures move out of the dark and into the street lamp's light circle. The back door opened and Dodee was shoved in, followed by a second figure.

"You okay?" he asked her.

She was shivering, perhaps not just from the cold. "Yes, shaken up, but—"

"Shut up," the voice wasn't disguised now and he swung around to stare into Ramon's Juan Valdez look-alike face. "Why in the hell did you park under the light?"

"You didn't tell me where to park."

"Get going," the motel night manager said, scanning the area through the windows. "Drive straight ahead."

"No, I don't think I will. Let go of Dodee—"

Ramon brought up his right hand, raising a gun over the back of the seat and into Jim's face. It was about the size of a tank cannon.

"Get going."

"Right."

Jim turned on his lights and headed up Bay Drive.

"Turn left here," Ramon ordered after they had gone six blocks.

He did as he was told. They took another left on Ocean Boulevard, heading north again, Ramon's head swiveling in constant surveillance, Dodee held close to his left side. They took another left on 69th and drove over a bridge to the mainland. Unlike the deserted barrier island, there were lights here, and cars parked at the curbs. They wound around some streets into a less affluent neighborhood and headed south on tree-lined Pine Road.

"Stop!"

He jammed on the breaks in an intersection, throwing both Dodee and Ramon into the back of the front seat.

"Fuck," Ramon spit.

Jim swung around to Dodee. "You okay?"

She nodded, but the frightened look on her face contradicted it.

Ramon again showed him the gun, as if he needed a refresher. "You try something like that again—"

"You told me to stop."

"—and your girlfriend gets it." He nodded out the windshield. "That house with the crummy lawn? White house? See it?"

In the middle of the next block a square bungalow sat on two-foot-high brick columns with an open crawl space underneath, a peaked attic above. It shared the same architecture as other seashore bungalows stamped out up and down the tree-lined street, but this one was more run down, with peeling white paint, overgrown shrubbery spilling onto the sidewalk and hiding the front door.

"What about it?"

"Twenty-three twenty-one." Ramon said, scanning the road both forwards and back. "Turn right and drive on."

He eased his foot onto the accelerator and cut right. "Who lives there?"

"No one now. Turn left at the intersection."

He did as he was told. "Billy? Did he live there?"

"He owned it," Ramon's head nodded in the rearview mirror. "He had an apartment, but this was his big investment," he said, emphasizing "big" with sneer.

"You're in with him on the blackmail," Jim said, like he knew, and waited for Ramon to deny it. And waited. "Right." He drove through another intersection. "I figured that out. Billy would need someone to help him."

No answer from the back seat.

"Billy was sly," Jim continued, passing yet another intersection, "the way he handled things, but he needed a leg man—"

"Leg man! The dumb shit didn't have an original idea. I had to tell him everything. Not once, but five times. Circle the block."

Jim took a left at the next intersection, passing a service

alley that separated the backyards of the houses on each
street. "But you got greedy—"

"No. He got greedy. Play it cool, that was the idea. Always keep the tape player on record. When something interesting popped up, we'd bug the room. Nothing big. Just
take each person for a one-time reasonable payoff. Keep
the evidence as insurance so no one got chummy with the
cops and move on to the next mark. That was the plan.
Build up enough capital to start our own motel. I told him
over and over, that was the plan."

"So, what happened?"

"What happened? How the hell do I know? He was always dime and nickeling everything. We were doing all
right, but he was always trying to make little deals on his
own, for peanuts, or to get into some broad's pants, and
then brag about it afterwards. He put everything into jeop-
ardy. Turn left."

Jim swung the Lincoln back onto Pine Road, heading
towards Billy's house. "Then why didn't you just stop
him?" He glanced in the rearview mirror. "Or did he record you, too? Is that why you couldn't stop him from ha-
rassing Consuelo? He had something on you—"

"Pull over to the curb and cut the lights."

He parked in a dark spot between street lamps, one block
up from Billy's, the only car on his side.

"All right," Ramon said, "leave the keys and get going."

"You want me to break into his house? Suppose the
neighbors—"

"Suppose my trigger finger gets nervous with your girlfriend here? If you see the police, anyone sitting in a parked
car, keep moving. Circle around and get back here. I see
the cops, and your girlfriend gets it."

"Yeah, and what if I get you the tapes?"

"You get me the tape I need and I drop you both off on a deserted sand dune to give me enough time to get away."

He continued to stare at the night manager.

"What?" Ramon's mustache turned down. "Think I won't keep my word? What have I got to gain by harming you? Nothing."

Jim glanced at Dodee to see her shake her head.

But there was a certain logic to what Ramon said.

Besides, it was not like he had a lot of choices.

"I'll be back as fast as I can."

He cut over to the opposite sidewalk, pulling up the collar of his car coat, and hiked down the street in leopard-spotted shadows cast by the trees overhead, keeping an eye out for people in parked cars. If they were there he didn't see them. He hesitated outside 2321 Pine Road, scanning the nearby houses for signs of life. Nothing there, either.

He glanced at his watch.

Nine forty-five.

Either people went to bed early or some of houses were used only as summer homes.

He sucked in a lungful of air and let it out, a white fog dissipating into the frosty night, then hurried up the walkway, squeezing past the shrubbery onto the porch, steps resonating over the crawl space below, and tried the front door.

Locked.

Big surprise.

He flicked on the penlight and immediately snapped it off as something rustled around inside. He held his breath and listened.

Nothing.

Not even the sound of crickets or night birds.

Too damn cold for that.

He switched on the penlight again.

Two locks, one for an old skeleton key under the door-knob, the second a shiny new Rabson dead bolt about six inches above. New or old, without tools it might as well be a castle gate with a moat of crocodiles.

He glanced at the surrounding homes again, then flicked off the penlight and started around the house. Overgrown shrubbery slapped him in the face as he tried navigating under the black overcast sky. Twigs cracked like gunshots under his feet.

Just great.

He was making enough noise to wake—

A new sound from the rear of the bungalow froze him in his tracks.

The squeak of a door opening.

Something clattered on the back porch. Clumping feet charged across the hollow floor. An instant of silence. Then he heard branches snap and a dull thud.

"Fucking horseshit."

A second pair of clumping feet, only lighter, "Come on, come on," from a feminine voice, then both of them raced for the back alley.

Doors slammed.

A masculine engine roared to life.

Tires spewed gravel as a car peeled off into the night.

Jim stood gaping at a world on fast forward. He swung around, peeking through the bushes at the dark houses, waiting for lights to pop on, windows to fly open, but it was like throwing a rock in a still pond, creating a few ripples only to settle back, tranquil and serene.

But at least it put an end to Ramon's worry about the police hanging around. Just as well; he wasn't ready to face Belinda Smith in the middle of the night. Again.

He flicked on the penlight and picked his way to the

porch, and kicked a broom and mop aside, probably what
had clattered to the floor.

He turned towards the alley.

So who the hell were they?

The car sounded like the Crew's Mercedes. And that
would make sense. If Tiffany got hold of the right tapes,
her fifty thousand was in the bag. But how did they know
this was the right house unless Billy told them? Like before
he stared into eternity.

Either way, if he interrupted their search it probably
meant they hadn't found them, and with the jamb broken
and the door wide open, they certainly had simplified his
entry problem.

He stepped into a small kitchen, the warmth of the place
enveloping him—at least Billy had paid the heating bill—
but a taste of rancid grease hung in the air. A center hallway
led toward the front of the bungalow, lost in the shadows
beyond his penlight. To the left, a pantry with a few cans
of beans and jars of spaghetti sauce looking lost on the
empty shelves. He brought the light around to the kitchen.
Metal cabinets, white and chipped, with tarnished chrome
handles on most of them. A dripping faucet left a rust stain
on a porcelain sink with a drain board. An unwashed frying
pan on the stove. Two lonely six packs of Budweiser, minus one, inhabited an old refrigerator. A red telephone hung
on the wall.

He picked it up and got a dial tone.

So, Billy had paid the phone bill, as well.

He stole into a small dining room with a sturdy old oak
table and a credenza with its drawers open and ransacked.

Maybe those guys were just common burglars.

The dining room opened onto the living room, a thread-
bare rug covered the wooden floor, dust balls in the corners,
a striped couch, two easy chairs, the arms worn, one clear

through to show stuffing under green material, but all of it facing—he whistled softly—an entertainment center of stereo components, CD-ROM, VCR, and a fifty-inch Hatachi Ultravision with external speakers, everything smack up-to-date.

Forget about Ramon's one-time reasonable payoff.

The tapes represented big bucks.

And forget about the common burglary theory; the entertainment center would have been long gone.

He moved on to the other side of the bungalow, two bedrooms sandwiching a bathroom.

Ramon had just moved up to number one on his list of murder suspects. With Billy dead, he had the blackmail business to himself. Except that Ramon was making a getaway.

So who did that leave?

Who else knew about the tapes?

How about everybody.

He entered the bathroom and used the commode.

Whatever Billy had on Ramon, it had to be pretty damn heavy for him to justify kidnapping Dodee and bringing the FBI into it.

He zipped his pants and stared in the mirror.

Ramon was stupid if he thought they wouldn't tell the FBI.

He blinked.

Or unless asshole Ramon never intended to get away. Like once he had the incriminating tape, what was to keep him from continuing the blackmail-as-usual business? In which case, when Ramon dropped him and Dodee off on that deserted sand dune, would they be in any shape to walk out?

TWENTY-FOUR

HE PUNCHED 911 on the red wall phone in the kitchen.

He should have seen this from the beginning.

The only logical reason for Ramon upping the ante from blackmail to kidnapping is that he figured no one would be around to tell about it.

What mattered now was getting Dodee out.

"Police emergency," came a voice he recognized as belonging to tall, shit-for-brains Sonny Raines.

Damn, the last thing he needed was for that donkey to come flying down the street with full bells and whistles.

"I need to talk to Detective Belinda Smith."

"This is the emergency line. If you want to talk to her you'll have to call on another line."

"This is an emergency."

"Then I need some information."

"I'm only talking to Detective Smith."

"Then you got to call on another line. And Detective Smith has gone home already. This line is only for an emergency—"

"Sonofabitch, this is an emergency! It's a matter of life and death. And if you don't call her... Isn't this conversation recorded?"

Small pause. "Maybe."

Maybe shit.

"If you don't call her, and someone else is killed, guess who will be prosecuted for neglecting his duty?"

A small silence on the other end while Sonny chewed on that, probably wondering what he had bit off.

Jim gave him a taste. "It's about the murders at the hotel."

"Who is this?"

"James P. Dandy," and he read the number off the wall phone. "Get hold of Belinda. Have her call me immediately or there'll be another murder," and gave the number again.

"Tell me where you are."

"No way. I'm only talking to Detective Smith," and he hung up.

Suppose Sonny didn't call?

Suppose Belinda didn't call back?

Either way, he had to figure how to get Dodee out. He searched through the kitchen drawers, finding an eight-inch filleting knife in the cabinet by the sink. Not the best of weapons. A gun would be better. A forty-ton tank better yet. But if he could get a jump on Ramon, the knife might work.

Sneak up the alley for a couple of blocks, circle around to the back of the Lincoln, yank open the door, and stab the guy in the arm before he knew what hit him. The gun falls on the floor. The police show up, and it's goodbye Charlie.

Or in this case, goodbye Ramon.

He jumped as the phone rang.

"Hello?"

"This better be damn good," came Belinda's high-pitched little girl voice. "This better be goddamned—"

"Ramon has kidnapped Dodee." He heard the other side go silent. "Ramon, the night manager at the Windswept Dunes Motel? He has her right now up the street in my car."

"Your car?"

"It's a long story, but he brought us across the bridge on Sixty-ninth Street. You know where that is?"

"Yeah, go on."

"And brought us to a house on Pine Street. I'm suppose to search this place for the tapes. He's in with Billy on the blackmail stuff."

"You in the house now? What's the address?"

"Twenty-three twenty-one Pine Street."

"Okay, and he's got Dodee out front?"

"No, up a block."

"Which way?"

"Lower numbers, I think. It's the only car on the opposite side in that block, at least it was when I left them. My car, a blue Lincoln."

"Know the plate number?" He gave it to her. "Okay, sit tight—"

"I'm heading down there, just in case."

"Stay out of it! This is our job now."

"The key is in the ignition. I'll try to stop him from running off, but you guys keep an eye out in case he gets away."

"Stay out of it. I can't be responsible—"

He hung up the phone, grabbed the knife, and headed out, taking the alley, pitch black under the overcast sky, praying there were no potholes lurking to trip him up as he raced for a street light shining at the end of the block, trees and houses passing like looming ogres on either side. He hesitated at the corner, stumbling on some loose gravel, checked both ways for traffic, then sprinted across the road and slowed down to a fast walk in the darkness on the other side. A dog barked in one of the houses—sonofabitch!— and he started trotting again, puffing white breath like a steam engine on an up-grade, partly from excitement, mostly from exertion.

Yeah, buddy, he was in good shape.

But yeah, buddy, he wasn't twenty-one anymore.

He took a left at the next street and hurried down to the corner of Pine, easing behind a tree, catching his breath and staring down at his blue Lincoln.

The car was two years old now.

An impulse buy.

More car than he needed, but it sure was comfortable to drive. Great for the long road. And good-looking inside and out. Which is why he bought it. He needed a thing of beauty to replace the beauty that had been ripped out of his life.

Except, as a substitute for Penny, on a scale of one to ten, it turned out to be a minus eight million.

He took a fresh grip on the filleting knife.

Damned if it was going to be a hearse for Dodee.

He charged across the road, huffing fog clouds as he raced through a street lamp's spotlight, through filigree shadows on the sidewalk, and on into a deep gloom close by the bungalows on the other side.

So far so good.

He searched the Lincoln's rear window for signs of life, but the car was too deep in darkness. Still, if everything were the way it was suppose to be, Dodee and Ramon would be studying the road ahead, not waiting for him to sneak up behind.

Otherwise it was going to be shit city.

He cut across lawns, staying in the funereal shade by the houses, eyes glued on the Lincoln, careful not to snap any twigs or trip over any bushes.

One house away a dog commenced to wake up the dead.

He dove for the dirt, like at the sound of an incoming during the war, and landed with a grunt. His breath was gone and he sucked to get it back in. God, he didn't remember the ground being this hard in Korea.

Nor did it smell so bad.

He waited facedown for the barking to stop, not the yap-yap of a terrier, but the deep woof woof woof of something the size of a pony. Which fit a piece into the malodorous jigsaw puzzle that labored his nostrils.

Great, just great.

Ten to one he had landed in dog doodoo.

Ten million woofs later, when he felt the barking had become part of the landscape, he raised his head and studied the Lincoln.

If anything had changed, he couldn't see it.

He inched up to his hands and knees, and the fragrance became overpowering.

Yep, talk about shit city!

It clung to the chest of his car coat like a glob of sewer muck. He used the back of the knife to scrape it off, then jammed the blade into the dirt a couple of times to clean it.

Then he shook his head.

Right, like when he stabs Ramon he's really going to worry about giving him dog germs.

He crept up to the car, coming up against the rear fender and listening.

Nothing.

Then again, the Lincoln's soundproofing would mute a jackhammer. So maybe they hadn't even heard the dog.

He switched the knife to his left hand and grabbed the door handle with his right, said a silent prayer it wasn't locked, then jammed the button, yanking open the door and diving inside. Knife out. Jabbing into the semi-darkness of the dome light.

But the only target was Dodee's navy-blue tote bag.

He shoved forward to glare over the seat back, as if they could be lying down, or hiding on the floor. Then he panned all the windows.

Where the hell had they gone?

The car that spun out of the back alley? They could have circled back and taken Ramon and Dodee.

He swung around to the windshield.

But more likely, impatient and suspicious, Ramon was heading for Billy's bungalow. What would happen when they found he wasn't there?

He tossed the knife in the front seat, hopped out of the car and immediately got back in behind the steering wheel, reaching for the ignition.

No keys.

He searched the dash and the seat, feeling the ignition again, then checked his pockets just to make sure.

Ramon had taken the fucking keys.

He leaped out of the car and started running down the street.

Where the hell was Belinda with the posse?

He hesitated at the corner.

Trouble was, what would Ramon do when he found the house empty? Tear ass back up the street for the car? Or figure Jim had called the cops and slink out through the darkened alley?

He opted for the alley, sprinting down to it and feeling his way in the gloom, concentrating more on audio than visual, but hearing only the blood throbbing in his ears and the wind coursing through his chest.

Then he froze and held his breath.

Footsteps scuffled toward him.

He inched towards the side, ran into a bush, and backed around it.

The knife!

Sonofabitch, he'd left the knife in the car.

The scuffling came closer, two figures huddled together,

a four-legged blob moving in the darkness. He waited, not sure of what the hell he was supposed to do.

He had no weapon.

Ramon had a gun.

Did that sound even-Steven?

Where the hell were the damn cops?

He watched Ramon and Dodee pass, held on for a minute, then stole along. They staggered, shuffling feet on loose stone, regained their balance, and moved on.

Shit, he had missed his chance. He should have been ready.

They hesitated in the light at the edge of the road, Ramon looking both ways, left arm wrapped around Dodee, gun visible now over the man's left shoulder, pointed at her head.

So, chop Ramon in the neck and hope he would be too stunned to fire? Or go for the gun and hope to yank it away before it went off?

Not a lot of choices.

Incongruously a Yellow Pages television ad played back in his mind, James Earl Jones demanding more choices.

They started to cross the street.

This was it, Charley.

He charged, choice still undecided, but coming up fast. He shifted to come up on Ramon's blind side, hit some gravel and stumbled.

Sonofabitch!

Ramon swung at the noise, bringing the gun around.

Jim hurtled on, lowering his shoulder, nailing Ramon in the chest and driving him backwards. The gun went off, blasting in his ears and bouncing around in his brain like high noon in a clock tower. And then they were fumbling and flailing and falling and crashing down hard against the pavement.

Tiny dots danced in his eyeballs.

He shook it off, aware he was gripping Ramon's wrist, the one with the gun, the one trying to twist around to blow his head off.

Another shot blasted the night.

Welcome back to the clock tower.

And a woman screamed.

He saw Dodee's face, pale and calm, peaceful and lifeless, lying on the white silk bed of a casket...only...it was Penny, not Dodee.

A third shot, louder and more powerful, cleared his eyes.

Blaring spotlights had materialized out of the night, a massive figure standing in the glare, twenty feet tall, hands clasped together, a gruff voice recognizable from some ancient memory.

"Freeze! Police!"

Shit-for-brains Raines.

Beautiful, wonderful, magnificent shit-for-brains Sonny Raines.

"Toss the gun."

He felt Ramon's arm stiffen for a moment, then go limp as his gun clattered across the pavement.

"Kick it away, Ms. Swisher."

He heard more clattering and relaxed, turning to see Ramon's dark eyes glaring back at him, disgust in the Juan Valdez look-alike face.

"Dog shit," the night manager said. "You stink like dog shit."

Funny, he thought he'd just come up smelling of roses.

TWENTY-FIVE

SHADOWS OF TREES and shrubs, outside, raced across the bungalow walls, inside, a surreal flashing between the red and white of police car domes.

Not that he could see it all that well, seated on the ratty living room couch, a male medic on a chair in front of him painting orange stuff on his face with a Q-Tip.

"I must look terrible."

"Not to me you don't," Dodee whispered at his side.

"Well," the medic said, "you might look terrible, sir, bruises and maybe a black eye tomorrow won't help, but aside from some minor aches and pains, you'll live."

"I guess I can't complain, considering I thought I was dead there for a while."

"I was convinced I was." Dodee put her arm around his. "And would have been if it hadn't been for you. I guess that makes you my hero."

"Um. Do any benefits come with that title?"

She raised her eyes to the ceiling and shook her head. "Sunday you couldn't even ride a bike, and now, half dead, you want to fly?"

"How is he?" Belinda Smith hove into view, her little girl voice raising over the cacophony of police troopers. "You taking him to the hospital?"

"Nope." The medic snapped his bag shut. "He's okay." The man stood and looked down at him. "You might want to check with a doctor for peace of mind, or if anything gets infected."

Jim nodded. "Thanks."

The man waved it off and headed out the front of the house. Belinda took the medic's place on the chair, handing Jim his car keys. "How you feeling?"

"I'd be feeling a lot better if you hadn't taken so long to get here."

"Hey," the lips turned down on her chocolate face, "you're lucky we even made it, Dude. You told me Pine Street."

He stared into her dark eyes. "So?"

"This is Pine Road. And we also have a Pine Lane and Pine Court."

Something crashed in the attic crawl space above.

"Find any tapes?" Dodee asked.

"Not yet."

Two New Jersey State policemen with crowbars crossed the room.

"According to Ramon," Belinda said, "Billy owns this place under an assumed corporate name. Persuasions Unlimited. How's that for a kicker? All we had was the address of his apartment." She glanced around. "Not much here, except for the electronics, but it was his hideout in case someone came looking. Not a bad idea, considering his business. And we also found an address book with Bixby Boyd's name in it, so we got a lot of things to sort out." She turned to Dodee. "How about filling me in on what you know?"

"Ramon kidnapped me, you know that. Met me in the hall, I think he was on his way to my room, and said you wanted to see me in the parking lot."

"Me?" Belinda's eyebrows arched.

"I thought it was strange, but what did I know? He believed he could force Jim to get him the tapes."

Belinda shifted her gaze to him "Did you find any?"

"Not a one, but—"

"That's when Ramon got the idea to search here. He told us he would let us go after he got the tapes," Dodee shook her head, "I didn't believe it."

"That's not what he claims," Belinda said, glancing around as state police used the living room as a thoroughfare. "I could sure use some coffee."

"What does he claim?" Jim asked.

"Claims he was only trying to scare you. Says there's some incriminating sex stuff on the tapes and he was desperate to get hold of it."

"He was in on the blackmail," Jim said. "Told us he was the brains of the operation."

"Well, well," Belinda's eyebrows rose again. "You're both lucky you're alive," Belinda put on a stern face. "Next time I hope you'll leave police matters to us, knowwhatamean?"

"I don't want a next time," Dodee shook her head.

Belinda turned on him. "You should have called us the moment you heard she was kidnapped. You could have gotten her killed, almost did. And suppose someone was here in the house and took a shot at you?"

"There was someone here."

Belinda blinked. "Say what?"

"There was someone in here. When I came around the side of the house, they ran for it."

"Who were they?"

"They didn't leave a card."

"Hey, I've missed too much sleep the last few days for some smart Jim Dandy answers. Do you think they got the tapes?"

"They went charging out of here, so I must have interrupted them. I would guess not. But," he held out his hands. "A lot of people are looking for those damn tapes." He toyed with telling her what he found out, but he wasn't ready to confess that he had searched the rooms. "Did you know Tiffany Crew is a private detective?"

"How did you find this out?"

"And that car that roared out of here? I'm pretty sure it was the Crews' Mercedes."

The ends of her lips turned down. "I wonder how she found out about this place? You're sure it sounded like their car, or pretty sure?"

He shrugged. "Pretty sure."

Belinda leaned back in her chair and rubbed her eyes.

"Did Ramon kill Billy?" Dodee asked.

"He says he didn't." She yawned. "But he had motive. He was a suspect in another murder in Pennsylvania. Maybe that's what Billy had on him. And maybe this time we'll get lucky."

"How about Winifred Harmony? Why did he kill her?"

"Well, if there is a connection, and if you believe her husband—" she bit her tongue "—which I'm not sure I do—there are some other things in the background there— but if you believe him, he says she was out wandering the halls with insomnia. My guess is Ramon thought she saw him kill Billy, whether she did or not." Belinda pressed her lips together, shook her head, and yawned again. "You two can go. But—" she wagged her index finger at them "—stay out of police business. Don't go looking for any more tapes. Anything suspicious, call. Preferably during the day, thank you very much."

They put on their coats and left by the front door.

"You know," Dodee said, "Ramon was right, you do smell like dog poop."

"I dove into it when I was trying to rescue you from the car."

"How did you know we'd be coming out the back way?"

He put his arm around her. "It was a guess. I figured when he didn't find me he'd want to slink out of there as quietly as possible."

"I'm ready to slink into a nice soft bed. Except I'll probably have a nightmare—ow!" She twisted away from him to rub her neck.

"What's wrong?"

"Ramon must have wrenched something when he was dragging me along the alley."

He moved her hand out of the way and gently kneaded the base of her neck between his fingers. "When we get back I'll try to work it out for you."

"Do I get another massage?"

"Do you want another massage?"

"It was different. I never had one before."

"Then I should give you the full bore treatment."

"I thought you already gave me the full bore. There's more?"

"Don't get crude. I'm talking about the massage."

They almost got lost driving back, but then found the bridge to the barrier island at 69th Street, and as they rolled down to Ocean Boulevard, following it to the motel, he told her what he'd found in the Crews' room, and the stethoscope, and of Sana and Kelly next door, and of Okawa's and Lee Sullivan's name tags.

"Why didn't you tell all this to Belinda?"

"What difference would it make now that they got Ramon? Besides, the police take a dim view of breaking and entering."

Consuelo was dusting tables in the lobby as they came in. She dropped her dust rag and rushed over to them.

"No one knows where Ramon is," she said softly.

"The police have him," Dodee said, briefly telling her about it.

"Ramon killed Billy?" Consuelo asked, wide-eyed.

Dodee nodded. "That's what the police say."

"He could have," Consuelo hesitated, eyes shifting between them, "he could have done it because of me." She wrung her hands. "Yes, he must have been trying to protect me."

Jim stared at her.

He couldn't see Ramon going out of his way to protect anyone. Especially if it jeopardized his golden egg. "You know Billy was blackmailing a lot of people?"

"I know you told me he had a lot of tapes—"

"And you knew Ramon was his partner?"

She bit her lip at that, eyes growing wide.

Dodee put her arm around her. "Don't feel sorry for Ramon. He's not worth it. Worry about your husband."

Consuelo leveled her wide waif-eyes on Jim. "No more tapes were found?"

"They're still looking," he said, and bit the side of his lip. If they weren't in the storeroom or at the house, and not in the rooms... "Do you have a pass key?" he asked.

"For the rooms, yes."

He told her about searching those on the ocean side. "Maybe you could look in the rooms across the hall?"

"Tonight. They would be asleep—"

"Not tonight. How about at dinner tomorrow?"

She glanced at Dodee and back again, opened her mouth to say something, then shook her head. "I come in early tomorrow. I could look in the afternoon when I bring towels."

The back door to the restaurant opened and the red-headed desk clerk came out with a coffee cup.

"I have to work," Consuelo said, going back to her dusting.

They rode the elevator to the second floor.

"I'll be right back," Dodee said. "If you're going to protect me from nightmares, I'm getting my nightgown."

"Here," he opened his door and handed her the key. "Let yourself in. I need a shower."

He stripped down and popped a Samuel Adams, taking a healthy slug and carrying it into the bathroom. He got into the shower, washing off the grime from the scuffle with Ramon, wincing as the water stung his battered face, then turned it off, pushed back the shower curtain, and almost had a heart attack.

"You scared the crap out of me."

Dodee looked up from washing the dog poop off his coat. "Um. You look like you're recovering nicely."

He snapped a towel off the rack, wrapped it around, and jerked his thumb to the shower. "Get in."

She raised her eyebrows. "Do I smell—"

"Hot water. Step number one." He grabbed his beer. "Let it soothe your muscles. When you get out you get step two, a full bore massage."

She took hold of his hand and twisted it to take a swallow of his beer. "Okay, Doctor," she turned him around and pushed him from the bathroom. "When do we get to step three?" But she closed the door before he had a chance to answer.

He dried himself off, climbed into his bathrobe, took a long slug from the bottle, and panned the room.

Suppose someone searched in here while he was gone? There was no sign of it, but would he know if it was Tiffany Crew who did the searching? Not unless she did something totally obvious, like take all his beer. Which would have at least shown she was smart enough to search the fridge.

He stepped out onto the balcony. His feet, even still

warm from the hot shower, felt like they would freeze to the concrete floor.

God, what a stupid idea.

What was he going to do, use X ray vision to see around corners into the fridges? The only fridge he would get out here was to fridge his balls off, something he sure in the hell didn't want to do just now. He gave a quick look over the railing and scurried back inside.

When the bathroom door opened, Dodee stood in it wrapped in a towel. "Would you hand me my nightgown?"

He patted the bed. "Lie down. On your stomach."

She looked across to her gown. "But—"

"It will only get in the way. Lie down."

She did as she was told. "I'm not so sure I want step two after all."

He started on her feet, working his thumbs into the muscles of her arches, and moved up to the smooth calves and thighs, kneading the firm muscles, softly at first, then more deeply as he felt them yield. He had done this a bazillion times before, but always with dressed people, clients with whom he maintained a professional detachment.

Now he was horny out of his mind.

Especially after pulling off her towel and working his way up from her buttocks to the small of her back to her neck, gently but firmly massaging the muscles to the accompaniment of little pleasure groans escaping from her lips.

He slapped her on the rump.

"Turn over."

She did, looking up at him a moment, then reached up to pull his head down and kissed him. "Turn out the light. I'm ready for step three."

It wasn't much of a bike ride.

As keyed up as they were, it seemed more like plunging

off a thousand-foot cliff, gasping and crying out on the
screaming ride down, but fortunately coming to a soft landing, like on a five-hundred-foot stack of fluffy pillows, lost
in each other's arms and legs and bodies, where, without a
word, he heard her labored breathing shift into regular, then
spread out into the long cadence of sleep.

He wondered if he was protecting her from nightmares,
but hardly had the thought formed when he left it behind,
along with the world's problems, oozing down, like thick
pancake syrup on a cold camp morn, into a downy slumber.

TWENTY-SIX

HE EASED OUT of the downy sleep, aware of the soft caress of Dodee's smooth body pressed against his back, legs curled up against his, her hand curled in a more immediate caress.

"Don't tell me," he said, seeing daylight seeping under the draperies, "you're an early riser."

"Um, I see you are, too."

"You're being crude again."

"That bothers you?" She rolled over on top of him. "You don't like me when I'm crude?"

"I like you when you are genteel," he put his hands on her shoulders and did some caressing of his own, "and when you are crude, and all the stops in between."

She kissed him, quick at first, and again, and then full bore. "You think you're up to another practice this morning?"

"You seem to have everything well in hand, you tell me."

Whereas last night had been a plunge off a cliff, this morning was a slow jaunt through the park, partially because it took him a while to come all the way up the hill, and partially because she brought him along that path, but the end result was pretty much the same, like two sprinters racing towards the finish line, and arriving in a dead heat, gasping and falling all over one another and laughing more like children than those old enough to, well, know better.

She lay with her cheek against his breast, her arms under his shoulders to end somewhere beneath the pillow. "You know,'' she raised her head and rested her chin on his sternum, ''I've been thinking about Ramon.'' Her head bobbed as she talked, chin jackhammering his chest.

''Oh.'' He made little circles on the small of her back, keeping his eyes closed, luxuriating in her presence, the smell, the smoothness of her body, the warmth, not really wanting to get into the Ramon business, half listening to the morning birds holding court out the balcony window, and half thinking he might be able to slip back into a golden sleep, even though his bladder was sending out the first messages that it had other ideas.

''That's it? Oh?''

''Your chin is digging into my chest.''

Her arms slipped from under his shoulders as she raised up on her elbows. ''Better?''

He opened his eyes to see her glaring intently down at him. ''Okay,'' he sighed. Forget about golden sleep. Dodee hung onto the thought like a bulldog chomping on a rag. ''What about Ramon?''

''Suppose he didn't kill Billy?''

''Okay, suppose he didn't?''

''Well, if he didn't, that means someone else did.''

''Duhh, profound statement, sweetie.''

The blue eyes flashed down at him. ''You're being sarcastic.''

''You don't like me when I'm sarcastic?'' He watched her
bite her lip. ''You're suppose to say, you like me when I'm nice and when I'm sarcastic, and—''

''You think we're in danger?''

That whacked away any lingering thoughts of sleep.

''No. Why should we be in danger?''

''The tapes. Ramon thought we knew all about them. So

did Consuelo. Maybe someone else does, someone who wouldn't mind putting us through some pain to get 'em.''

That was crazy. But then he would have thought the same of Ramon kidnapping Dodee.

"You said so yourself," she went on, "there's a lot of people looking for the tapes."

He nodded.

No doubt about that.

She laid her head back down on his chest, stretching her arms under his shoulders again. "You searched all the rooms on this floor?"

"All the ones I could get to by hopping balconies."

"And you found nothing?"

"Just what I told you." He turned down his lips. "Well, not completely. I forgot to look in the refrigerators."

She thought about that a minute. "Why would anyone put recording cassettes in a refrigerator?"

He smiled. "So they would have some frozen assets." Nothing. "I said, so they would have—"

"Oh, that's a Jim Dandy joke."

He slapped her on the rear.

"Ow. Don't get wise, buddy. You're much more vulnerable than I."

He was?

With her legs wrapped around his?

He decided not to chance it and caressed the spot he had slapped. She stretched like a cat and he expected her to start purring.

"Maybe we're missing something," she mused.

"What do you mean *we?* We're not the police. You heard Belinda. Stay out of it."

"Um."

"No, um. We're out of it."

"Um."

He might as well save his breath, but she'd play hell getting him into anything else.

"Think the tapes could be in a refrigerator?"

"I'm not going back into those rooms."

Yeah, buddy. Especially not in the daytime. Late at night, he might have a chance, but in daytime—

What the hell was he thinking?

"I'm not going back into those rooms."

"You said that."

"I'm emphasizing it. I want to make sure you hear."

"I suppose if Ramon killed Billy, it would make sense he'd kill Winnie if she saw him do it. But if she didn't report it, he probably only thought she saw him. Poor Winnie."

He shrugged.

Even more, poor Clarence.

He knew what the man was going through, and would be going through for the next few months and years, add to that the business with the police and it wasn't happy days.

"For that matter," he shifted slightly, easing her off his bladder, "why kill Billy?"

"Billy I could see." Her voice came up from his armpit. "Everybody was pissed off at him. Why else jam a tree in his chest?"

"Maybe it's not Billy at all," he grinned. "Maybe they just didn't like Okawa's bonsai."

"Very funny."

He stared up at the ceiling, spikes of fire sprinklers sticking out. "The thing that intrigues me is not the cassettes, but the tape recorder. If it was on the floor when we found the body, as you said—"

"It was on the floor. I saw it."

"Then why would the murderer come back and put it in

Billy's pocket?'' He spread his hands across the bed. ''Why would he take that chance?''

She raised up off his chest, blue eyes wide. ''How do we know it was the murderer?''

He blinked. ''You mean someone else? To get the cassette?'' He nodded. ''I suppose, but that would mean the killer didn't know the recorder was there, if he didn't take it. Maybe he didn't even know about the blackmail. Then why did he kill him?''

''I don't know. But say someone comes along afterward, finds the body and takes the cassette?''

''You mean like Ramon. But why put the recorder back?''

She stared down at him. ''Not Ramon. If it was Ramon he would have taken the recorder along with the tape. But someone, knowing about the blackmail, could have taken the tape, leaving the recorder on the floor. That's the way we found it. But then, thinking it over—I have to go to the bathroom—he guesses Ramon, or someone, would know who it was who took the tape, so he sneaks back in and replaces the recorder.''

''Then why not the cassette with it?''

''I don't know.'' She rolled off the bed, grabbing her nightgown off the night table, then shrugged and tossed it aside. ''I'm really glad I brought that with me,'' and entered the bathroom.

He went in as she came out, and when he came out she was dressed.

''I have to get back to my room before the whole hotel knows we're sleeping together.''

''Like there's someone who doesn't?''

She put her arms around his neck. ''Oh God, you think so?'' She cocked her head. ''I guess.'' She kissed him. ''See you at breakfast.''

He showered and shaved, careful around the bruises, relieved he hadn't ended up with a black eye, put on sage-colored cords, brown loafers, an oatmeal pullover, and went downstairs.

The conference room was open and he glanced in, surprised to see tables set up with white linen and glasses and water pitchers. The carpet had been scrubbed so only a knowledgeable eye could pick out the blood stain. Up front were charts and easels. Apparently a group was going to have a sales meeting. He wondered how they'd feel if they knew about the murders.

He continued on to the restaurant and went through the buffet, passing on the bacon and eggs this morning, deciding on bran flakes and sliced melon, and turned, surprised to see Clarence, thick arms sticking out of a short-sleeved shirt, sitting forlornly with his daughter and son-in-law at an isolated table, playing with his food.

He nodded, but they weren't looking his way.

Were they waiting for Winnie's body to be released?

Or was Clarence still under suspicion?

He carried his tray to the table at which the crowd had become more or less permanent, people being territorial as animals. Two seats were empty. He sat in one, the other Aunt Alice had saved for her niece.

"Good morning."

"Good morning," everyone returned.

"Ms. Alice was just now telling us," came Sana's singsong English, "that Dodee was kidnapped last night."

"She's not down?" he asked Aunt Alice.

"She's still putting on her face," the old lady answered.

The female Miettlinen leaned forward. "Is it true, *ja*," the Finlander said, her haughtiness giving way to curiosity, "vat Ms. Alice said? That is how your face got banged up?"

He nodded, scanning the table.

His almost-roommate, Barney, sat across from him, next to the Miettlinens on one side, and Sana and Kelly next to them on the other; to his left was Tiffany and Simon Crew, taking the place of the Harmonys.

If Ramon hadn't killed Billy, like Dodee said, any one of them, calmly eating breakfast, could be a murderer. Including the thick-armed Clarence, for that matter. At least four were sniffing for the tapes, and might even have them stashed in a refrigerator. How many others didn't he know about?

"Well," Kelly said, hardly containing herself, "go on. Did you really rescue her?"

"Huh?"

He wondered what Dodee had told Aunt Alice, who had obviously regaled it to the group. Hopefully not about searching the rooms. But then the lady herself put in an appearance, dressed in a spruce plaid shirt, midnight blue sweater vest, blue jeans, and ankle high, suede walking boots, her wheaten hair neatly in place, cornflower-blue eyes clear and bright, and she gave them all a white-toothed smile. "Morning everyone."

"Jim was just now about to tell us of the kidnapping," Sana said. "You were indeed scared?"

Dodee sat down in the empty seat, flashing questioning eyes on Jim.

"It wasn't me." He nodded at Aunt Alice.

"Well, everyone was so anxious to know, dear," the old lady said.

Dodee labored over her cereal box. "If you'll pardon the expression," she said sweetly, "I was scared shitless."

"Vat did he vant?" asked the male Miettlinen.

She dumped the cereal in her bowl. "He wanted some cassette tapes that Billy recorded."

"Excuse me," Kelly pounced, "did you find them?"

"I didn't," Jim said.

"Ramon, eh?" Barney's lips turned down and he nodded. "So he killed Billy. Yes sir, and Winnie, too."

"So, tell us how it happened," said the female Miettlinen.

Jim outlined the story.

"He left out that he saved my life," Dodee added.

"I wonder what happened to those tapes?" Tiffany Crew stared across at Jim, then added, "I wonder what was on them that was so important."

"Blackmail," Barney blurted out, then shrugged when everyone looked at him. "What else could it be?" No one answered, so he nodded. "Yes sir, blackmail. That's why Ramon killed Billy and Winnie."

"That doesn't make any sense." Dodee put down her coffee. "How could Winnie be involved in blackmail? She just got here like the rest of us."

"Winnie must have seen something, Dodee," Barney nodded again, a self-made expert on the thing now that no one had questioned his theory. "Clarence said she couldn't sleep and was roaming the halls. Probably saw Ramon killing Billy, when the police get to the bottom of it. Or maybe taking something from the body." Barney clapped his hands. "Yes sir, Ramon did it. Killed Winnie, too. And blackmail was the motive."

That was that.

Jim sipped his coffee.

Barney had spoken.

TWENTY-SEVEN

AUNT ALICE wanted to see the Victorian houses down at Cape May. Dodee decided to play hooky and drive her. So Jim also decided to play hooky and drive them both. But between breakfast time and departure time, the clouds that had hung around all night spilled over big time, so they decided to pass on venturing out into the cold world and go instead, sheepishly late, to bonsai class.

Okawa was giving a styling demonstration of plantings on a rock. The rock in question was flat, an inch or so thick, with some ridge lines and indentations, a little like a piece of slate.

"Where do you think Ah found this?" the Georgian asked, big smile on his puckish olive face.

"In Japan?" Barney barked.

"Noooo," Okawa lifted it on edge for all to see. Two-and-a-half-feet long and eighteen-inches wide, gray with rust-red spots. It looked like something pried from a rocky outcropping. "Anyone else want to venture a guess?"

"In the Smokies?" Simon Crew asked.

Okawa pointed a finger at him. "That's a good guess."

"But it's not right?"

"Not quite," Okawa smiled. "But almost. It's a trick question." He sat the rock flat on his turntable. "The truth is, I made it."

Dodee reached out and ran her hand over it. "It feels real. How did you do it?"

"First you need a real rock." Okawa nodded to Simon. "That one I found in the Smokies, when I was camping.

It was in a national park where Mr. Rock says to me, you can't take me, partner, or take anything else for that matter, so I made a latex mold of it, don't you know. The park still has their rock, and I have some copies.''

"But how did you do it?" Tiffany asked, reflecting the same amazement as Dodee.

"You give the rock a coat of latex every day, put it on with a brush. On the third day you brush some on, then stretch some panty hose over it. I get old panty hose from my wife—I think she suspects I wear them for a boyfriend I have on the side." Big grin.

Jim shook his head.

He didn't want to contemplate Okawa's powerful body wearing panty hose.

"You brush another coat over the panty hose, then two more coats the next two days, five days in all. You let it sit on the rock for a week before you peel it off and, shazam, you have a mold to make your own rock."

"How long was your camping trip?" Aunt Alice asked, also feeling the rock, as if it had to be touched to be believed.

"A week. I had to go back to peel off the molds, but I had fifteen working, so it was worth the trip. Now you mix a mortar of fine sand and cement fondue from a place in Virginia, add some rust-red dye, keep it splotchy, and work it into the mold. Then embed a piece of fiberglass window screening for reinforcement, cover with damp rags and plastic, and let it cure for a week or two. Shazam. One rock that's difficult to tell from the real thing."

"God, what other tricks you got?" Dodee asked.

"I'm not God," he grinned, "just a high up saint, don't you know." He gave a wave of his hand. "I'll have some books for sale here this afternoon that will explain a lot."

Okawa spent the rest of the morning on the rock planting,

using Kingsville boxwoods for specimens. He carefully styled and planted each tree, and when everything was in place he allowed Sana, Kelly, and Tiffany to help work soil around the roots with pointed chopsticks, all three of them talking and laughing together.

Jim watched, wondering how well they would be getting along if Sana and Kelly knew Tiffany was a detective working for their husbands. He peeked around to the others, people he had come to know over the past few days, maybe not ones he would choose for lifetime companions, but for the few days of the Elderhostel he was happy to be part of them. Even the grumpy Barney. And the Miettlinens, by sharing the same dinner table, he had come to know their strangeness was more culture than snobbery. And Aunt Alice, so enthusiastic about learning new things.

Then his eyes landed on Dodee, sketchbook resting against her arm, drawing pencil in the other hand, making swift, deft strokes, using the white of the paper as much as the dark of the pencil to make the picture. The light glinted off her wheaten hair, and at that moment the blue eyes chanced his way, a quick smile accompanying it, before going back to the sketch.

What was he going to do about Dodee?

What could he do about Dodee?

He could live with it if he never saw the others again. But Dodee was something special. You can't make rational decisions based on four days, although, after all they had been through together, it seemed like a month. And yet, he knew when tomorrow came he didn't want to just say good-bye. Like forever.

So what did that leave?

And how did she feel?

Here he was, first time out of the chute since Penny had died, and instead of being casual and frivolous, it had left him wary of where to step next, afraid to go on, not wanting to turn back.

Okawa had everything in place on the rock now. To give it depth, he had planted the thinner trunks in the back, and added a little swale in the soil, hinting of a dry stream bed like Dodee's, the back lost in a winding curve so that in the mind's eye it continued on forever. Then he added some short grass, *eleocharis radicans,* and three miniature azaleas for accent plants, to make the trees seem bigger than they were.

And it came to Jim that bonsai was not just about what was there, but also the things that were missing, like in Dodee's sketches. Reason told you it was only dark lines on a white pad, like it was only, say, a six- or twelve-inch plant in a pot. If you locked onto that reality, that's all it remained, perhaps why some people didn't care for bonsai.

But once you allowed the imagination to click in, it became a tree at the beach where you could feel the steady wind, like salty sandpaper, abrading the trunk and branches as smooth as a baby's butt. Or it was a venerable old oak from childhood, begging for a swing or tree house or just to be climbed.

Or it became Okawa's artful illusion.

A mountain grove resting on a rocky outcrop that plunged into an unseen crevasse. Breathe in its musty smells. Peer into the darkened tree hollows. Listen to the *joie de vivre* of the birds singing and squabbling as they flitted among its branches.

It was a glen in which he would like to take a walk.

Kick off his shoes and air out his toes.

Linger awhile with Dodee at his side.

Maybe make love on a summer's day.

Thank God for being alive.

HE WAITED for Dodee in the lobby.

Since he started thinking about her and the end of the Elderhostel, he felt the need to talk. Besides, he wanted a respite from the motel's buffet table.

She showed up in a red rain slicker with hood to cover her head. She tied it under her chin as she smiled up at him. If she thought he was crazy for wanting to go out in the pouring rain, for lunch in Bolder Harbor, she didn't say it.

He drove the Lincoln up under the portico to the front door, shoving a cassette of Rimsky-Korsakov's "Scheherazade" into the tape deck as Dodee hopped in, and they went squishing off, whisper smooth wipers clearing the windshield, undulating music evoking images of nubile Arabic maidens going through titillating gyrations.

"I hope you're not suggesting something with this cassette," she smiled.

He blinked at her. "Suggesting—"

"I don't know the Dance of the Seven Veils, and with the droops of my body I don't think you'd like to see it even if I did."

"I like the droops of your body. You can droop it over me anytime."

They ran into more traffic than he had seen since coming onto the barrier island, and would have had to circle the Colonel Bolder statue except a car pulled out from in front of the liquor store. He swung right in and they entered the eatery next door on the seaward side.

Maxie's had tables to the right of the entrance, a bar on the left, subdued lighting, a lunch-time crowd giving the place a pleasant buzz, and the aroma of frying onions and bubbling soup garnished the air. They were lucky to get a still-cluttered table by the front window, maybe relinquished by the same people who had supplied the parking space, and gazed out on the rain-pocked sidewalk where men in yellow slickers were trying to hang a banner across 130th Street.

The waitress looked like she was thirteen, a short skirt, light blue sweat shirt, and a white bowler hat setting in a nest of black hair. She cleared the table and took their order—Reuben and fries for him, tuna salad for her—and in a few blinks was back with a couple of Samuel Adams's.

"Is it always this crowded?" Jim asked her, taking a sip on his beer.

"It's Bolder appreciation weekend," she smiled. "It doesn't actually start until tomorrow, but a lot of people start coming in on Wednesday. It's sort of the pre-season for people who have places here. They come down and open up, get the water running and air out the rooms, if it isn't raining." She nodded out the window to the guys hanging the sign. "We'll have a parade on Saturday, just local high school bands and some clowns and a string of old cars, but most of the people are from the city and seem to dig the hokey scene."

She left to turn in their order and the old man from the hardware store came through the door.

"Hey, there you be," he said, sniff-sniffing with his cold or allergy. "Good thing you bought that last miniature tape recorder when ya did."

"Someone else looking for one?" Dodee asked.

"Not someone," sniff, sniff, "three someones came in after you did. Don't understand. Suddenly the whole town wants 'em. Enjoy your lunch."

"Well," Dodee arched her eyebrows to Jim, "what do you think of that?"

He raised his glass. "In spite of the murders and landing in jail and being shot at, it's been a hell of an adventure. There's no one I'd rather have shared it with."

"Likewise, I'm sure," she said, putting on a New York accent, and clinked his glass. She sipped the beer and put it down. "There were other things."

He nodded. "Great other things. I wouldn't trade the other things for anythings. I just hope all the bad things are over for awhile."

She gazed out the window. "They just added spice to the other things."

He stared at her profile, glowing in the muted daylight, and wondered again about tomorrow. How to approach her about it? Maybe she was wondering the same thing. Maybe that's why she had agreed to come to lunch. To give him a chance to ask her to...

To what?

"So," she said, "what do you think?"

He blinked.

Had she read his thoughts?

The silence stretched out like a rubber band and threatened to pop.

"What do I think?"

"Three other people trying to buy a tape recorder?" She turned from the window. "Any of them the one who put the recorder in Billy's pocket?"

He let out an audible sigh.

Her eyebrows rose. "What did you think I meant?"

"Nothing. I was just wondering." He stared into the questioning blue eyes and shrugged. "To tell the truth," he bit the inside of his cheek—did he want to tell the truth? Well, it was one way to get it out in the open. "I was thinking about tomorrow."

Her eyes searched his face. "Tomorrow?"

"The Elderhostel is over tomorrow. What happens to our adventure?"

Her eyebrows rose again, as if the thought had newly

dawned on her, then she lowered her eyes to her beer, taking a sip and setting it down. "I've been concentrating so much on the murder and the tapes, I guess I never stopped to look past tomorrow."

He glanced down at his own beer, like he could read tea leaves in it. "I mean," he rubbed his chin, "is this just a beach fling that washes up on the shore tomorrow when you head home? Is that the end of our...friendship, or whatever it is?"

"I don't know. What do you think?"

He raised his eyes to hers. "What do I think or what do I want?"

"Okay, then, what do you want?"

He ran his hand through his hair and let out another sigh. "I don't know what I want, except that I don't want it to be the end of us."

She reached out to take his hand. "That's the way I feel. Why don't we think about it some more? We still have a day."

He nodded, and the waitress arrived with their food, breaking the heaviness that had settled on the table.

"So," he said, putting a couple of fries in his mouth, trying to steer a course out of deep waters, "who do you think came back to put the tape recorder in Billy's pocket?"

She shrugged, forking tuna salad into her mouth. "I'm wondering if anyone came back."

"You mean you made a mistake when you saw the recorder on the floor? Oh, you mean someone was hiding behind the door when you found the body?"

"That's what I'm wondering."

He took a big bite out of the Reuben and chewed on both the thought and the sandwich. "Was the recorder on the floor when you first discovered the body?"

She grimaced and shook her head. "See, I don't know. It could have been only when I came back down with you." They ate in silence for a few minutes, he retracing the ground they covered that morning, then Dodee pointed her fork at him. "Suppose someone discovered the body after I did, and took out the tape recorder, heard us coming back, panicked, dropped it on the floor and hid behind the door."

"Okay, then he had to know the recorder was there. And if we go with your theory that he took the tape, but put the recorder back because Ramon would guess who it was, who does that leave?"

Her lips turned down and she wagged her head. "Someone who knew about the tape."

"Everyone knew about the tapes, Kelly and Sana, and the Crews, but who knew that Billy always carried the recorder, that's the question. And someone who was around at that hour. Someone prowling the halls—Winnie was prowling the halls."

"Yes," Dodee nodded, "but how would she know about the tape?"

He shrugged.

They seemed to be back where they started.

He munched on some more fries. "Wait a minute. There was someone in the lobby who knew about the tape."

She squinted her eyes for a moment, then opened wide as they said the name in unison.

"Consuelo!"

TWENTY-EIGHT

THE RAIN had stopped by the time they pulled up outside the motel, brightening clouds reflecting in the opaque mirror of the wet parking lot. He turned off the key and popped the "Scheherazade" cassette out of the player.

"Damn," he said, staring at it.

"What?"

He opened the built-in console between the seats, rummaged through the tapes, and held up a miniature cassette, the one from the storeroom floor. "I should have gone to the library and given this to Harry while we were in Bolder Harbor."

"It's still police evidence. We really should give it to Belinda."

He turned it over in his hands a couple of times. "I'll think about it," he said, replacing it in the console.

"You're leaving it here?"

"Who's going to break into the car?" Yeah, buddy. Like no one's going to hop balcony railings and search motel rooms. He slipped the cassette into the pocket of his coat. "Feel better?"

They strolled hand-in-hand into the Windswept Dunes Motel. At the desk they found out Consuelo wasn't scheduled to report to work for another hour, so they went up to the classroom, draped their coats on a free chair, and looked over Okawa's finished rock planting.

For their last meeting, a question and answer session, Okawa had laid out all the trees he had styled, along with tools and bonsai books he had for sale.

Jim started picking through the books, glancing at the authors—John Naka, Yuji Yoshimura, Jerome Meyer, John Ainsworth—until he admitted to himself that at the moment he could only concentrate on what they would learn from Consuelo. And wondered if he should call Belinda and tell her about it.

"Have to get some of these, Jim," a voice barked at his side and he turned to see Barney motioning to the books. "Have to get a check from my room first, but I want to soak up everything I can. We need to pick Okawa's brains while he's here, right?"

Jim nodded.

After an hour, Okawa drawing different styles of bonsai on an easel and answering questions, Jim gathered up their coats, tapped Dodee on the arm and ushered her out. They found Consuelo pushing a cart with towels along the open hallway between the front desk and the elevators, her face brightening as she saw them.

"You found the tapes?"

Jim shook his head. "We haven't. I don't know about the police."

Some of the eagerness left her and her voice dropped. "I am going to search through the rooms now, like you said."

"Consuelo," Dodee put an arm on her, "where were you when Billy was killed?"

The woman quickly glanced from one to the other. "I was not in that night."

"Um," Dodee wagged her head. "It was just a thought."

"Wait a minute," Jim pointed to the cleaning woman, "we saw you. Remember, you were crying when we came into the lobby from the police station."

"That was Monday night."

"Nooo," Dodee stood in front of her, "Jim's right. It was Sunday night, or Monday morning. Before we found the body."

"I did not do it!"

"No one's saying you did," he said.

"If they find the tape of me, the police will say I am in on it with Ramon."

"If Ramon was going to implicate you he would have already done so. He's not the type to spare anyone. What we're looking for is a missing cassette."

Her expressive face turned hard. "What has this to do with me?"

"Consuelo," Dodee's voice soft and soothing, "sometime after I discovered the body, someone went into the room and took a cassette from Billy's tape recorder."

"Then after we went to call the police," Jim continued, "that same person replaced the empty recorder in Billy's pocket."

"No! I did not do it. I was cleaning another place when you found the body. I know nothing about a tape recorder."

"Okaaay," Dodee stretching it out, as if to give Consuelo a chance to change her mind, but the woman's jaw had set. "We were just guessing. So we're wrong."

Jim sucked in a breath and let it out.

Dodee didn't sound like she thought she was wrong.

And Consuelo didn't sound like she was right.

But she did sound like she wouldn't talk.

"The police are on their way," he said. Consuelo's eyes narrowed and he nodded. "They want to search the employee lockers. That's why we wanted to warn you. Do you have a locker?"

"I tell you I know nothing about it."

"All right," he shrugged, "then don't worry."

Consuelo pushed her cart towards the elevators.

Dodee put her arm around his. "You weren't too heavy-handed," she whispered.

"Heavy-handed? I thought I was extremely subtle."

"Oh yeah, like 'do you have a locker?'"

"Anyway," he motioned down the hall as the cart came rolling back.

Consuelo stopped beside them. "If someone gave the police the tape, would that make them happy?"

He nodded. "Yeah."

"They would not come looking for the person who had the tape?"

"If we had the tape," Dodee said, "we wouldn't have to tell the police who gave it to us."

Consuelo bit her lip for a moment. "I have the tape. I saw you rush from the room and when I looked in I saw that pig. I knew about the recorder. The pig always had it turned on. I got it out of his pocket and tried to play it, but the recorder was broke. The button was stuck. So I took the tape. It did not want to come out. I twisted it and turned it over and it popped out when I dropped the recorder. But then I hear you outside and hid behind the door. When you left I put the recorder back in his pocket. I thought the tape was the one he was using to try to get me to," she waved her hand, "you know."

"Was it?" Dodee asked.

Her lips turned down, eyebrows arched and her shoulders hunched. "The recorder was broke. When I tried to buy one at the store they were all gone. If I get it I will not be in trouble?"

"I promise you," Dodee said, "we won't tell who gave it to us."

Consuelo nodded and headed for the lobby.

"Why don't you wait for her," Dodee said, "and I'll run and get our recorder."

He watched her rush off towards the elevator.

Would they find the killer on the tape?

That would make it easy.

The elevator doors opened, and as Dodee got on, Barney escorted Sana and Kelly off. "Coffee, Jim?" he barked. "We're on a break upstairs."

"In a little bit. I'm waiting for Dodee."

"I've learned so much from Mr. Okawa," Kelly said in her husky voice. "I can't wait to try some of these things at home."

They turned the corner in the lobby, chatting away as they headed for the back door of restaurant.

Instead of the killer, suppose Consuelo's cassette had Sana and Kelly's husbands on it, say the information they wanted for their divorce? The same sought by Tiffany Crew, only at cross purposes.

He followed them down to the lobby.

Maybe they were both on the tape, different things on different sides.

He laid Dodee's jacket over the back of an easy chair and felt in his coat pocket for the Harry cassette. There were two sides to this one, as well. Maybe he should listen to it before giving it to Harry.

Consuelo arrived seconds after Dodee, handing her the cassette. "You promise the police will not know I had the tape?" she whispered, dark eyes darting toward the red-headed clerk behind the check-out desk.

"Promise," Dodee whispered back.

"I have to go to work," she said loudly, for the redhead desk clerk's benefit, then lowered her voice to Jim. "I will search the rooms for the others."

Dodee turned to him after Consuelo left. "Let's play this thing."

He glanced towards the desk. "Let's take it somewhere we can't be overheard."

As if to underscore the point, Sana, Kelly and Barney came out of the restaurant with foam coffee cups.

"Dodee, Jim," Barney said in his general's voice, stopping the parade, "come back upstairs. There's more bonsai to learn."

Dodee looked up at Jim.

"We were thinking about going for a walk," Jim said.

"Is it not raining out?" Sana turned towards the front door. "Oh, no, it is stopped. Ah, but indeed it must also be cold?"

"It's warmed up a bit," Dodee said.

"Well, I am going back." Barney made it sound like a religious obligation. "First I want to get my checkbook. You should purchase some of those books, Jim," he called back as the three of them headed for the elevator.

"Do you really want to go for a walk?" Dodee asked.

He held her coat for her. "At least no one will hear us."

They cut across the patio toward the beach.

"Which way do we go?" she asked.

He shrugged.

When they reached the packed semi-wet sand, Dodee turned her suede walking boots north and they trudged on for half a block. "Now?"

He looked back toward the motel and saw a couple of people out on the hospitality room balcony, but it was too far to make out who.

Did anyone suspect what they were doing?

Not likely. For that they'd have to know Consuelo had given them the tape. They'd probably put it down as crazy lovers out for a stroll on the deserted beach. If they even noticed at all.

He put his arm around Dodee and pulled her close.

"Okay, play it now."

TWENTY-NINE

THEY WALKED ALONG, huddled together, Dodee holding the recorder between them, and listened as the waves trounced and spit and gurgled, foaming tentacles sizzling up the shelf in a feeble attempt to entrap them, fresh breeze blowing damp and salty into their faces.

"Turn it up," he said.

"I have it all the way up."

"Here." He took it from her, looked at the volume, and shrugged. "It's all the way up."

"See."

He pushed the Fast Forward and let it race ahead. "Maybe there's something in the middle." He stopped it at a couple of places to listen, but the only sound, and that only when sheltered up close from the surf and wind, was a soft hiss.

"Maybe we have the wrong side," Dodee said.

He opened the recorder and reversed the cassette and pushed the play button.

Billy Dack's nasal voice blasted forth.

Hey, if I get me a little poontang, what's the skin off your ass?

Then a second voice, muffled slightly, as if the recorder were in Billy's pocket.

Goddammit, you stay away from her.

He looked into Dodee's wide-open eyes.

Hey, you got a little piece of ass, now it's my turn.

I order you to stay away from that woman.

Look, General, you might have been king shit when you were in the army—

"Oh, my god," Dodee said.

"Barney!"

See, ya ain't got no bargaining chips here. Either I get the money or I get the old broad to gimme a ride. She give you a good ride? Hey, stay back!

I'm warning you—

Oh ho. I don't think so.

Goddammit, I'll call the police.

Yeah, and Mr. Harmony finds himself a little present.

You think that bothers me?

Oh no, but what about your girlfriend? And what if the garbage man decides he's gonna trash you for takin' his woman? No, I don't think you wanna call the police.

A small silence.

Something going on?

Tell you what. Twenty-five hundred. I give you the tape and we say no more.

I'm not letting you bloodsuckers get into me—

Then I get into Winnie.

Goddammit, I told you—

You told me what? I'm tired a talkin'. I gotta get back to work. My boss finds me missing—

I'll inform your boss!

Oh, you will. Ha, that's a laugh. See, I'm laughing, ha ha. Not if you don't want old Clarence getting an earful. Twenty-five hundred. Bottom line.

Another break, tension in the silence.

I told you, not a penny—

No sweat off my balls. Maybe I'll go for a BJ.

You go near her and I'll kill you!

Yeah, she looks like she got soft lips. She got soft lips? Hey, what d'ya think ya doin' with that? Hey, get away. You crazy or somethin'. What d'ya think you're gonna do—

Goddamn sonofabitch, I told you I'd kill you—

With that? Ha ha. I'm laughing see, ha ha. You try anything and your ass— Hey, get away! Mr. Big Shot. Mr. Big General in the Army. Well, excu-oooze me! I gotta see about getting a BJ, a be-ee-ee ja-aa-ay— Hey, you crazy! Hey get away— NO!

A soft thud, like something landing on the carpet.

Billy?

Or the bonsai pot?

Then a loud whack, something banging against the tape recorder, like the floor. Followed by close-up wheezing. Gurgling. Air and blood bubbling in and out of Billy's laboring chest, then a long discharge.

And silence.

Barney's voice, more muffled, more distant.

Now, you bastard, tell it to the devil.

Then only the soft hiss of the tape.

"Oh God!" Dodee nudged him. "Look."

He jerked his head up to see her gazing inland.

They had traveled down the shore, engrossed in the tape, to where motels had given away to deserted houses; to where a shaft of sunlight broke through clouds to shine on a car parked in the middle of a street, dead-ending at the edge of the beach; to where a figure, straight and tall, trudged towards them across the sand, something hard and black in his right hand.

Jim pulled Dodee close and slipped the tape recorder into her coat pocket.

"We don't know anything," he whispered and caught her nod.

He glanced over his shoulder.

Walled-in by a somber sea to the east and faceless buildings to the west, a sandy ribbon drawn taut to the cloudy horizon, the same forward as back, with only the mournful cries of a few scudding gulls to break up the solitude of wind and waves, the world had ebbed to Dodee and him and the advancing general.

Barney stopped ten feet away and brought up his hand, eliminating any lingering doubts about the gun. It looked like a military-type forty-five.

"Give me the tape, Jim."

"The tape?" He put as much incredulity in his voice as he could muster.

"The tape Billy had when he was killed."

"I don't know—"

"You have it. Consuelo gave it to you."

He hesitated.

Was Barney guessing, or—

"Caught her going through my things, Jim, and after a few threats, she sold you out. Have you listened to it?"

"How could we?" He gave up on denying possession, but hung onto the ignorance. Barney had killed two people already. Why would he hesitate now? "We don't have a recorder."

"When we went to buy one," Dodee added, "they were sold out."

Barney nodded, seemingly satisfied; apparently he had looked for one himself. He reached out his free hand and wiggled his fingers. "I'll take the tape now."

Jim nodded.

He might be about to get himself killed, but he could only come up with one solution to save Dodee. He only hoped Barney was just as much of an amateur in this situation as he, except, of course, for the forty-five.

"Toss it here," the general said, as if to confirm Jim's suspicions.

He pulled the Harry tape out of his pocket, and pitched

it, high and wide, twirling in the air, buoyed like a bird by the wind, and Barney suckered for it.

And Jim charged in right behind.

Head down. Arms out. Hitting him waist high, smashing his shoulder into Barney's gut, forcing a grunt. Churning legs driving him back, but the guy refused to go down.

Then the world crashed upon Jim's head.

Tiny dots swam in a black sea before his eyes.

And he felt Barney slipping from his grasp.

"Hang on," yelled his own voice from the edge of time, and he did, blinking away the dots, and got his sluggish legs churning again, driving Barney back until the steel gun smashed down again behind his ear.

And Barney was falling.

But so was he.

Not only into a hole of swimming stars, but down onto the ground to trench up a mouthful of sand.

He felt Barney break free.

His eyes cleared into a kind of tunnel vision, filled with the muzzle of the forty-five. A dumb cliché popped full-blown into his mind: goodbye cruel world.

But a foot flashed into view, ankle-high walking boot racing toward the forty-five and then both disappearing from his circle of vision.

He blinked and his eyes snapped back to wide angle.

The gun flew through the air toward the water, with Do-dee going for it. Barney lunged and tripped her up, and she landed spread-eagle on the sand. Then the big man lumbered to his feet and stumbled for it himself.

Jim struggled upright and shuffled after.

He felt like an old fart, trudging after another old fart, two dinosaurs lumbering across a beach of chewing gum after a forty-five which lay on the slick surface of freshly washed sand.

Barney bent for the gun.

Jim tackled him in the butt.

They both crunched hard down on sand and shells, the world closing in again, wet and frigid this time as a wave crashed over him, stinging his eyes and tasting of salt.

Hang on, shouted one part of his brain, even as the other announced he was out of air.

The wave sucked back to the sea and he blinked out salt to see the gun, lying exposed in thin water and foam, Barney's big hand stretching out for it. Jim grabbed Barney's leg and pulled him back. And the ocean returned, crashing and pounding and scraping his face over a sandpaper bottom, freezing his balls and shriveling his penis.

When it sucked away this time the gun was gone.

Barney wrenched free and sat up, and flung something seaward.

It arched, black and tumbling, glinting as a shaft of sun broke through, a miniature cassette swirling in the air, then plunked into the sea.

"Good arm," Jim's own voice came through his popping ears.

"You are too late." A half mad grin spread on Barney's face as another wave almost threw him off balance. "Your evidence." He panted. "Out there." Pointing. "Being buried, even as we speak." Puffing steam. "Without it, you have nothing."

Jim sat up beside him, sand in his shoes and socks, weighing down his pants like a lead apron, chilled not only from the water swirling around him and foaming up his crotch, but from that evaporating on his face and in his hair. Chest heaving—breath coming in painful gasps—no matter what, he was too old for this shit.

"What about Winnie?" he gasped.

"Winnie." Barney jerked around, face muscles tighten-

ing, body stiffening, ready for combat once again, then everything seemed to flow out of him, shoulders slumped,
head sagged. "Winnie." And he started to cry. "I loved
her." Big heaving sobs now, as if he had been pressing her
death down so tightly, that the tiny fissure of mentioning
her name had become the chute for an entire eruption. "She
was such a good woman—" tears rolled unbidden down
his cheeks "—always willing to go along." He shook his
head and wiped his nose. "Except for Billy's death. I
couldn't sway her on it." Shaking his head again. "I killed
that bastard because of her," his voice gained strength,
"and I couldn't sway her. Had to tell the police, she said.
Couldn't let her do that, Jim. We were arguing in the conference room. Someone came by. I grabbed her mouth, just
to keep her quiet, just holding her close, and when I let go
her neck was loose and her head just—" he raised a hand
and let it fall "—flopped." The sobs came back, wracking
his body, blubbering like a hurt little boy.

"You got to tell them, you know."

Barney glared at him, tears rolling down the granite face,
then he bent his head, stared down between his legs for a
moment, and suddenly picked the forty-five out of the water, waving it in Jim's direction. "I did meet her in Japan.
I guess you figured that out."

Jim nodded, but only to agree, his attention on the gun.

"Been seeing her ever since. She was smothering under
fat Clarence, Jim, him and his garbage business. This was
suppose to be *our* week away together, a week to ourselves,
but suddenly Clarence decided to come along and ruined
everything. I would have had to get a separate room, so it
was nothing against you, Jim, but I couldn't have a roommate. Even so, it turned into a shabby affair." Barney
pointed the gun at him. "You understand what I'm saying?"

"I guess," Jim stared at the muzzle of the forty-five, no longer worried about his labored breathing and freezing balls. "Why not put the gun down?"

Instead Barney raised it, pointing dead at Jim's chest, and pulled the trigger.

Click.

"It's not loaded," Barney said, shaking his head.

And Jim felt glad for the water swirling around his crotch.

"I never meant to kill anyone." Barney threw the gun on the ground. "I just wanted to destroy the tape. Couldn't think past that."

Jim struggled to his feet, searched for Dodee, and saw her rushing toward him with Belinda and three uniformed policemen, cars with red lights whirling on the edge of the beach.

How did they get here?

Consuelo?

He turned around and grabbed Barney under the arm. "Come on," he helped him up, almost lifting him, and then held on as the general swayed like a drunken sailor. "The police are here. You have to tell them the truth."

Barney shrugged.

"No," Jim went on, "you have to tell. It's the only way you have a chance of getting out of this thing. That tape you threw out into the water?" Barney's eyes locked onto his. "It wasn't the tape of you and Billy. That's in the recorder in Dodee's pocket. The police probably have it now."

Barney glanced out to the water and back, a glaze coming over his eyes. "It was all for nothing?"

"Listen," he guided Barney up the slope of the beach, towards Dodee and Belinda and the cops, "get a lawyer and make a clean breast of it. The tape will show that Billy provoked his own death. If you can get them to realize Winnie's death was an accident, things could work out.''

Suddenly he had to let go of Barney and bend over, hands on his knees, as he coughed up a lungful of ocean. When his chest cleared and he straightened up, Barney stood mummy still, arms limp, jaw slack, glazed eyes fixed on the advancing police.

''Hang on, Barney. It'll work out.''

THIRTY

HE HELPED Aunt Alice to the car, dropped off her suitcase, and went back up to the room for Dodee's, entering to see her sealing brown-bag wrapping around a flat package with cellophane tape.

"This ready?" he asked, hefting her suitcase off the rack.

"Just a minute."

He set it back down. She came across and set the package next to the bag, and reached up to put her arms around his neck, brushing a hand through his hair.

"All the sand out?"

"Ow!" he said as she hit one of the military-style forty-five lumps on his head.

"I'm sorry, I'm sorry."

"It's okay." He put his arms around her waist. "I guess it's all out. I don't know about my clothes though. I pulled a ton of sand out of my jacket pocket this morning. It's probably ruined."

"Um." Cornflower-blue eyes gazed into his. "I thought we might say our goodbyes before we went down."

"Goodbye. That sounds final."

She shook her head, wheaten hair swishing with it. "Not goodbye." The blue eyes glistened now. "Wrong word. Until we meet again. So long. *Auf Wiedersehen. Adieu. Ciao, arrivederci*—"

"Okay, okay. I got the picture." Then he stared sternly at her. "*Ciao?* What a phony word."

She put her finger on his lips. "There's nothing phony

about you. You are a real—" a malicious smile spread on her lips "—Jim Dandy."

He smacked her on the rear end. "Smart ass." He kissed her, long and warm, and not the kind he should be giving if she was leaving. "When am I going to see you again?"

"We can write and phone. Maybe one day you'll come to Kansas City. And maybe one day I'll come visit Maryland."

"How about next week?"

She smiled, and ran a finger over his face again, as if to commit it not only to visual memory, but like a blind person, to feel as well, and they kissed once more.

"I know—" she let him go "—maybe we can go on another Elderhostel. Only this time I won't bring Aunt Alice."

"An Elderhostel?"

"Uh-huh." She picked up her pocketbook and package. "They have them all the time. We can find one we like and meet there. You said yourself, this has been an adventure."

He picked up the bag and followed her into the hall. "An adventure would be an understatement for the last five days." They rode the elevator down. "Okay, an Elderhostel. It's a fantastic value for the money."

"When you get home, start looking through the catalog and I'll look through mine. When we find something we both like, we sign on."

They strolled out into the warm midday sun—yeah right, now that they were leaving, spring had come on in earnest—and were surprised to see a police car in the parking lot, door open, engine running, Belinda Smith leaning against the fender of Dodee's car, talking to Aunt Alice.

"So," the detective gave them an ivory-toothed smile, "you're finally going?"

"Looks that way," Jim said, putting Dodee's bag in the trunk and clicking it shut.

"All good things come to an end," Dodee added.

Belinda's grin broadened. "Even nightmares. I think I'm finally going to get a good night's sleep." She shook Dodee's hand and then Jim's. "For two pains in the butt, I have to admit you made a difference on this case." She looked from one to the other again. "Now tell me, you really are leaving?"

Dodee nodded.

"Okay. Have a safe trip home." She walked around to the door of her police car and looked back at them. "Yeah, what the hell," she shrugged, "if you ever want to come back to Bolder Harbor again, I want you to know you'll be welcome to…go straight on down to Cape May." She gave them a wave and drove off.

Jim hugged Aunt Alice. "Nice meeting you, Aunt Alice."

"Yes, and you too, Jim. We'll have to do this again, only next time I want to be your roommate."

"Fat chance, Aunt Alice," Dodee said from her side of the car.

"You have to come visit us in Kansas City," Aunt Alice said. "Dodee has her little house fixed pretty as a button."

"Okay with me." He helped her into the passenger seat. "How about tomorrow?"

She held onto his hand. "Permit an old lady an observation on life." Her watery blue eyes stared up into his. "It starts out like being in a room full of lights, so many you can't discern one from the other. But they slowly blink off. Oh, you don't notice them so much at first, but after a while black holes begin to appear, and the holes spread so that each individual light becomes a shining entity of its own." She shook his hand for emphasis. "Cherish each of your lights while you can, treat them as priceless treasures, for every blink off is a reminder of just how precious and irreplaceable they really are, until in the end we are left with only one Light, the one that never goes out, the one we have to follow home." She smiled and nodded. "Come see us when you have the chance."

He bent and kissed her on the cheek and shut the door, then hurried around the car to give Dodee a last kiss, more innocent than up in the room, and quicker than he wanted it. "*Ciao,* baby."

Her eyebrows rose. "What a phony." She got in the car and handed him out the flat package she had been working on. "This is for you."

He watched them pull out onto Ocean Drive. Dodee circled around the concrete island in the warm sunshine, waving out the window, then was lost to sight as they disappeared behind the motel wing, heading towards Bolder Harbor.

He missed her already.

Would he see her again?

Or was the package a goodbye gift?

He ripped it open to see, mounted on a cardboard backing, a sketch of himself. Only the face looked younger than the one he saw in the mirror every morning. This was more like the one he saw in the mirror of his mind. And she had signed it in the corner—*Love, Dodee.*

Yeah, buddy.

He'd see her again.

At some Elderhostel across the country, he'd see her come walking through the door and they would meet and kiss, and go bike riding.

He gathered his things from his room, packed the Lincoln, putting his bonsai plants from class on the floor of the back seat, along with the two they'd collected together—more proof he would see her again—and rolled onto Ocean Drive, made the circle around the concrete island and gave a last look back at the Windswept Dunes Motel.

People would sleep a lot easier there with no one around to tape their private moments.

Traffic picked up as he turned down 130th Street, the wide banner—BOLDER HARBOR APPRECIATION WEEKEND—stretching high across it. He found a parking place and went into the library.

Harriet Bleacher's full face and dark hair popped up from behind the counter. She gave him an easy smile. "Back again?"

"Yeah," he looked around to see others browsing through the racks and came up close to the counter. "I found a cassette tape with a couple of people talking on it," he whispered. The smile dropped from her face. "One of them named Harry."

"I don't know what you're talking about," she said, hard eyes staring at him.

"I didn't think you would. But what I wanted—"

"I'm not interested."

"—to tell you, is that the cassette is resting a hundred feet out in the ocean, probably buried under a ton of sand by this time. If you happen to run into someone who cares, you might pass it on."

Her eyes were still hard as he turned for the door.

"Excuse me," she called out as he reached it, and he turned to see the easy smile was back. "If I ever run into that person, I'm sure Harry will be thankful to hear it."

He smiled and nodded and went out, climbing back into the Lincoln, slamming the door on the noisy world outside, leaving only the lilting, undulating strands of "Scheherazade" to caress his ears as he drove the whisper-smooth, richly-appointed, and perhaps slightly ostentatious car over the connecting bridge to the mainland, heading out in the warm sunshine, the lone vehicle against all the traffic coming in for Bolder Harbor's Appreciation Weekend.

HARVEST OF BONES
A VERMONT MYSTERY

NANCY MEANS WRIGHT

Ruth Willmarth, busy working to keep her rural Vermont
dairy farm in a manageable state, is plunged into a mystery. It
starts with a finger bone, and leads to a skeleton.

New neighbor Fay Hubbard has just opened a farmhouse
B&B and finds her home invaded by its original owner, a
gutsy septuagenarian who announces the dead body is that of
her husband—whom she murdered twenty years ago.

The bizarre discovery puts Ruth and Fay in the middle of a
twisted history of hatred, blackmail and murder, as deep and
dark as the rich Vermont soil.

Available October 1999 at your favorite retail outlet.

Take 2 books and a surprise gift FREE!

SPECIAL LIMITED-TIME OFFER

Mail to: The Mystery Library™
3010 Walden Ave.
P.O. Box 1867
Buffalo, N.Y. 14240-1867

YES! Please send me **2 free books** from the Mystery Library™ and my free surprise gift. Then send me 3 mystery books, first time in paperback, every month. Bill me only $4.19 per book plus 25¢ delivery and applicable sales tax, if any*. There is no minimum number of books I must purchase. I can always return a shipment at your expense and cancel my subscription. Even if I never buy another book from the Mystery Library™, **the 2 free books and surprise gift are mine to keep forever.**

415 WEN CJQN

Name	(PLEASE PRINT)	
Address		Apt. No.
City	State	Zip

Ronald Weber

The Aluminum Hatch

A MICHIGAN MYSTERY

Link Pickett's tourist season ended before it had even begun. The fishing guide met his grisly end as he canoed down the Borchard River and was nearly decapitated by a wire strung across the river.

Most have decided that Verlyn Kelso—Link's fierce business rival—is the killer. Department of Natural Resources agent Mercy Virdon, who happens to be Kelso's ex-wife, thinks otherwise.

Soon Mercy is up to her neoprene chest waders in a mystery as turbulent as the churning river waters—and twice as deadly.

Available October 1999 at your favorite retail outlet.